PENGUIN BOOKS

AFTER SHOCKS/NEAR ESCAPES

Stephen Dobyns is the author of *The Two Deaths of Senora Puccini*, *Cold Dog Soup*, *A Boat Off the Coast*, *The House of Alexandrine*, and a series of detective novels set in Saratoga Springs. His seventh volume of poetry, *Body Traffic*, was published in 1990. Mr. Dobyns is a professor of English at Syracuse University and also teaches in the MFA program at Warren Wilson College in North Carolina.

AFTER SHOCKS/
NEAR ESCAPES

STEPHEN DOBYNS

PENGUIN BOOKS

PENGUIN BOOKS
Published by the Penguin Group
Viking Penguin, a division of Penguin Books USA Inc.,
375 Hudson Street, New York, New York 10014, U.S.A.
Penguin Books Ltd, 27 Wrights Lane,
London W8 5TZ, England
Penguin Books Australia Ltd, Ringwood,
Victoria, Australia
Penguin Books Canada Ltd, 10 Alcorn Avenue, Suite 300,
Toronto, Ontario, Canada M4V 3B2
Penguin Books (N.Z.) Ltd, 182–190 Wairau Road,
Auckland 10, New Zealand

Penguin Books Ltd, Registered Offices:
Harmondsworth, Middlesex, England

First published in the United States of America by
Viking Penguin, a division of Penguin Books USA Inc., 1991
Published in Penguin Books 1992

1 3 5 7 9 10 8 6 4 2

PUBLISHER'S NOTE
This is a work of fiction. Names, characters, places, and incidents either are the
product of the author's imagination or are used fictitiously, and any resemblance to
actual persons, living or dead, events, or locales is entirely coincidental.

THE LIBRARY OF CONGRESS HAS CATALOGUED THE HARDCOVER AS FOLLOWS:
Dobyns, Stephen, 1941–
After shocks/near escapes / Stephen Dobyns.
p. cm.
ISBN 0-670-83914-0 (hc.)
ISBN 0 14 01.5358 6 (pbk.)
1. Earthquakes — Chile — History — 20th century — Fiction. I. Title.
PS3554.O2A69 1991
813'.54 — dc20   90–50920

Printed in the United States of America
Set in Bodoni Book
Designed by Cheryl L. Cipriani

In learning about the Chilean earthquake of May 1960, I received great assistance from my wife, Isabel Bize, her parents, Ricardo Bize Borquez and Adelina Brintrup Schwerter of Santiago, and their brothers and sisters, their children, their nieces, nephews and cousins. To these people I dedicate this book. All the characters and their stories are my own invention but most of the details and events surrounding the earthquake itself are accurate.

AFTER SHOCKS/
NEAR ESCAPES

EVEN BEFORE the earthquake my grandmother liked to say how wonderful it would be if we could all die together. She would make this statement on Sunday afternoons when her sons and daughters and their families would be visiting and her unmarried sisters had made cakes, and often there would be cousins and uncles and aunts depending on the weather and how far they had to travel. As a child, I saw nothing strange in her wish and was moved by the idea of togetherness more than by the idea of death. Nor was my grandmother an excessively morbid woman but she saw her family as ill-prepared and ill-suited for the world and she worried about how we would get along without her. In retrospect, I think she saw Heaven as one extended Sunday afternoon with endless cups of tea and cake and gossip and farm talk.

Now I imagine there must have been raised eyebrows and quick looks between her sons, but at the time I only thought of being taken up to St. Peter as a group, as if in one of those great buses that travel between Santiago and the south and which are called "coffins" because of the accidents. It made me happy to think of us being always together, forever joyous and without rancor, and sometimes my grandmother would speak of this glad possibility and put her arm around me and squeeze me so hard as to crumple the pleats of my Sunday skirt.

My family was made up mostly of German farmers whose ancestors had come from Bavaria in the 1850s to settle around Puerto Varas at the edge of Lake Llanquihue. Miles across the water the two volcanoes of Calbuco and Osorno push toward the sky like a pair of snow-covered breasts. Successive generations from all over Europe intermarried with these early immigrants but the names for the most part remained German and Spanish. My grandmother's name was Pilar Schiele Grob and as a young woman she married my grandfather, Héctor Droppelman Gebaur. Together they had six children but the oldest, Gabriel, was killed as a child when he was kicked by a horse. But to my grandmother he was still with us, alert but invisible, and she would tell me and my brothers and cousins how Gabriel watched us play and longed to join us. And after the first earthquake when it seemed certain we would die, she told us how Gabriel was waiting for us in Heaven and how he would be the first to welcome us. During those weeks I wandered through my grandparents' house and imagined Gabriel in Heaven as on some upper story I hadn't reached yet, wearing a white nightgown and beckoning to us impatiently.

My grandmother was a heavyset rectangular woman whose entire face was wrinkled except for the tip of her nose. She wore dark dresses and silver brooches and kept her white hair in a bun. She had some problem with the toes on her right foot, or perhaps it was with the toenails, which made her walk like a sailor, rolling from side to side. Her shoes were black and masculine with thick soles and on her cheeks were red circles of rouge. She was big without being fat and her dresses always looked stretched as if ready to burst. She had very small hands with short fingers, almost a child's hands, and even now I can feel them within my own, hot and dry, although she has been dead for many years. Her parents were from town and one of her disappointments was that she had married a farmer, instead of living in town, living in society, even though she seemed to have no interest in society. But she liked to give the impression that she was too refined for the farm and when she ordered her perfume, it came from Santiago. At the time of the earthquake her eyes had grown weak and she was frightened of being alone. She had, I believe, a terror of isolation and she spent her life making her family think they could not survive without her, that their excursions into the world were destined to fail. But I did not know that then. To me the way her arms seemed to stretch out and embrace us all was something I loved about her. She would summon me from across the room for a hug, then squeeze me against her large bosom so I would gasp for breath and her silver brooch pressed coldly, even roughly, against my forehead.

Her husband always seemed to escape these embraces. I never wondered about their marriage. It was not a child's question. I can't remember ever seeing him converse with his wife but nor do I have any memory that he seemed to dislike her. He was a small, rather thin man, smaller than his wife. In his sparseness and compactness, he reminded me of a walnut or pecan. He had long thinning white hair and blue eyes. His face had an alert and pointy quality: narrow skull, straight nose, a narrow pointy chin like a trowel. He always seemed to have several days' growth of beard which gave him a white and grizzled look and I remember him often chewing on a small stick or twig which waggled up and down from the corner of his mouth. He wore farm clothes for the most part: gray woolen trousers that were old and stained but clean, with suspenders and blue shirts. Always he wore a gray fedora and when he took it off there was a shallow indentation around his skull. He was soft-spoken and taciturn and stubborn in his ways.

After he died, people spoke of him as being one of the best farmers in the south. At the time of the earthquake, he was growing deaf. While my grandmother's decreasing sight was an affliction, my grandfather's deafness was probably seen by him to be a blessing. Even then I was struck by its unevenness, that he was deaf to his wife and children, but seemed to hear me and my brothers and cousins without difficulty. The main consequence of his deafness was that he spoke more loudly and I remember him stamping the ground and laughing and saying, "It's hollow. It's all hollow underneath."

My grandparents had a large yellow farmhouse on a hill overlooking the town. From their front porch one could see all of Puerto Varas, the great yellow church with its red tin roof and three red steeples, then the lake and the volcanoes and the rough edge of the cordillera crossing the horizon like the rough edge of a torn piece of paper. Down the hill in the field in front of the farmhouse stood a huge eucalyptus which shaded the cattle. On either side of the house were gardens with flowers and fruits, berries and vegetables all mixed together. A tall palm rose from the center of the garden on the north side of the house. Behind the sheds and barn was an orchard with cherries, plums, apples and pears.

During those years my parents lived on the second floor of a house across from the hospital, about two kilometers from my grandparents' farm, but still it seemed that most of our time was spent in that farmhouse, exploring its many rooms or playing in the outbuildings. I wonder now about my father and what he thought about his wife spending so much time in her parents' house, as if in some way she hadn't grown up. My brothers and I certainly preferred the farm and as for my father, Plinio Recabarren Opitz, I never knew him well. I was eight years old when he died in the earthquake. For years my mother claimed he was killed rescuing an elderly woman from a burning building. Much later, when I met his mistress, she described how they had run from her house in their underwear when the earthquake struck. They crouched in the street and my poor father was hit in the head by a chunk of brick thrown from a chimney. The woman, his mistress (by the time she told me, she was middle-aged and fat and I could hardly imagine it, although perhaps she was no older than I am now) sat on the curb with my father's head in her lap, wiping away the blood with her brassiere and crying and crying, while the street rocked and buckled and the town collapsed around them.

That afternoon my brothers and I were playing in the yard. It was Sunday, May 22, 1960. Thirty years ago. May in the south can be very cold. Although it almost never snows, except in the mountains, it rains nearly every day. There are still a few flowers: chrysanthemums, marigolds, laurestinos. The leaves of the oaks turn brown and fall, but the elms stay green and of course the palms and eucalyptus and pines. The air is smoky and for weeks at a time the tops of Calbuco and Osorno are hidden by clouds. Even now the smell of wet wool can bring my whole childhood back to me. Wet shoes, the clammy feel of wet socks bunched between the toes, the dusty smell of my grandmother's parlor stove and the pinging noise of hot metal, the two farm dogs crouched in their shabby houses with only their black noses poked out into the murk, the constant drumming on the roof.

It had rained all week and that Sunday morning as well. Then by early afternoon it began to clear. My older brother, Spartaco Recabarren Droppelman, who had turned ten that fall, hated to be indoors and dragged us out to the yard the moment the rain stopped. I most likely was reading, while my younger brother, Manfredo, who was six, had been with my mother, helping her bake a cake to take to my grandmother's later that afternoon. I can hardly think of Spartaco without tears coming to my eyes, he was so dear to me. Two years older, he was a boy who yearned to be a hero and was constantly looking for occasions to exercise his heroism. Since his idea of heroism came from children's books, his sense of these occasions also came from children's books and I doubt that he ever left the house without expecting to encounter a runaway horse with some poor girl desperately clinging to the saddle. He loved Robert Louis Stevenson and he had a wooden sword which he often carried in his belt. Sometimes I would look out the window and see him standing in the yard. He would draw the sword and hold it up and ponder it almost impatiently, as if wondering why it hadn't already called him to some higher purpose where his bravery would be constantly tested and each test would be a victory. He was a tall boy and black-haired and his face had a slightly Indian cast, which, according to my mother, had come from my father's side of the family, since on her side there was still talk about the precious gift of European blood.

Neither my younger brother nor I went outside willingly. It was cold and damp and I was afraid of getting mud on my dress. But such was my affection for Spartaco that probably he only had to ask twice and I put down my book and began pulling on my rubber boots. With Manfredo he had to work harder since Manfredo hated to be separated from my mother and liked nothing better than to sit with her while she was baking and perhaps stir something or sift something and get flour all over his clothes. That day Spartaco offered him a bribe. If Manfredo joined us in some military game, Spartaco would let him play with the pistol that my father kept in his desk. This had serious consequences but on the other hand if we had stayed inside that afternoon we might have been badly hurt or even killed.

In those years Manfredo was extremely timorous. He had

been born nearly three months early and was small for his age, and his teeth were slightly pointed. Because he was delicate, he had also been protected, perhaps overprotected, and the result was a nervousness that kept him often at my mother's side. He was happiest when we were together and when we weren't he was always asking where I was or where his father or mother was or where Spartaco was. He was also happiest in my grandparents' house and liked nothing better than to have us all in the parlor on a Sunday afternoon, the grown-ups gossiping and eating cake while he played behind my mother's chair. He was a watcher and constantly sought out explanations as to why things were the way they were. Once when Spartaco explained to him about the volcanoes across the lake and the explosive qualities of volcanoes in general, Manfredo had nightmares for a week. He frightened easily and distrusted adults who were always telling him what to do or tickling him or tossing him roughly into the air. This was especially true of his uncles. His nervousness was like a barrier between himself and all the world and he would peek around it with his large eyes. Small and dark and with his pointy teeth he looked like some pretty little animal. It seemed that Spartaco and I were always looking out for him. But he loved my father's little revolver with its silver barrel and ivory grip and sometimes my father would let him play with it. He would sit on the rug in my father's study, spinning the cylinder and pulling back the hammer. Of course my father wouldn't have wanted him to play with it outside but he was gone that day and my mother wouldn't have noticed and Spartaco was desperate to have his brother play in his game after a whole week of rain, and of course the revolver was unloaded.

Who was I in those years? I hardly know. Now I have a daughter as old as I was then and I look at her and try to find myself within her, but I catch only glimpses and I think how strange it all is. I see myself as quiet and studious, someone watching from the edges of the rooms. I loved my wilder cousins and the games we played but perhaps I loved my own company best of all, sitting in my room reading and hearing the activity of the house around me. My father would call me for dinner and I would try to read a little faster. Then he would call a second time and a third. "Lucy, I'm going to give your food to the poor." I would run to the kitchen and by the time I arrived grace would be over and they would have begun to eat and Manfredo would give me a sly little grin.

I was a very romantic little girl and moved through my days with great amounts of curiosity and wonder. But it is hard for me at thirty-eight to see past that sexual barrier, to imagine myself before puberty. What could I know about my parents' sexual frustration or my father's mistress? What could I know about how my two uncles were in love with the same woman, my eldest uncle's wife? One of the reasons the world was mysterious was because a major piece of information was missing. I knew nothing about that desperate hunger and disappointment which I would only discover in my teens and which would clarify so much of the behavior of the adult world. At eight years old I was thin and dark and tomboyish and my long brown hair was kept in a ponytail. That space between my legs was a vague question mark and deep in the forest rode a young man on a white horse, who I imagined looked much like Spartaco, and some bright morning he would gallop up to my parents' house and take me away.

My father rented the top floor of the house from an old woman, Mrs. Moedinger, who lived downstairs and whose husband had been lost at sea shortly after her marriage. She was kindly but reclusive and we rarely saw her when we played in her yard. It was a white stucco house with a roof of wooden shingles and next to it were half a dozen gnarled apple trees.

From their branches we could see into the windows of the hospital across the street or south across the fields toward my grandmother's house. The hospital wasn't very interesting except when an ambulance arrived, but we would see men and women in white standing at the windows and we would wave and they would wave back. Spartaco had once visited the morgue and had offered to take me as well but I chose not to go. He spoke of bodies covered with white sheets. It sobered him tremendously and for days he saw their outline in the rough edge of the cordillera.

My father was partners with my uncle, Hellmuth Droppelman Schiele, in a business that bought and sold cattle, and looking out from the branches of the apple trees toward my grandmother's house we could see the pens along the railway tracks where these cattle were often kept. They were mostly Belgian cattle, brown and white. I can't remember their name now. Once Spartaco tried to ride one and was thrown. But I would sometimes visit the pens when they were full of calves and they would lick my hands with their sandpaper tongues. I would find an especially pretty calf and scratch his ears and imagine his long trip to Santiago and how lonely it must be.

Spartaco's game that afternoon was a kind of hide-and-seek with revolvers. Since my allegiance to him was complete and I didn't need to be bribed, my revolver was a broken-off stick. Spartaco had some sort of cap pistol. Mostly we hid while Manfredo crept about the yard. But he was so dazed with the responsibility of carrying my father's revolver that his concentration was focused on it rather than us and I would see him wandering through the wet grass, staring at this silver thing in his hand as if in a happy trance. Several times he walked right past Spartaco who finally hissed at him in irritation so that Manfredo turned and guiltily muttered "Bang, bang." Then, with great relief, Spartaco crumpled dramatically to the ground.

He never found me and when it was Manfredo's turn to hide, Spartaco spotted him so quickly—abstractedly standing behind a tree spinning the revolver's cylinder—that Spartaco wanted to shake him.

But as the game progressed and Manfredo grew accustomed to the revolver's privilege, he began to play more efficiently. And of course he wanted to please Spartaco. We played for about an hour. Then, at three o'clock, everything changed. It was as if all our definitions were suddenly proven false and we moved forward not into another moment but into another world. Both Spartaco and I were up in an apple tree. It still had leaves and a few apples and we thought ourselves well shielded from the ground. Occasionally through the branches we saw Manfredo prowling back and forth, more attentive now and beginning to grow irritated that he couldn't find us. Across the street people were going in and out of the hospital for visiting hours. A few cars were parked along the sidewalk. Through the windows I saw groups of people sitting around the beds. In one room a man was playing the guitar. In others I saw great bouquets of flowers. Looking out across the fields toward my grandmother's house I saw that the air was full of birds. We have a large bird in the south called a bandurria, with a long syringe-like beak, that makes a cry that sounds like someone hitting a clay pipe with a wooden mallet—*tock, tock, tock*—and the air seemed full of that cry. But also there were the small green parrots that always fly in pairs and queltehues with their piercing screams, and swallows and sparrows, a whole skyful of birds. The cattle were bunched together in their pens and lowing and shuffling about. All this time Manfredo was pacing back and forth beneath us, holding the silver revolver out in front of him, preparing for his shot. Spartaco was grinning down at him.

Then another glitter of silver caught my eye, but way off to

the south. Then it flashed and brightened. Then I saw it was
the railway tracks, but not lying motionless, a pair of silver
parallel lines running straight and flat with hardly any deviation
for a thousand kilometers from Santiago to Puerto Montt. Now
they had come alive as if dancing. They were heaving and
rearing up in the dim afternoon light and resembled two silver
serpents cavorting and rushing toward us at the same time. I
must have made some noise because Spartaco turned and he
too saw these great silver snakes undulating and intertwining
and rollicking toward us, their movement growing ever wilder
as we watched. And then we saw how in the distance the ground
had turned to water, not like the river or lake but like the
ocean itself, great waves of water rushing toward us, but it was
not water, it was the land. It was all the fields to the south
with one wave in front rushing toward us and then all motion
and turmoil and turbulence behind, with the trees heaving
back and forth, and the line of pines leading to the cemetery
looked like a line of galloping horses. And then the bells began
to ring. First off in the distance, a wild tinkling that rose above
the noise of the birds. But then coming closer with the heaving
train tracks and turbulent ocean of the earth. Farm bells. The
bells in the convent. The bells in the German school. The fire
station bells. The bells by the lake. School bells. The bells in
the Church of the Sacred Heart of Jesus. And all this time
Manfredo was searching for us down in the yard as we watched
the trees caught up in this stormy confusion be flung back and
forth, back and forth until their trunks snapped with sharp
explosions. And the cattle burst through the fences of their
pens by the railway as the wave struck the sheds and the sheds
swung back and forth and collapsed. And to the bells and noise
of the birds and the bellowing of the cattle and the explosions
of the trees were added the sounds of wood being bent and
bricks being torn asunder and metal being twisted and all the

plates in the houses at the edge of town and all the chairs and the furniture and the pictures on the walls and the religious statues and all the windows and all the broken fragments of glass were thrown up and back and up like pebbles being shaken in a great tin can. And as the wave of earth came ever closer we saw several parked cars being tossed up and onto their sides and all the chimneys disappearing and flurries of bricks and wooden shingles springing into the air above the houses, and still the wave rushed toward us, and the panels of concrete which made up the street were flung up like playing cards and the façades of the houses toppled or disappeared like curtains being ripped aside and the electrical wires were whipped up and around like skipping ropes, while behind, stretching into the distance all was motion: train tracks, houses, cattle being tossed in the air and the hysterical trees. And still the wave rushed down the street toward us flinging a pickup truck and several farm carts and Luis Castro's Model A Ford, ploughing the concrete and jostling the houses. And suddenly beneath us Manfredo saw where we were hiding, and over all the noise and destruction he shouted, "I see you, I see you! Bang, bang, bang!" And at that precise moment the earthquake struck our yard and Spartaco and I toppled down from the tree, falling from limb to limb, as if the tree had gone crazy and was trying to shake us from its branches like a man shakes water from his hands.

Three minutes. It lasted three minutes. The time it takes to brush one's teeth or recite a poem or drink a glass of milk. We tumbled to the ground and the ground tossed us up again. And in the way that watercolors can blend to solid brown on a pad, so all the noises joined into one roar: Manfredo's yelling, our house collapsing, glass disintegrating, the hospital breaking apart, people screaming, the earth opening, the hospital

ambulance being bounced down the sidewalk on its roof. The
front of our house pitched forward into the street as if the stones
had become liquid, the stucco was flung from the walls, and
such was the noise around us that the collapse of our house
seemed as silent as the raising of a curtain at the start of a
play. And there was the old Mrs. Moedinger downstairs
crouched under her dining room table. And there stood our
mother perched on the high cliff of our kitchen wearing a white
apron and clutching a large white bowl to her breast with a
wooden spoon sticking straight out of it and her mouth open
in a perfect O, and then she fell back and disappeared. There
above me was also my room and my bed with its blue cover
which I had made so carefully that morning and, as I watched,
my bookcase bumped and skipped across the floor and leapt
out into the yard and my books flew into the air and scattered
like a flock of stiff-winged birds. I stood and tried to run but
was immediately thrown to earth again. And all around us
things were falling and striking the earth: branches, bricks
from the chimney, shingles from the roof. Across the street we
saw people in white nightgowns leaping from the third-story
windows of the hospital and their mouths were open and they
were yelling but we heard no sound. And some were naked
and some wore pajamas. And we saw women with newborn
babies jump from the windows as the hospital swung back and
forth tossing bricks and glass from its front like beads of sweat.
And an old woman in a white gown and with thick white legs
ran through the hospital doors and across the yard, hop, hop,
hopping away, while a big white stone, the same color as her
legs, hopped after her. And several blocks away the Church
of the Sacred Heart of Jesus was thrown two feet into the air
and came down again with almost no damage except for broken
windows and toppled pews. And across the street in the Grotto
of the Sacred Virgin, the life-sized statue of the Virgin Mary

fell forward and toppled all the way down the hill, head over feet over head and it was a miracle because it landed on its feet in the road and was undamaged. But a big house next to the church, the house of Omar Valdevenito Teuber, who was rich and had no friends, also fell down the hill and burned and the people inside burned up as well. And Spartaco and I and Manfredo kept trying to run to the house where our mother had disappeared but we kept being thrown to the ground, as if the earth were a blanket whose corners were gripped by four giants and they shook and shook and we all tumbled within it. And now the fires started as the chimneys fell and the cooking and kerosene stoves were overturned. And the convent school collapsed and the German school collapsed completely and if it had been any day other than Sunday many children would have been killed and my grandmother said that was a miracle as well. And downtown my aunts Carmen and Josefina Recabarren were attending the wake of their good friend Florencia Veliz, who had died of cancer, and they fled from the chapel as the lights crashed down around them and the saints fell from their niches, and as they crouched in the street, they turned and bounce, bounce, bounce, the coffin came bouncing out of the chapel and into the street as well. And Nancy Risco fell into a crack in the ground and screamed and screamed until her brother Conrado pulled her out and the crack snapped shut like the teeth of a beast. And the great metal pier extending into Lake Llanquihue collapsed and the water retreated, leaving the sailboats and rowboats stranded in the mud or piled in a heap. The water retreated several hundred yards and many strange things were seen there: the skeleton of a horse, a moss-covered grand piano, a sunken fishing boat that had disappeared in a storm years before, a rust-covered bus that used to travel between Puerto Varas and Puerto Octay. Along the Costanera by the beach the ornate front of the Hotel Playa collapsed and a side wall of the Hotel Bella Vista fell into the parking lot crushing the cars including Pedro Bahamonde's American Buick. And all the windows broke, and all over town all the windows broke. And still the three minutes continued as the fabric or blanket of the earth was snapped and flapped and yanked tight. And at the Odeon my cousin Luis Quintas was seeing Doris Day and Rock Hudson in the movie *Pillow Talk* and part of the ceiling fell and killed his best friend Hugo Opazo sitting right by his side and he dragged Hugo's body into the street and rested his head on the curb. And after that day people didn't want to go into the theater anymore even though the owner kept lowering the price of tickets—it was too dark and the roof was not safe—and so the Odeon went bankrupt and was turned into shops. And the tanks of milk at the dairy burst and flooded the streets. And the roulette wheels were thrown across the big room in the casino at the Grand Hotel of Puerto Varas and never worked right again. And above my grandmother's house the four-thousand-liter concrete water tank crashed to the ground and the barn fell down and the granaries fell down and the house moved a foot on its foundation and the walls cracked. And a locomotive in the train station tumbled onto its side and the great kitchen stove at the Club Alemán burst into flames and the huge gasoline tank of the Copec station on Santa Rosa fell and burst into flames and the great pyramids of apples and pears and winter squash at the market collapsed and rolled down the street and the dogs ran in circles and bit their tails and the cats hid and people stood and were thrown to the ground and stood and were thrown down again and on the corner of Puente and Bio Bio my father in his underwear crouched in the street with his mistress Elisa Anabalon Schwabe and a piece of brick flew toward him and smashed his head and took his life and then it was over, the earthquake was over, the noise stopped and for a moment everything was silent except for the sounds of falling things and the air was full of the crying of the birds, and then came the screams of the people.

I was crouched in the yard and Spartaco had his arms around me. Manfredo crouched near us still clutching my father's revolver and the moment the earth stopped tossing and jerking us he jumped up and took the revolver with great rage and terror and he threw it back toward the remains of our house shouting, "No, no!" and after that he did not speak again for he felt the earthquake had been his fault, a punishment for taking and shooting the revolver, and his knowledge was a rough hand pushing against him, a thick finger pressing down on his tongue. And then my mother came running out of the front of the house and swept us up and we were all crying but I also felt glad because I was alive. I felt I had been given something important because everything around me was torn or broken yet I was still whole.

The yard was full of clothes and papers and bits of furniture and leaves. Spartaco ran into the house of old Mrs. Moedinger, ran to where she was still hiding under the dining room table which was covered with plaster. Gently he helped her out of the house, stepping across the ruins of her living room wall with its picture of her dead husband lost at sea, and she stared around her as if this were her first moment on earth and all was new to her and she hardly seemed to notice Spartaco's hand upon her arm. My mother was crying and kept turning this way and that. She seemed uncertain about what she should do and took a few steps in one direction, then a few steps in another and after a few minutes she began gathering up the clothes in the yard, not putting them down but pressing them to her chest so she seemed to grow bigger and bigger. Mrs. Moedinger stared around her and she at last pulled free of Spartaco but kept her hands stretched in front of her, like someone moving through the dark, and then slowly she began picking up bricks and carrying them to the edge of her house, but almost mindlessly as if her brain were empty except for some muddled tidying instinct.

All this time there were screams from the hospital. People were lying all over the grass and parking lot as if randomly tossed there and many had blood on their faces and arms. Others were wandering around and the thin rivulets of blood crisscrossing their faces made it seem they were wearing masks. Doctors and nurses were calling to each other. The street was full of rubble, several overturned cars, broken pieces of wood. I saw my books everywhere. The air smelled of smoke and eucalyptus. We heard fire sirens and their wailing blended with the crying of the people. The trucks, as we learned later, were unable to leave the fire station because the concrete panels of the roads had been tilted up and down until they resembled a line of *W*'s. Many buildings were on fire and pipes had burst and electrical wires hung broken from their poles.

After Spartaco had helped Mrs. Moedinger from her house, he hurried across the road to the hospital and I stood up to join him but my knees felt so weak that I could hardly walk. People were crying and moaning but in a stunned sort of way as if they needed to hear the sound of their own voices and be reassured by them, and their surprise seemed equal to their hurt. A young woman in a white hospital gown had fallen near the buckled sidewalk and her leg was bent back beneath her. Spartaco tried to turn the woman over to free her leg and she cried out and tried to push him away. A man with a black beard hurried up to help him. The yard was covered with glass and mud, and the white and bloody gowns of the patients were becoming filthy. I felt dazed by the noise, by the crying and screaming, but slowly I crossed the street as well. The ground was wet and the air cold and raw. Nurses were carrying blankets out of the front doors of the hospital. No one wanted to go back inside. During the next few minutes the doctors and nurses began shifting people so they lay in long muddy rows and to each one they gave a blanket. I lost sight of Spartaco who had hurried off with a nurse. I found a chair in the road and sat down on it until my legs felt stronger. The road was so disrupted and upheaved and filled with stones that I didn't see how it could ever be used again. Even a donkey would find it difficult to walk. At best the road had become one of the few dry places to sit.

I found it strange how some houses had suffered no damage while others were completely collapsed, a random punishment that cared nothing for the people involved; for why was our house destroyed while next door the house of Mr. Luttecke, who threw stones at us whenever we crossed his yard, was undamaged except for broken windows? Along with the cries of the people it sounded as if every dog in town was barking, and off in the fields the cows, too, were still bellowing and full of protest. I saw my mother standing next to a pile of our clothes, not knowing what to do with them. Mrs. Moedinger was still picking up stones. People were wandering around as if they had a thousand errands, a thousand tasks, and didn't know what to do first. A spotted horse galloped through our backyard and its eyes seemed huge and white. Glancing up I saw my favorite doll hanging from a branch of an apple tree. The doll's name was Isabella and she wore a red gown and went to many balls. I asked Manfredo to help me get her down from the tree, but he would neither answer nor move from his place on the ground.

It was growing colder. The street filled with more and more people and some were hardly dressed but no one made any move to go back indoors. People stood in small groups and spoke quietly to each other. Some wept. Some were angry. One man was laughing. A woman walked by cradling the plaster statue of a saint as one might hold a baby. Their behavior frightened me: no one was acting as they should. All their assumptions had been swept aside. All their plans for the next moment and the moments after had been made irrelevant. Many people had clumsy bandages around their heads or hands or arms. Their clothes were dirty. It was hard not to think of the earthquake as a punishment inflicted because of something we had done without knowing: some wicked action which had seemed innocent to us and which we might keep doing, unaware of the additional punishments which were even then preparing themselves.

A half hour after the earthquake there came a tremor which lasted about ten seconds. A few bricks fell. Despite how brief it was, I was amazed at the panic it caused, the crying and screaming, the uncertain running around. Even the badly injured wrapped in their blankets tried to crawl or hobble toward the street. But where could they go? I suddenly recognized the several dead lying in the hospital yard for they were the only immovable ones, the ones who didn't try to escape. I was with old Mrs. Moedinger and she fell down at my feet and began to shiver and it surprised me that someone at the end of her life should have such terror about the passing of her life, as if there were so many things she still wanted to do. I didn't realize that life's sweet taste is always with us. I thought it was mine only because I was young. But I sat with her and patted her back and told her not to worry, and to console her made me feel very grown up.

She refused to be consoled and it was Mrs. Moedinger whom I first heard express the idea that one later heard everywhere. "It's just the beginning. The earth will swallow us all."

I had nothing to say to this, but continued to sit with her

until I was distracted by the sudden appearance of a young Mapuche girl named Rosa who often worked for my parents. She was crying and she ran to my mother and said something and then my mother began crying as well. They were standing by the corner of the house. My mother pushed her hands into her hair and began pulling it violently and I could see the white of her teeth and eyes as if her whole face were shaking and moving very quickly. Abruptly my mother ran off down the street and Rosa ran after her. I started to follow but they were running too fast and I knew I would lose them. Besides, I was afraid of leaving Manfredo who was still crouched on the ground. It was only later that I learned that Rosa had told her of my father's death, and it was years before I heard the true circumstances: how my father was lying almost naked in the street with Elisa Anabalon Schwabe, who had removed her brassiere to wipe the blood from his face. My mother never mentioned any of this to me. Even now she contends that my father died while rescuing an old woman from a burning house. But others told me how my mother drove Elisa Anabalon away and tried to hit her with a stick and how she screamed and threw rocks at her.

My mother had been afraid of my father when he was alive, but in death he was sufficiently docile and so she appropriated him at last. Finding a wheelbarrow, she and Rosa loaded my father into it and wheeled him through the broken streets to the house of the mortician who had buried my father's mother. And although many people died that day my father was the first to arrive at the mortuary, the first to be prepared for burial, the first to be put into the ground. And Spartaco said it was as if our father had had the privilege of leading the others into Heaven. But my grandmother shook her head and disagreed and clearly she did not believe that Heaven had been his destination.

The afternoon was ending. There was no electricity and I was worried about the night and what we would do in the darkness. Manfredo and I were sitting by the pile of clothes that my mother had collected, as if to protect them from thieves. Although I tried to talk to him, he refused to answer and his eyes were full of guilt. I was afraid he would be cold so I dressed him with clothes from the pile, as if he were one of my dolls, so that he wore one of my father's sweaters and my mother's short fur coat. Across the street I would occasionally see Spartaco busy with a doctor or nurse. Most of the people still looked distracted and many wandered around aimlessly. They called to each other or shouted and occasionally there would come a crashing as stones fell or part of a wall gave way. A red-haired fireman hurried down the street with a megaphone and warned people not to use their stoves because the chimneys were cracked or destroyed. And some people laughed at the idea of going back into their houses or going under any roof at all.

I was growing increasingly anxious and was still waiting for my mother to return, when I saw my uncle, Alcibiades Droppelman Schiele, walking quickly toward us down the street. I jumped up, waving and calling his name, and he ran across the yard toward me. Before I could even speak he gathered me up and squeezed me to his chest.

Alcibiades was my favorite uncle and my mother's younger brother. He was then about thirty-five and he worked as manager and part owner of a clothing store right downtown on San Pedro across from the post office. He had wonderful blond wavy hair that was fine like a girl's and a blond mustache. I thought he was terribly handsome but his chin was small and it gave his face an uncertain look. He was tall and thin and very kind. Whenever he talked to me, he would sit down or kneel so that our eyes were on the same level. His eyes were gray, the color of stone, and sometimes looking into them I felt lost in their depths.

"Where are your parents?" he asked.

I told him that I didn't know and explained how my father had been away and that my mother had run off with Rosa and how she had been weeping. And I was weeping, too, although I didn't know why, and the sobs kept catching in my throat until I could hardly talk. And then Manfredo began to cry as well. Spartaco had joined us and we all stood around my uncle, who was bending over us, touching his brown leather jacket or arm or shoulder as if he were the one safe place.

"We'll go to your grandmother's," he said. "Put on something warm."

It seemed that all the clothes in the pile belonged to my parents and not to us. Spartaco put on a dark leather coat of my father's that was much too big for him. Manfredo continued to wear the fur coat and I found a blue wool coat of my mother's which was so long that it dragged on the ground. So we set off and in our grown-up clothes we looked like three adults who had been suddenly shrunk, as if this shrinking were just another effect of the earthquake. As we left the yard, I picked up my bruised copy of Louisa May Alcott's *Little Men*, which I had already read twice but knew I wanted to read again. Manfredo picked up a little statue of St. Christopher carrying the Christ Child, which had stood on my parents' dresser, and as we walked he carefully wiped the mud from the tiny faces.

We walked down the street making constant detours around fallen trees, broken wagons, furniture, the disrupted panels of concrete. Many people stood as if they had absolutely nothing to occupy them, no place to go. A few were rescuing their possessions from their destroyed houses, making little piles of property in their yards: a bed, a radio, a lamp, some clothes. Some people were bandaged or had crutches or canes or even an old broom to prop themselves up. Some stood as if asleep. One man lay on a narrow cot in his front yard and he wore a new blue suit and his hands were crossed on his chest and his eyes were shut and his wife and five children stood around him weeping, all except the smallest boy who was staring up into a tree.

Many houses had lost their façades and I found it fascinating to look into these rooms. It was like overhearing secrets. Some were neat, some messy. Some had expensive furniture, some were shabby. In one exposed living room hung the tilted painting of a very pink and very naked woman lying on a couch, while across the street several men with heads tilted at the same angle stared up at it in respectful silence. But in most rooms the pictures had fallen and on the walls were arrangements of lighter colored squares where they had once hung; and often the wallpaper had come loose and hung rumpled on the walls just like colored bed sheets. The rooms suggested a sort of domestic tranquillity, a coziness, which seemed not simply distant but bogus, a lie which had once held our attention. One house was burning ferociously while people watched and did nothing. The heat made my face flush and the fire's crackling and popping was like a noisy conversation. Elsewhere in town I could see smoke from other fires. Dogs ran by on nervous errands. It was hard not to see the houses as if they had been constructed from blocks or cardboard or playing cards which some bad child had cast down. Manfredo and I held our uncle's hands while Spartaco walked some yards ahead. People were looking at everything very hard, staring hard, and it seemed I could feel their eye muscles ache. There was so much to see!

After several blocks we turned and crossed the railway tracks toward the fields that led to my grandmother's house. The tracks were all bent and had been ripped loose from their beds. In places they resembled silver corkscrews. Sheds had fallen. A cattle car was lying on its side. The cattle pens were all broken open and the cattle gone. One cow was lying dead and Alcibiades said that it probably had had a heart attack. He said many chickens had had heart attacks as well.

"It's harder on the animals," he said. "Their sense of betrayal is much worse."

"We might have been like that if you hadn't come," I said, and I tried to picture myself lying rigid with fear until the life passed from me.

"I thought of you right away," he said. "I was at the store and came as soon as I could."

Alcibiades was unmarried and that probably encouraged the romantic feelings I had about him. The previous summer he had broken off with a woman to whom he had been engaged for as long as I could remember, although perhaps it was only for several years. She taught school and was very nice. His life, as I came to realize, was governed by a kind of indecisiveness and a fear of diminishing options. He had had several girlfriends, several jobs, had lived in several different apartments, and whenever he did something long enough so that it appeared to be growing permanent he suddenly broke it off.

Even so, I think he fantasized about the perfect wife, the perfect job, the perfect place to live. And maybe that was the trouble. Imperfections haunted him and it seemed he could stay with nothing if there were the slightest chance that it might not work out, that his choice might prove to be the wrong one. His mother, as I came to understand much later, had somehow convinced her children they were not destined for success and that even leaving home was a kind of betrayal. She had also taught them that disappointment came to every person and it was useless to struggle against it. The result in the case of Alcibiades was that he had grown hesitant and many times he let the occasion make the choice rather than letting himself choose the occasion. He didn't seek out jobs, he took the one that fell open at the right moment. He didn't seek out a place to live, but took the place that suddenly fell vacant. He didn't pursue women but was seduced by the one who cared enough to penetrate his shyness. Even so, he was full of hope and in those days he had a sort of enthusiasm that the right job or place to live or woman was waiting only a few days ahead in his future.

Although Alcibiades was stunned by the earthquake, he also felt exhilarated. We were alive and our lives felt like a gift. Other people had been packed off to Heaven or Hell, but for the time being we remained safe. Alcibiades had also come to hate his position at the clothing store and the fact the store had been destroyed was very liberating to him. It had been open for inventory that afternoon and he had been working when the earthquake struck, counting shirts and stacking them in tall piles. He laughed and said that when the building began to shake five of the women clerks ran to him, grabbed his arms and begged him to save them.

"I told them to get out fast," he said. "You should have seen them scamper. The moment we got outside the ceiling caved in. Of course the windows went, too."

"And were you hurt?" I asked.

"Not a scratch. One woman fell and twisted her ankle but I think she's all right."

When Alcibiades talked to children, he always spoke as if we were contemporaries, and he had a way of touching people lightly when he talked to them, both children and adults, touching a shoulder or arm, maybe straightening a collar, which felt very intimate and special. That day he was wearing gray pants and a white shirt and his brown leather jacket was spotted with patches of light-colored dust.

As we proceeded up across the field we became aware of the strangeness of the sky. The air was dusty and it gave the day's last light a yellow quality. Looking back down the hill toward town, we saw it as through a yellow filter. I had the feeling that it wasn't my town but a strange ruined place that had been hastily switched with my town. There were clouds of steam, smoke and dust. There were more than a dozen fires. We saw the rubble of the convent school, the overturned locomotive in the railway yard, destroyed office buildings, collapsed houses, the ruin of the streets, the snapped and broken trees. The water from the lake had come back, but it hadn't stopped at the shore, but had continued into town several hundred yards to the town square, putting out the fire at the Copec station and flooding the ground floor of three of the hotels. We could see bucket brigades getting water for several fires, especially for the one at the Club Alemán. I had many school friends down there and I wondered what they were doing and even if they were alive or had bandages around their heads like people I had seen at the hospital. Several lived not far away and I looked for their houses and couldn't find them. Above us in the field the great eucalyptus had lost one of its two trunks which had crashed to the ground and the air was full of its smell. In the distance to the south I could see cattle running. Vultures were descending in sleepy spirals. When we crossed into the sheep meadow we found the first of a number of dead sheep.

"Is that also a heart attack?" I asked. But then I saw the blood and saw how the sheep's throat had been ripped out and my question seemed foolish.

"I don't know what it is," said Alcibiades.

We came upon a second sheep and a third. Their throats were torn out as well and their legs looked bitten.

"Maybe there are wild dogs," suggested Spartaco and we all moved a step or two closer to Alcibiades.

We were halfway across the meadow when another tremor took us by surprise. Suddenly it was shaking us like a bumpy ride in a wagon. At first I thought it was another earthquake, a big one, because this one was stronger and it became hard to keep on our feet. The birds were all screaming and from the town, too, we heard a distant shouting as people were overswept by terror. I turned to my uncle and was surprised by how rigid his face looked. Manfredo began to whimper and pressed the small statue of St. Christopher to his forehead. Spartaco's eyes got very big. I bent my knees and thought I would fall. Perhaps it lasted thirty seconds. The eucalyptus shook as if in a storm and more of its leaves swirled off into the air. I saw a sudden puff of dust downtown where a wall or building collapsed and there was a rumbling noise like a faraway avalanche. I imagined the panic at the hospital, the nervous running, and I wondered where my mother and father were.

The moment the ground became quiet we began hurrying up the hill toward my grandmother's house. From the field in front we could see the tops of the six downstairs windows divided equally by the front door. All were broken and several shutters were missing but at least the house was standing and the roof looked solid. The house was shingled with yellow wooden shingles and many had fallen which gave the front wall a freckled look. Although there were no dormers, the second floor was quite large with six rooms as well as storage rooms and a large open windowless room in the center where we often played on rainy days and where there was a radio. Another long storage room, used for storing wheat, formed a third floor or attic under the ridgepole of the pitched roof. The house had a wing in the back for the kitchens and pantries and which extended into the farmyard like the short leg of the letter *L*. An ornately carved front door formed the town entrance and a plain back door was the farm entrance. As we approached the front gate Spartaco saw that the water tank which usually rose up to the left of the house had disappeared. A few feet from the gate we discovered another dead sheep. The front gate stood open as did the door of the house. It was windy on the hill and the wind made a whispering in the grass. Leaves and bits of paper were caught up in little spirals on the front porch. As we passed into the yard, Alcibiades glanced back over his shoulder.

"Look," he said.

A great black cloud was moving toward the town from the south, not like a storm cloud but truly black, a piece of midnight broken off from the darkness and floating into the twilight of early evening. Beyond the lake the volcanoes were invisible. Under the shadow of the cloud, the water of the lake appeared black as well.

"What is it?" asked Spartaco.

Alcibiades tilted back his head to survey the sky. "Maybe dust," he said.

In the strange light Puerto Varas looked very fragile and I almost expected a great hand to come out of the black cloud, grasp the town between its fingers and crumple it as if it were constructed from paper and tin. It made me want to get indoors even though indoors wasn't safe anymore.

But I couldn't think that of my grandmother's house and I hurried up the steps and crossed the porch. Then I stopped and what I saw filled me with dismay. Beyond the door was the hall that ran to the back, equally dividing the house. Like the rest of the house, it was always immaculate, no dust, nothing out of place. The hall was very dim but as I looked into it I saw broken tables and chairs, religious pictures fallen from the walls, broken glass and bits of wood. Again I felt that this was some false place, a changeling place which had been traded for the house I had always known. Then I heard voices ahead of me and, catching my breath, I hurried into the hall toward my grandmother's room, kicking and stumbling over the rubble on the floor.

My grandmother's room was on the left beyond the stairs and looking onto the farmyard. Reaching the doorway, I paused. The room was full of bright candles. There was my grandmother, my two great aunts, then my aunt Dalila as well, then two of the maids all kneeling in the center of the room and praying in strained and nearly hysterical voices. It was like a wake, but their voices were too loud and their words came tumbling out in a rush. The twenty or so candles flickered in the draft from the door while the floor around them twinkled with broken glass and jewelry.

My grandmother in a black dress was kneeling before a statue of the Virgin Mary which stood on the seat of a chair. Statues of saints surrounded the Virgin in a half circle and candles stood behind them. Hearing me at the door, my grandmother turned and cocked her head like a bird. Then she pushed herself up to her feet, scrunching her eyes in order to see. She took a few rolling steps and when she recognized me she began to smile a wonderfully warm and beatific smile. Her whole face was wreathed in happiness as she held out her hands and hurried toward me.

"We're going to die," she said, bending over so I could kiss her cheek. "Your father's there already."

2

FOR MY FIFTH birthday my father gave me a cow: not a real cow and not quite a toy cow, but a creature made from cow hide with a foolish head and real horns and a tail that must have been real, at least it smelled real and after a few days my mother made my father throw the tail away and replace it with a piece of braided rawhide. My cow also had real hooves and they smelled as well but at least they stayed. The cow was on a sort of platform with wheels and I could ride it if someone pulled me. My mother wouldn't let it inside the house and it lived in the shed in the backyard for about a year until some dogs ripped it to pieces. I named my cow José and I was always after my father or Spartaco to pull me. Once my father attached José to the back of his car and drove very slowly, but when I fell off he didn't hear me and drove away, leaving me sobbing in the street and my mother was furious.

And when I was six my father took Spartaco and me camping in the national park Vicente Pérez Rosales in the hills above the Lake of All the Saints and almost under the shadow of the volcano Osorno. We camped for three days and cooked over a fire and slept in a tent and on the third day I fell and sprained my ankle and my father carried me out many, many kilometers because he thought it was broken, and as we walked Spartaco sang my favorite songs to distract me from the pain. My father was wearing a sheepskin coat and I can smell that mixture of lanolin and sweat even today. It took him all afternoon to get to the car and he never complained and I kissed his cheek and told him I loved him and felt the bristles of his three-day beard scrape my mouth.

And now he was dead and I understood this to mean that he would be forever absent. His smell was dead, his laugh was dead, the peculiar softness of his hands was gone forever. He had often left on trips to buy cattle; now he wasn't coming back. There was no way to write or to telephone, no one to carry messages except the saints. The peculiar rasping of his voice had joined the silence of the air. Now he was memory and I thought that if I had had any warning I would have looked at him much harder. He had gone out that day around noon. He was in a bad mood and he and my mother had been quarreling. When he left we had only looked at each other. At first he had given me a dark look, then he shrugged and tried to smile. I had hurried to the window and watched his back depart down the street through the rain. He had a tweed jacket on but his head was bare and as he turned the corner he pulled up his collar. A smudge of black hair, the wide expanse of his shoulders and now he would be absent forever. The hole in the air at the corner through which he had disappeared had closed tight, leaving him on one side and me on the other. The sound of the air closing up was the sound of the earthquake itself and people said it was a sound like a gigantic freight train, but it wasn't that: it was the sound of my father going away.

When the meaning of my grandmother's words grew clear to me, it felt like something hot and suffocating was being pressed over my mouth and I couldn't breathe. I pulled away and ran into the farmyard. Someone had come from town with the bare fact of my father's death and at that time my grandmother still thought of him as a hero: that her son-in-law had gone to join her son Gabriel in Heaven and soon the ground would open up and the rest of us would joyously follow. Later, when she learned that my father had been with his mistress, she stopped talking about him and it became as if he had never existed, as if my mother had had her children in some way free of sexual intercourse and male assistance.

The farmyard was enclosed on nearly all four sides with space only for a driveway between the back of the kitchen and the line of sheds. The rear of the house and kitchen formed a right angle while the sheds and barn formed another right angle to make an almost complete square. One of the sheds had fallen and the barn was tilting dangerously. In the corner farthest from the house was a gate leading into the orchard. On either side of the gate was a doghouse, each with a captive dog. These dogs, as far as I remember, were never set free from their chains and so had become a little crazy. There was a large gray dog and a small orange one. The large one was old with a deep bark that sounded like "Ouch, ouch, ouch." His name was Peppo and he bit people. The smaller dog was called Margarita. She had to be tied because when she got loose she chased the chickens and killed them by lying down on top of them and suffocating them. Margarita had no bark at all, most likely, according to my great-aunt, because of all the feathers that had gotten stuck in her throat. Instead, she had a sort of squeak like a rubber mouse that one might squeeze over and over. These dogs were my good friends.

That afternoon, however, they refused to leave their houses. I could hardly even see their noses. I crouched down next to Peppo's door and cried and cried for the death of my father, while Peppo crouched inside and made nervous growling noises. And as I grieved for my father, so he grieved for the confusion of the earth, and really it seemed that our grief was very similar. I tried to think what it would mean for my father to be gone forever and I worried that I would become like my four cousins who lived on a farm and whose father had drowned in the River Maullin. Everyone called them wild and their wildness was blamed on the fact that they had no father. And that was true. My cousin Otto was the wildest; he once brought his horse into the house and rode it around the dining room table. He was a year older than Spartaco and liked to do nothing but ride and hunt. He had many dogs and once when we were visiting he sicced one of his dogs on me and made me squat down perfectly still. If I tried to run, he said the dog would bite me. Then he got on his horse and galloped back and forth, making the horse jump over me. I remember its hooves cutting the air only inches, it seemed, above my head. And now we might become wild as well and I wept and wept. I did not know what happened to wild children, but I knew they had neither friends nor peace of mind.

I had been crouched down by the doghouse for about five minutes when Anna, a Mapuche Indian girl who worked in the kitchen, came out to comfort me. She was about fourteen and, like many Mapuches, she was short and squat as if something big had pushed down on top of her and squashed her. Her hair was black and shiny.

"Why do you cry?" she said, kneeling down beside me and touching my shoulder. "Soon you will be with him again."

"But he is dead."

"Your grandmother says that was just the beginning. Soon the ground will open up and we will be taken up to Heaven and we will all eat cake, even me. Look, perhaps it is starting again."

"What do you mean?" I asked.

"The chickens," said Anna.

As I looked, the chickens came squawking from all over the

yard and pushed and heaped up together into a noisy group near my uncle's mustard-colored Opel. Immediately afterward the ground began to shake and deep within his doghouse Peppo made a mournful howling noise. The tremor lasted about ten seconds but it showed me how animals could feel it coming before human beings, and whenever we saw the chickens all crowding together or the horses and cows suddenly lie down with their legs splayed out in all directions or the birds fly into the air we knew that another tremor was coming.

This time, as the earth shook, my brother Spartaco came running out the back door of the house. He was red-eyed and I could see he had been crying. Manfredo elected to stay with my grandmother who had taken him under her wing, and he chose to stay with her even though the house might fall down around them. Alcibiades hurried out as well, followed by my aunt Dalila, who was married to my oldest uncle, Hellmuth Droppelman Schiele, even though she was nearly fifteen years younger than he. My aunt was very fearful and she threw herself on Alcibiades, who had to comfort her and speak to her soothingly. Dalila Muñóz Irribarra was an exceptionally beautiful woman, as I see now, although in those days I was mostly struck by her masses of black hair. She had married my uncle when she was only seventeen and at the time of the earthquake they had been married fourteen years. They had no children. I came to realize that my uncle Hellmuth saw this as her fault, that she was a barren woman, although much later when she was married again she had several sons and daughters.

I had known her all of my life and heard about her for long after the earthquake as well. Now she has been dead for many years and, because of all my wondering about her and the destruction she caused, it seems that I now see her best of all. What did I know of her as a child, just that she was talkative and laughing and plump? But even then I had the sense that it didn't matter whom she talked to, that she talked for the sake of talking and not to say anything in particular. Later I decided that she used speech in the same way a porpoise makes noises to test its sonar: she talked simply to bang the noises off the surrounding walls so she could recognize where they were and move between them. She also talked to keep people's attention from moving too far away from her, to summon their consciousness back to her again. Her talking was like the tug of a leash. I came to believe that she could just as easily count out loud or read the obituaries out loud or name all the countries of the world and all the kinds of fish. She didn't talk to convey information but to register her presence. Her talk was like the squeak of a motor and one had the sense that one could stop the noise simply by oiling her.

But she was very beautiful, a kind of sexual beauty that I had no sense of but that even Spartaco recognized, and many times I found him standing near her. She was also, I came to see, one of those people who work very hard to make you like them. The way they touch you or speak softly to you or look at you—all their gestures are intended to draw you to them. But once they have captured you, then that is enough, their vanity has been satisfied. There is nothing more they want you to do and, indeed, at the point you become enamored of them, you even become dangerous, you threaten to compete with their self-love, you become the weaker leg of a love triangle and they hurriedly push you away.

Dalila had masses of black hair which she constantly fooled with and which dominated her face, as if her hair had grown a head and not the other way around. Her father was a barber in Puerto Montt and she had once learned to manicure nails. Consequently, she judged everybody by how well their nails were done, even my grandfather, whose nails, as she often said, were a sight. I think she was afraid of my grandmother and rather overwhelmed by her. Her husband, Hellmuth, loved her very much but she exasperated him and he often thought her a fool. On her part she pretended to ignore him or tried to embarrass him, although I came to realize that she was completely under his control. It is often hard to arrive at a clear understanding about couples and their lives together, since that sexual dimension, which dominates most of their existence, remains hidden from us.

Dalila was terrified by the earthquake. She had a vivid sense of the incompleteness of her life and was frightened of her days coming to an end before the world gave her what it owed her, or what she felt it had promised. Additionally, the earthquake was an occasion for drama. Dalila wept with her head on Alcibiades's shoulder and he seemed almost lost in her hair. He stiffly patted her back.

"It's nothing," he kept saying. "It's over now."

Dalila had a fear, which I came to see was very common, of the earth opening up, of falling into a crack or fissure and having the earth snap shut again, of being buried alive.

"Let me stay with you," she said. "I'm sure it's going to happen again. Oh, look at my shoe, it's all scuffed. Everything's so dirty."

We looked down at her shoes, which were white sling-back pumps. Across the vamp of the left shoe was a black smudge. Because of the indignation in her voice one felt that despite the damage done to the house, the destruction of the town and the many deaths, here on her shoe was a devastation which she could at last comprehend.

"A little water will take care of that," said Alcibiades.

"They're ruined. Everything's ruined. And my nice house, I don't even want to think of it. My closets must be a mess." Here she began weeping again and Alcibiades resumed patting her back, but in a stiff-wristed sort of way, as if his hand burned when he touched her.

Even I, at eight years old, was struck by her self-obsession and I was surprised at my uncle for paying attention to her. But Alcibiades was a shy man and he was grateful to Dalila for pushing aside his shyness. In truth, I doubt she noticed. She dealt with men by flirting with them, even the local priest. It strikes me that she had no women friends, while I, of course, was nearly invisible to her. But she had a special smile for Spartaco and I expect even Manfredo, as *homo en potencialis*, had made a mark upon her eye. If someone, however, had accused her of flirting or of dressing seductively, she would have been indignant. Men were simply the environment she moved through and her coquettishness was the grease that eased the movement. It existed almost, but not quite, for its own sake—in that the attention she received flattered her vanity—but it was not intended to lead anyplace or entangle her with other men. Alcibiades, I expect, saw her as romantic and liberated and in control of herself, as being above convention: all those things which he was not. And of course this led to problems.

But on that evening of the earthquake with the sun setting and with so much confusion about where people were and what had happened to them, with my own grief over the death of my father and our sense that our world had not only changed but actually might be coming to an end, our behavior was vague and thoughtless and we had no idea of consequences. All we had were our feelings for each other. And the moment that Alcibiades disentangled himself from Dalila, he hurried to me, picked me up and embraced me, sharing in my grief. And even Dalila dabbed a handkerchief to her eyes and admitted there had been many losses.

My grandmother then came out of the house with her two sisters, followed by Manfredo and one of the farm workers. The chimneys in the kitchen had collapsed, meaning that the stove couldn't be used and something had to be constructed outside so that food could be prepared and water boiled. Additionally, everyone except my grandmother was afraid of staying in the house. Although they were ready for the earth to open up and take them away as a group, they didn't like the idea of having the ceiling come crashing down on them.

My great aunts, Bibiana and Clotilde Schiele Grob, were eight and fourteen years younger than my grandmother. They had been her little sisters as children and they were little sisters still. Neither had married; my grandmother hadn't permitted it. Bibiana was round and quite lazy. She was in charge of the garden, but, as my father used to say, she gardened through the window, telling the servants where to dig, what to prune, what to pick. Consequently, she was very happy.

All her life Bibiana had been under the thumb of my grandmother and as a result had remained rather childlike, constantly deferring to my grandmother and being almost unable to think and act on her own, as if her older sister were also her tongue and muscles and feet. But she was good-natured and forever laughing and she found the fact of the earthquake quite funny, except when there was a tremor. Now I believe she was unable to see the seriousness of any situation, unable to imagine any future event. She was rather chubby and red-faced and perpetually out of breath. She kept a man's white handkerchief pinned to her bodice and whenever she laughed, she unpinned the handkerchief and first wiped one eye and then the other. Her laughter bore some similarity to the earthquakes themselves. As the earth always seemed on the verge of a tremor, so Bibiana seemed on the edge of laughter and when she began to laugh all her surfaces were overthrown and she had to sit down. We children liked her very much, although we knew better than to count on her for anything.

Her sister Clotilde was very different, both in shape and manner. She was thin and dry, like a dry piece of fruit, and she was a great complainer. Clearly, she had been very much the baby and at fifty-seven there was still much baby about her. She had twice nearly married and once nearly became a nun, but had done neither because, I think, of the interference of my grandmother. One man who had been her fiancé now owned a restaurant in Puerto Varas called the Asturias and whenever he held a banquet or catered a large wedding or did something that obviously brought him a lot of money, my great-aunt Clotilde would darkly refer to their former intimacy as a great financial loss to the family, although I doubt they ever did more than hold hands. Clotilde had a thin, expectant face with dark, suspicious eyes as if everything she had received in life were somehow substandard. In fact she always expected to be cheated and was constantly going over tradesmen's bills for discrepancies. And if ever she found one, she became such an avenging angel that the very mention of her name would cause many local shop owners to shake their heads and look depressed. Her fingers were long and thin with long red nails and she had several rings with red stones. The fingers had a rapacious quality and if she was angry at one of the children she would catch hold of one of their arms and squeeze and I still remember the bite of her fingernails pressing against my skin.

Clotilde's best quality was that she told marvelous stories. Most, if not all, dealt with disappointment—brides left waiting at the church, money that came too late, illnesses that were not diagnosed in time—and she sighed wonderfully, raising herself up and then diminishing with a great release of air, getting smaller and smaller to the accompaniment of a falling cry, which, according to my father, was like the distant cry of someone falling from a cliff. Spartaco would imitate her sigh and my mother would laugh until the tears came to her eyes.

Even though my grandmother was the first to hurry into the farmyard, she seemed to surround the others. Wreathed in smiles and with her sailor walk, she looked somewhat mechanical, as if she might have a key protruding from the middle of her back. Immediately she began giving directions to her sisters, the workman, Alcibiades and even Dalila. Bricks had to be collected from the fallen chimneys in order to make an open stove in the yard. Tarpaulins had to be taken from the shed and some sort of shelter erected. Dry firewood and lanterns had to be found. As she issued these orders she also kept making irritated yet anxious asides as to where her husband might be and what had happened to her other two sons and two daughters. Didn't they know their mother needed them? What kind of children would leave their mother at a time like this? And her husband, had she ever been able to count on him? My grandfather had driven that afternoon to an *asado*, or ox roast, out in the country. Now, of course, the roads were impassable. As for her older daughter, Miriam, she lived in the city of Puerto Montt twenty kilometers to the south with her four children and her husband, Freddy Piwonka Gray. They had been planning to come that afternoon for tea, all except Freddy who was often busy. "Aren't we good enough for him?" my grandmother demanded. "He has too many plans. He knows too many pretty women."

Although my grandmother seemed to love her two sons-in-law and one daughter-in-law, she also made it clear that her children had married against her best advice. However, it wasn't the spouses she disapproved of but the institution of marriage. It robbed a mother of her children and my grandmother disliked anyone moving away. She didn't see the point of it. She was the sworn enemy of fragmentation and dispersal. My grandmother was still alive when I married sixteen years later and, although totally blind and not entirely coherent, she focused herself enough to tell me that it was a bad idea. And considering how it turned out, perhaps she was right.

She was also worried about the whereabouts of her two other sons, her oldest and youngest children, Hellmuth and Walterio. Both lived in town and both had been expected for tea. Dalila had driven up earlier and Hellmuth had been intending to walk. "And where are they now?" asked my grandmother. "Don't they realize that tea time has come and gone?"

"The earthquake," suggested Bibiana.

My grandmother dismissed this inadequate excuse. "This is their home and I need them."

She grieved, too, I think, for the death of my father. But it wasn't his death that bothered her so much as that he had died before the rest of us. He hadn't waited. He shouldn't have been fooling around in town. He should have brought his wife and children directly to my grandmother's house where they could have prepared themselves for the final calamity. Didn't he realize that major earthquakes were always signaled by tremors? Well, the earthquake that afternoon had been such a signal and a worse earthquake was obviously coming. Mixed with these ideas were my grandmother's religious convictions, which were quite passionate. I expect that she and her sisters attended mass at least five times a week besides doing volunteer work at the German convent where they had all gone to school. My grandmother seemed to believe that Jesus and Mary and her favorite saints lived on some platform not very high above us, maybe fifteen or twenty meters, and that they patrolled this platform like guards on a prison wall keeping an eye on the convicts. This at least was the idea she gave to us children. As for God, he was on an even higher platform. When the final earthquake came, the saints would let down ladders and we would all scramble up. "That's why there are so many saints," my grandmother would tell me, "just because we're going to need a lot of ladders."

I am not sure to what degree I believed this, but I loved my grandmother and felt safe with her. I also still felt stunned by the earthquake and the memory of the wreckage of our house and my books lying all over the yard. And then there was the death of my father and that knowledge was like a knife that kept sticking me over and over. Spartaco, too, felt overwhelmed by our father's death and he stayed by my side and looked miserable. But he was also trying to act bravely, and he would turn away whenever he began to cry and shake his head and feel angry with himself. When he had stopped crying, he would look at me crossly and I would lay my hand on the sleeve of my father's leather coat which Spartaco kept buttoned right up to his neck. It was all so confusing that I wanted nothing so much as to climb into the doghouse with Peppo and say "Ouch, ouch, ouch," but didn't he have his sadness as well? And even the word *sadness* brought me again to my father's absence as if the fact of his death were the destination of all my language and thought.

Despite her weak eyesight, my grandmother must have realized how upset we were because she began to give us tasks.

"Go into the house and collect all the candles and oil lamps," she told us.

Her sister Clotilde thought this a bad idea. "What if there's a tremor? The ceiling might collapse."

"Nonsense," said my grandmother. "They're small; they can jump out of the way."

And so we went inside. Spartaco had a scout flashlight which he had the presence of mind to bring from home, as well as his Scout knife, a first-aid kit, ten meters of line and two fish hooks. Manfredo stayed with my grandmother and seemed so mixed up with her long skirts as to become part of them. He still wouldn't talk and whenever I glanced at him, he refused to meet my eye and instead looked up at my grandmother or stared guiltily at the ground. He was very frightened, I think, that either Spartaco or I would tell my grandmother that he had caused the earthquake with my father's pistol, that this entire disruption including our father's death had been his fault. And he desperately wanted to make it better, even to help clean up, but he didn't know where to begin. He still wore my mother's short fur jacket and looked more like a little creature than a boy, as if in his guilt he hoped to surrender his human nature and become a bear.

Except for several candles left burning in my grandmother's room, the inside of the house was very dark. Spartaco went first and I followed him. Directly in front of us were the stairs to the second floor which were dusty and strewn with paper and bits of wood. Spartaco pointed his light up into the darkness. Neither of us wished to investigate that murky space so we skirted the stairs and made for the door to the dining room on the left side of the hall. The eight-inch yellow boards and thick beams on the ceiling had remained in place, but many boards had fallen from the walls. As we moved forward pieces of wood and broken glass crunched underfoot. My grandmother had had many little china figurines—men and women dressed in peasant costumes frozen in the act of milking cows or dancing or harvesting grain. Some of these were scattered across the floor. They looked up at us from the wreckage and their expressions of surprise or laughter seemed a commentary on where they happened to find themselves and their good humor struck me as very brave.

Something was blocking the door to the dining room and we both had to push against it. After a moment we managed to open it just enough to slip through, then Spartaco swept his light across the walls. The result took our breath. My grandmother had had three huge china cabinets that reached to the ceiling and were filled with dishes, candlesticks, silverware and, in one case, jars of preserves. All three had fallen and the floor glittered with hundreds of fragments of broken china mixed with what appeared to be apricot and blackberry jam. Then there was the broken furniture: the cabinets, a sideboard, the dining room table and a dozen chairs which had not only fallen but had been violently bounced up and down for three minutes. The result was a lot of broken wood. Within the mess were half a dozen lanterns but four had smashed and the room smelled of kerosene. I retrieved the other two, trying not to step in the puddles of jam, while Spartaco held the light. Along with the broken dishes were religious pictures, crucifixes and palm leaves twisted into crosses and left over from Palm Sunday. Although I had seen plenty of devastation in town, the wreckage of my grandmother's dining room made the destruction truly palpable: it was the room where all my family used to gather for serious occasions, where, in fact, we were most a family. I kept stopping and looking around in amazement until Spartaco grew impatient and asked what I was doing. Then, clutching the two lamps, I made my way to the kitchen door in the far corner.

The kitchen area was a series of rooms which formed a wing extending off the northwest side of the house. The first room was about five meters by five meters but the rear third was blocked off by a partial wall that separated the stove and sink from a larger eating area which was the more informal social center of the house. The room was very smoky because the chimney had collapsed. Along one wall and under the windows looking onto the garden was a long table where most meals were eaten. Those windows were all broken. Beyond the section of the room with the great wood stove was another room with sinks and dishes, while beyond that was a third room where they made cheese and butter, stored the milk and stored food. Beyond that was a fourth room where they stored ropes, harnesses and saddles. All these rooms appeared to have been turned upside down while covering the floor was a great lake of coffee. A large can of Nescafé had fallen from a shelf and had mixed with the pans of water usually kept simmering on the stove. More cabinets had fallen and jars of tomatoes, beans, all kinds of vegetables, all kinds of fruit were scattered across the floor. Most were broken and the food had mixed with the broken glass, pieces of furniture, milk, coffee, religious pictures, Sunday newspapers, candles, salt, sugar, my great-aunt Bibiana's knitting, several hats and sweaters and a few more lanterns, all but one of which were broken. And of course there was more broken furniture. The walls and ceiling were covered with pale yellow boards with brown trim and several had come loose. I went to collect the one unbroken lantern. There was a side door from the kitchen to the farmyard. Unlocking it, I took the three lanterns to my grandmother, then returned to Spartaco. Together we continued to explore.

My grandmother and her sisters often spent their days occupying themselves with projects that had to do with food and through their efforts the farm was nearly self-sufficient. The house, in fact, was a great warehouse of things to eat. My favorite room was a small room on the second floor filled with shelves and shelves loaded down with cookies: hard German cookies that could seemingly last forever. My grandmother and her sisters dedicated five days every year to baking them and in that time they must have produced thousands. But there were other rooms with jars of preserves and vegetables, jars of butter, dried fruit, dried peas and beans, onions and garlic, potatoes and winter squash, smoked hams, barrels of different kinds of flour, barrels of cider and homemade beer.

For almost an hour Spartaco and I searched these rooms, occasionally stopping to take a handful of candles or another two or three lanterns out to my grandmother, although in almost every case the glass chimneys had been broken. In each room everything had been overturned. Onions were adrift in the cider, flour was mixed with beer, apples were floating in the molasses and glass, always glass crunching underfoot. Neither Spartaco nor I had eaten since noon and we kept nibbling the cookies and cakes we found on the floor.

At one point when I went back outside, I said something to my grandmother about the mess and how long it would take to clean it up. She was with Alcibiades and the workman, telling them how to arrange the bricks for the outdoor stove. She paused and kissed me as if I had said something charmingly original.

"Clean up?" she said. "We don't need to clean up. Soon God will gather us into his arms. Why should we leave a neat house behind us?"

I felt both frightened and relieved by her words. "When is it going to happen?" I asked.

She kissed me again as if I were full of unintentional jokes. "It can't happen before the whole family is together. That would be too unfair. But soon, very soon." She smiled and all her wrinkles deepened. Behind her my brother Manfredo peeped out at me, then ducked down guiltily. It struck me that he stayed close to my grandmother because she was the only one who saw the disaster as our immense good fortune. It made me want to pinch him.

I hurried back into the house to find Spartaco. "Grandmother says we are going to die tomorrow," I told him.

He had been poking around under a fallen sideboard in the dining room. When he straightened up, I saw that his face was filthy with dust and soot. "I'll protect you," he said. "If we get under a tree, maybe the tree will keep us safe."

"Grandmother wants us all to go to Heaven."

Spartaco looked at me skeptically. Our sense of Heaven was that we would be forced to play harps and keep our white robes clean. Besides that, Heaven would mean the end of Spartaco's ambitions. There were no heroes in Heaven, or perhaps they were all heroes.

"Nothing's going to happen to us," he said. "I'll make sure of that."

And I noticed that even in the house he was carrying his scout survival kit with its small magnifying glass and compass—tiny tools for any contingency—and I thought of his two fish hooks and wondered how they would save us.

We had had no tremors for over an hour and I had begun to think they were over, but we were not so fortunate. When the next one struck I guessed it was coming because the dogs started barking, then the birds began crying in the darkness and then came the bells. As the house began to shake, Spartaco dragged me to the doorway leading to the backyard and we crouched down within its frame. All the broken glass and furniture began bouncing and jouncing behind us, the noise getting louder and louder. Out in the yard, I saw my grandmother fall to the ground and saw Manfredo try to bury himself under her skirts. Alcibiades and the workman jumped back as all their bricks disarranged themselves and scattered. Dalila was across the yard but when the tremor struck she ran toward Alcibiades. But such was the shaking of the earth that she appeared to be hopping and dancing, as if her movement was gleeful and not terrified. Her mouth was open but we heard no sound. Above all the noise came the additional roar of the barn collapsing back into the orchard.

Close by in our grandparents' room, Great-aunt Clotilde was trying to jump out of the window with an armful of blankets and had gotten herself stuck halfway through. The shaking was so violent that it swung her back and forth as she straddled the sill. She was wearing a long light-colored dress and looked like a flag being waved during a parade. She was shouting and I could just hear the words. Even though we spoke Spanish, my aunts and great-aunts and grandmother and many others prayed in German because they had been educated at the German convent. And as Clotilde was swung outward to the yard, she prayed loudly in German; and as she swung inward into the house, she cursed loudly in Spanish. Back and forth: German prayers and Spanish curses and it seemed that as she prayed and swore she was undoing in one language all that she had gained in the other; the two languages, as it were, canceling themselves out, which kept her exactly in the center. In memory, the picture of Clotilde being swung back and forth has come to signify the basic division that I felt under my grandmother's tutelage: the appeal of Heaven and the appeal of the world as I was propelled violently back and forth between the two places with no clear idea where I would end up.

Hellmuth and Walterio Droppelman Schiele, my oldest and youngest uncles, appeared about nine o'clock. They had no light and had stumbled up across the fields from town. Both had been busy all afternoon and evening helping to put out the fires and digging people free from collapsed buildings. Their faces and hands and clothes were smudged with soot and dirt and in the firelight they looked, as Great-aunt Bibiana said, like ragamuffins. We had all been eating a thick stew made from the tomatoes and vegetables from the broken canning jars and with huge chunks of mutton which the farm worker had gotten from someplace.

Hellmuth and Alcibiades ran and embraced each other, grinning and loudly slapping each other on the back. Hellmuth was about ten years older than his brother. He was a big man, almost too heavy, and gave the impression of thickness and bullishness, which struck me as appropriate since he was in the business of buying and selling cattle, as if he were one of them in some way. It made me feel good to see Hellmuth and Alcibiades hug each other and I grinned, because Alcibiades was my favorite uncle and I was glad that he had a brother who loved him. Certainly, they were best friends and would sometimes go hunting together or fish for salmon in the River Maullín or sit together and play chess and tell stories and I liked to sit nearby and listen.

Walterio embraced his mother. He was the youngest of the adults, only thirty, and sometimes he seemed even younger. He had hurt his hand and was showing it to his mother, who began to wash it with water from a bucket. Walterio had a soft look, like a balloon full of water, and he was quite chubby. He was also growing prematurely bald and his hair was thinning rapidly. The hair was very light colored and fine, and it seemed like a child's hair. In fact, it seemed not as if his hair were falling out but that it was growing for the first time.

Hellmuth and Walterio were very different and, apart from the love they had for each other as brothers, they didn't particularly like each other. Hellmuth believed that Walterio was foolish and childlike; Walterio was afraid of his brother and felt burdened by his bad opinion. Walterio would have given almost anything for his brother to respect him, but he lacked the will to change himself.

Hellmuth was a very proud man and quite successful in the cattle business he had shared with my father. His Opel was brand-new and he had someone clean it every day. But despite his successes, he had a certain insecurity and shyness which inhibited him. As a result Hellmuth had a great sense of the person he might have become if he had acted differently or if a different series of circumstances had transpired or perhaps even if he had married differently or if he had been stronger. This imagined more powerful and successful self was so vivid to him that it was as if he were that bigger self's smaller friend. Truly, he acted as if he knew somebody famous, like those poor distant cousins of the rich, but that famous person was only the person he had hoped to become but had not. However, this sense of being well-connected made him act very proud, and he spoke slowly and with great deliberation. He always wore a suit and wore one now, even though it was filthy.

Hellmuth was balding and brushed his dark hair straight back, leaving a widow's peak and two great triangles of scalp that always seemed shiny. His eyes were weak and he wore thick glasses in heavy black frames. These frames so commanded his face that one imagined he didn't so much put them on each morning, but that some greater force raised him up and inserted him between the temple pieces. His features were also thick and his pores seemed big and open, almost as if one could see down inside them. He had a wide thick nose, like a bull's, and when he walked, he walked flat-footed so that the floor shook and the dishes rattled. I came to see that he felt trapped within this bullish shape and deep inside he saw himself as being light and unencumbered. But one glimpsed that part only rarely and perhaps only with Alcibiades when they were sitting together and telling stories. It was as if Hellmuth lived in a great box and that box was his lumpish body. He had partly married Dalila because he thought she would help him free this other self—after all, she had already brushed aside his shyness—but after a while he must have

realized that she was unable to see anybody but herself. And
so along with his pride and success was this sense that he had
been martyred to his own life, that he had suffered some loss,
like one of those adults one used to meet who had been tu-
bercular or suffered rheumatic fever as a child and spent
months in bed and whose lives were still touched by the seriousness of that time.

Walterio Droppelman Schiele was none of these things. In
truth he seemed not yet to have had a life, as if he were always
putting it off. Years before, he had left for college in Valdivia
only to return after several months. He had been homesick
and complained that the other students teased him. Then he
lived at home for some years until his father made him find a
job. My mother claimed that this created a great battle between
her parents. My grandmother saw no reason why Walterio
couldn't remain at home and not work, as if he had some
ornamental value which raised him above the others. My grandfather, on the other hand, kept dragging him out to work on
the farm. Walterio hated farm work. It made him dirty and he
hated to be dirty. So he moved into town and had a succession
of jobs, none of which he kept for very long. Slowly, however,
he got into the business of selling fabric and women's clothes
and, although he still changed jobs fairly often, the move was
always from one fabric store or women's clothing store to another, mostly in Puerto Montt, and my grandmother began to
speak of Walterio as having a profession.

Years later when I happened to see a nineteenth-century
painting of a Turkish harem, I saw my uncle Walterio in the
faces of the eunuchs. As a child, of course, I never saw him
as asexual or nonsexual or terrified of sex. I only saw him as
belonging to the children's side of the family. His softness was
also childlike and I doubt that he shaved, even though my
father claimed that he reeked of barber shops, a remark re-

ferring to his use of perfume. He was very pale and his face reminded me of the moon's. When he went away, one had a memory of whiteness and roundness rather than of clear features, except perhaps for a slight pout. Walterio was the sort of man to whom no one listened and he had fallen into the habit of never finishing his sentences. As a result he tended to begin his sentences with no particular destination in mind. After all, that closing period was a place he rarely had the chance to visit. And if someone happened to ask him what in the world he was talking about, he would grow flustered and say he didn't know. This often made me feel sorry for him. He felt most comfortable with the children and it was only with us that he was able to achieve some degree of eloquence.

When my uncles appeared and we were all greeting and hugging each other I was again aware of a kind of exuberance which I had observed several times during the day. Despite the destruction and the apparent dangers ahead, we were alive. Our time hadn't come yet. Not only were we alive but there was also the sense that we had been freed from the daily world. There would be no school and our places of work had been destroyed. Despite our losses and grief and our many fears, there was also a sort of giddiness. We ourselves had escaped destruction, while the world which held us in bondage had received a serious blow.

Both Hellmuth and Walterio said they were starving, and Great-aunt Bibiana gave them huge bowls of stew which they began to devour with wooden spoons as they stood by the fire. Dalila had fluttered around her husband while he had been embracing his brother and the firelight shimmered in her black hair.

"Our house," she kept saying, "did you see our house?" She and Hellmuth had had a house on Mirador overlooking the lake. Although only five rooms, it was very pretty with blue shutters and a large side porch.

After another moment Hellmuth chose to answer her. When he had arrived, he had shown little concern for her safety, as if thinking such a concern was a sign of weakness or assuming she was all right. In fact, he had greeted her with reluctance, for, as I came to understand, she was not only his pleasure but his burden. Yet, if she said foolish things and was rarely able to turn her mind from her own concerns, wasn't this to some degree his fault? They had married when she was still almost a child and if, after fourteen years, she hadn't changed, wasn't he partly to blame? Now she couldn't open her mouth without his wishing she would close it. Of course she knew this and it threw her back on herself and her superficiality and perhaps she made herself even more beautiful just to torment him.

"The house is gone," he said, as if it meant little to him. "The ground gave way beneath it and it slid down the hill. I even saw one of your dresses up in a tree." Hellmuth laughed, although it wasn't a real laugh, only a nervous one. Even though Hellmuth loved his wife, he felt she was his misfortune and so his love embarrassed him and he sought to conceal it. Besides, the house on Mirador was her house and one of her main preoccupations. For Hellmuth it was just the place where he slept. And of course, its destruction decreased her influence over him.

Dalila couldn't believe him. She took hold of her husband's arm. "It's not true," she said. "You're making a joke."

"I saw it myself," said Walterio. "It was, you know, just not there, as if it were just . . . absent."

"Totally destroyed," said Hellmuth.

Dalila stared suspiciously at her husband and Walterio as

if suspecting a joke. Then, as her suspicion diminished, her face seemed to separate as if she were rapidly aging or as if her face were falling inward toward its center. She turned away from the fire and began to weep, making a quiet hiccupping noise as if she couldn't catch her breath. I stood by her and took her hand. She truly had very little in her life—no children, no friends, hardly any respect—and her clothes and trinkets and furniture, all her pretty things took the place of family.

"Isn't there something?" she asked, turning back after a moment.

"Splinters and broken glass," said Hellmuth more quietly. "It slid all the way down the hill, leaving a trail of broken dishes, clothes, dining room chairs. The garage went as well. We're lucky the car wasn't there."

"All the houses along the hill went," said Walterio. "Not just yours. And the Beckerman family was killed."

"The radio says that Valdivia and Osorno and Puerto Montt are completely destroyed," said Hellmuth, glad to change the subject. "But a man came from Puerto Montt and said it wasn't that bad, although hundreds were dead. But Valdivia and Osorno have been wiped out. Everybody. And other towns, too: La Unión and Corral and Entrelagos. The earth just opened up and swallowed them."

Within a few days, of course, we learned this was not true, that although those towns had sustained great damage and there were many deaths, they had not been wiped out. But people from those towns told us how they had heard on the radio that Puerto Varas was completely destroyed, and each town had a similar story, so that for several days the people of all the big and little towns, including the people of Puerto Varas, all thought they were the only survivors, that everyone else was dead and only they were lucky enough to survive. Moreover, the radio said how we could expect more and even worse earthquakes, how all of the south could be expected to fall into the sea. And for years afterward the priests said they had never in their lives heard as many confessions as they had during this time of the earthquake and that for weeks outside the church there were long lines of anxious shopkeepers and farmers and laborers and teachers and housewives hoping to cleanse their souls before being swept off to Heaven.

"What about Miriam and her children?" asked Great-aunt Clotilde. "They're in Puerto Montt."

"I don't know," said Hellmuth.

"Miriam will come here," said my grandmother. "She knows I want her here."

Hellmuth and Alcibiades gave each other a look indicating they had little hope for my aunt Miriam and I was surprised because I thought what my grandmother said must be true.

There were now twelve of us in the farmyard, including Ana who worked in the kitchen and the workman who was her cousin and whose name was either Pedro or Pablo and who had ears so big that my great-aunts simply called him Mr. Ears. Tarpaulins had been strung on poles to make shelters and, along with the stove made from loose bricks, there was a large bonfire. Still, it was very cold and we all had blankets. Manfredo had fallen asleep and had been put in the front seat of my uncle's Opel. There was some talk of going into the house but part of the dining room ceiling had fallen during the last tremor and no one wanted to sleep inside. In fact, none of the adults wanted to sleep at all. They seemed too excited or restless or anxious. We sat near the fires and I sat on one side of Alcibiades and Spartaco sat on the other. Hellmuth had gone into the house and found wine and now they were drinking from wooden bowls. Hellmuth also knew something about the death of my father and when he spoke to my grandmother about it, I saw her face change and become cold and she never mentioned my father again. I begged Hellmuth to tell me what he knew, but he would only say, "He was a brave man. He died helping others." Then, when he saw how upset I was, he came over and put his arm around me and said, "He was my great friend. I know how sad you must feel." Then he moved away and pushed his glasses back up his nose and seemed embarrassed by his emotion.

"And me, too," said Walterio, bobbing his moon-like face. "I wept when I heard about him."

Dalila was somewhat removed from us and had made a nest of blankets under one of the tarpaulins. Occasionally, I would think she was asleep and then I would see her shoulders shaking and realize she was crying. What I didn't realize was that she was also very angry, as if her husband had somehow caused the destruction of her house or as if he could have saved it had he chosen, that its destruction was caused by the fact that he didn't care. Hellmuth and Walterio were full of what they had seen: burning buildings, people crushed when a wall collapsed, landslides, the sudden appearance of sulphur springs right in the middle of town, the lake receding, then coming back. The volcanoes Puyehue, El Carrán and Calbuco were all showing activity and sending up columns of steam. The chain of volcanoes, which included those three, was called the Belt of Fire of the Pacific and it was common during an earthquake for one or more to erupt. The volcanoes were all snow-covered and when they erupted, along with the lava, there were terrible avalanches caused by melting snow and ice.

Walterio had been working mostly with several bucket brigades which had drawn water from the lake. Hellmuth had been with a troop of explorer scouts digging into collapsed houses. As he described what he had seen, the firelight reflected off the lenses of his glasses and seemed to dance. Around us everything was dark and there were no stars.

"Conrado Carrillo must have been taking a nap," said Hellmuth, "because we found him on his bed with only his bare feet sticking out from under the plaster. We pulled and pulled and when we finally got him loose, his head was nowhere to be found. It must have been a sheet of glass or part of a beam, but the neck was cut cleanly and Jorge Yunge thought it wasn't Conrado at all but there was the tattoo of the naked girl on his shoulder which he used to make dance when he flexed his arm. When I was young, I wanted a tattoo just like that one. Remember how he used to show it to us at the beach?"

"Conrado Carrillo was a dirty man," said my grandmother.

"And Elsa Delgado had her whole room fall down around her," said Hellmuth, "but she was safe where she was sitting in her chair, just like she was in a little prison, and we could hear her in there praying and talking to her cat who was with her and when we finally dug her out, she asked us what took us so long."

"People were putting up tents in the park," said Walterio, with his mouth full, "you know, even people . . ."

"Even people whose houses were hardly damaged," continued Hellmuth. "No one wants to sleep inside."

"I would hate to be buried alive," said Alcibiades. "At least outside you have a chance."

"Wherever you go outside, you have to carry a long thick pole," said Great-aunt Bibiana, holding her hands far apart to show us. "Then if you fall into a crack, you can hang onto the pole and be saved."

"How could you hang onto any pole?" asked Clotilde. "Do you think you're an acrobat? You'd break the pole."

Bibiana laughed and unpinned the handkerchief from her breast and laughed some more. Then my grandmother told her to stop being silly, that people had died, and Bibiana tried to look serious but still she kept chuckling, even though she, too, felt grief and understood the calamity we had suffered.

"Is there looting?" asked Alcibiades.

Hellmuth reached out his hands to the fire to warm them. "I didn't see any but it's bound to start. All the windows in the shops are broken. Everything's there for the taking. The police are busy with the rescue work or helping to set up shelters."

"The army . . . ," said Walterio, licking something from his fingers.

"They're expecting to mobilize the soldiers," said Hellmuth. "They've done that in the past."

"In the earthquake in 1939 they shot many looters," said my grandmother.

"Everything's over for a while," said Hellmuth. "There's no electricity, the schools will be closed. All the businesses are closed. The roads are no good and the train tracks will have to be completely rebuilt. I can't see anyone buying or selling cattle for a long time."

"Dead sheep," said Walterio, "you know, the dogs . . ."

"That's right," said Hellmuth, "the dogs have gone crazy and are killing the sheep. We came across several on our way up."

"We did, too," said Spartaco. "I thought it was a puma."

"We should hunt down the dogs and kill them," said Alcibiades.

"Why bother, you know . . . ," said Walterio.

"If we're going to be killed anyway," said Hellmuth.

Alcibiades disagreed. "But we can't just let them kill the sheep."

"What's the difference if the dogs do it or if an earthquake does it?" asked Hellmuth. "Farming's over."

"At least we have lots to eat," said Bibiana.

"Cookies . . . ," said Walterio.

"I'm glad you are all here with me," said my grandmother. She was standing behind her three sons and she patted their heads. The firelight reflected off her cloudy eyes and she had a smile like an angel.

My own mother appeared a little later. Manfredo heard her voice and immediately woke up and came scrambling out of the front seat of the Opel. There had been another tremor and when it was over we heard her call from somewhere down in the field. Spartaco ran off with his flashlight and a few minutes later he returned, leading my mother behind him. Both Manfredo and I ran to her and embraced her and Spartaco put his arms around us and we all wept, except for Spartaco who was brave. My mother hadn't eaten but she wasn't hungry. She sat down next to my grandmother and put her head in her own mother's lap and her sobs kept us all crying. Even Dalila got up and embraced her. I think my mother loved her husband very much even though she was frightened of him and now that he was dead she didn't know what to do. My mother was a large woman with heavy features and she was often ill. Some days when we came home from school we would find her still in bed with a wet washcloth across her forehead. When she got old, she became thin, but during those years she was very solid and was clearly the sister of Hellmuth and Walterio, who were also oversized. The fact that she was thirty-eight, the same age that I am now, fills me with astonishment. She seemed old then and I don't feel old at all. She had long black hair and she often let me brush it while she sat and sighed and looked out of the window. Even though she was a big woman she had tiny hands and feet and her feet were even smaller than Spartaco's. Her hands were very white and her only ring was her wedding band. But even it looked out of place, like a wedding ring on a child's finger, and her hands looked fragile and sad.

She had stayed with my father's body at the funeral home. There was now a long line of bodies but my father was first. Many people were afraid that the bodies wouldn't be buried individually but would be put into a mass grave. In the cemetery was a Recabarren plot and there was a place in it for my father next to his parents and his sister who had died young.

"If I had left, they would have pushed him out," said my mother. "Some people were offering lots of money."

I'm sure I felt proud that my father would be the first to be buried, as if he had been chosen to lead the dead into Heaven. My grandmother looked angry but didn't say anything. I thought she too was grieving for the death of my father, but much later I came to understand that she was sorry that he couldn't be thrown into a mass grave along with the homeless and poor.

"And I had to wash him and dress him," said my mother. "I had to go back to our house and find a suit. The only suit was covered with plaster dust and I had to brush it clean." Then my mother began to weep again and lowered her head into her mother's lap. We children sat behind her and patted her and Manfredo cried because he still felt he had caused the earthquake and had killed his father and that when people found out they would yell at him.

"You must eat something," said Bibiana. "Plinio would want you to eat something."

And at the sound of my father's name, my mother again burst into tears and my uncle Hellmuth shook his head and admitted it was a bad business.

Not long after that we heard the sound of horses' hooves coming along the farm lane. Hellmuth called out to see who it was, but the workman with big ears already knew and he

ran into the lane, only to return minutes later leading an old
plow horse with my grandfather sitting on top and holding a
lantern. My grandfather first glanced at us, then looked around,
his eyes taking in the collapsed barn and shed and the missing
water tower. Slowly he dismounted and stretched.

"What a mess," he said. "We'll have to get this picked up."

I ran to him and embraced him and he patted my head.

"Where's your father?" he asked.

I began crying.

"Our father was killed," said Spartaco who had joined me.

My grandfather hugged us to him and his whole face looked
sad. Then he released us. "And Miriam?" he asked.

"We haven't heard," said Hellmuth.

"There are huge fires in Puerto Montt," said my grandfather.
"I saw their light in the sky." He went to his sons and shook
their hands, then kissed his wife's cheek and the cheeks of
the other women.

"Why are you crying?" he asked Dalila.

"Our house was destroyed. Everything was lost."

"Then you must build another," said my grandfather. He
turned and looked at the surrounding buildings, at the tarpaulins and makeshift stove. After another moment he went
off with the workman, poking into the house and sheds. At
one point I saw him slap the wall of the house and laugh as
if he were pleased with it. He was a small man whose clothes
looked too big for him and he wore a blue wool coat that hung
past his hips. His hat was pulled low on his forehead and it
was hard to see his eyes.

"They say Valdivia and Osorno are destroyed," said my
grandfather. "What a mess. In the country all the animals have
gone crazy. Every time there was a tremor my horse would lie
down. It's late. These children should be in bed. There's lots
we must do tomorrow."

"There'll be more earthquakes," said my grandmother. "Even worse ones."

My grandfather grinned and stamped the ground. "That's right. Everything's going to fall down. What a mess. There's going to be a lot to do."

"We're all going to die," said my grandmother.

My grandfather tilted his head toward her. "What did you say?"

"We're going to die," she repeated in a louder voice. "The earth is going to open up and we'll be swept away."

My grandfather stamped the ground and grinned again. He looked gnomish and sly. "There'll be a lot to do," he repeated.

They put me to bed in the backseat of my uncle's Opel and covered me with blankets. I lay there but didn't feel sleepy. Occasionally I would hear Manfredo stir in the front seat.

"Manfredo," I asked, "why won't you talk to me?"

Silence.

"Manfredo, I promise not to tell anyone anything."

Silence.

"No one cares that you had the gun. It didn't do anything."

Silence, then I heard him begin whimpering again. His foolishness made me feel cross. Around the fire, the adults continued to talk, telling stories, discussing the dead sheep, wondering when the next earthquake would strike, wondering if certain people were all right and grieving for the ones who had been injured or killed. My grandfather had ridden the plow horse across the fields because he said the roads were impassable. He said there were crevasses and hot springs and the air was full of birds. He said he heard the cries of animals and couldn't even recognize what kind of creatures they were. He said that once he had seen the moon through the clouds and it was bright red, like blood. In the distance I heard the howling of dogs. I thought I wouldn't sleep, that all night I would listen to my family talk about the strange things that had happened. But then I fell asleep and dreamed of my father and that he was reading me a story about the wide world, and in the distance, still in the dream, I heard a shouting and I woke up and I realized that the shouting was out in the yard. It was much later and the fire had died down. My grandfather had disappeared. My uncles were running around with lanterns. My great-aunt Bibiana was crying. My grandmother was certain that her husband had fallen into a crack in the earth.

"He's been swallowed!" she cried. "He's gone without us!"

After a while someone thought to look in the house and found my grandfather asleep in his own bed.

"Stubborn old man," I heard Hellmuth say.

"He has no fear," said Alcibiades. "He ought to be more careful."

"The ceiling," said Walterio, "it could, you know . . ."

"Come crashing down," said Hellmuth.

I went back to sleep. Later that night or early in the morning when it was still dark, there was another severe tremor. Everything rattled and there was a crash from somewhere. My uncle's Opel shook and jounced and creaked and I felt I was adrift in a ship at sea.

3

ALONG THE roadsides of my country one often finds little shrines where there has been a fatal traffic accident or where perhaps a pedestrian has been killed. It is believed that part of the victim's animating spirit inhabits these shrines and so they are called *animitas*. Most often the *animitas* resemble little houses with pitched roofs and a front door. In the south they tend to be made out of wood and in the north they are made from stone. Some look like the houses of very poor people: little falling-down houses about a foot high tucked back off the side of the road. Others can be several feet tall with fresh paint and even windows. Often there is a cross on top and a tin can with dead flowers. Some *animitas* clearly haven't been visited for years and years and are covered with dust. Others are painted regularly and have fresh flowers and may even have a little garden plot. They also may have flags and a stone monument and burning candles. Often they include the license plate of the vehicle in which the person was killed. Sometimes they include the dead person's photograph in an ornate frame. Occasionally they are surrounded by a white picket fence. Up near Chillán there is a place where a bus crashed head-on with a truck and along the side of the road are about seventy *animitas* of all different types and styles: rich and poor, cared for and abandoned, wood and stone. It looks like a miniature city, although no paths run between the houses, and when people drive by they cross themselves and drive carefully for a minute or two before returning to their reckless ways.

The highway between Santiago and Puerto Montt passed almost two kilometers west of my grandparents' farm and sometimes I would walk over to it. There was a large Copec station at the corner of the turnoff to Puerto Varas, and Spartaco liked to go there and listen to the truck drivers talk about faraway places and the hardships to be found in each place: the police, the women, the rough roads. A few hundred yards south of the station was an *animita* which occupied me for several years during my childhood. It belonged to a young man by the name of Jaime Alverez and his license plate said he came from Santiago. A man at the gas station said he had been killed in a rainstorm. A truck had jackknifed and Jaime Alverez had crashed into it. According to the man at the gas station, Alverez had been driving a brand new 1957 Chevrolet and it had been completely destroyed. I was five years old at the time of the accident and knew nothing about it.

I must have been about seven when Spartaco showed me the *animita* and right away I decided that Jaime Alverez was the most handsome man I had ever seen, even handsomer than my uncle Alcibiades. His photograph showed a laughing face with dark wavy hair and regular features: a thin face with a straight nose and full lips and a strong chin. He had a neatly trimmed mustache that made him look very distinguished. The man at the Copec station said he looked like an Englishman and perhaps it was that suggestion that bound me to him because although I knew nothing about Englishmen they were in all my best books. And even though the dead man's name was Jaime, I thought of him as James.

The *animita* of Jaime Alverez was made of white boards divided by thin strips of batting with a steeply pitched roof covered with wooden shingles which had been painted red. At the very top was a white metal cross. Around the *animita* was a little yard of crushed stone and around that was a fence with black metal railings and a gate. The yard was perhaps six feet by six feet and stood partway up a small hill above the highway. The *animita* had two side windows and each had a little window box with red flowers. I would lie on my stomach in front of the front door and look in at the license plate and the photograph above a little altar and I would think about the life of this young man who had happened to die so close to my grand-parents' farm. Sometimes the stories I told myself about the life and death of Jaime Alverez were so sad that I would begin to sob as the trucks and buses roared by only a dozen feet away.

In one of these stories the dead man was an orphan and all his life he had received money from some secret person who had paid for his clothes, his schooling and his new car. Then he learned that this secret person was an older half-brother who owned a copper mine far to the south. Jaime Alverez leapt into his car and rushed off to find him only to meet death in a rain storm near Puerto Varas. In another story Jaime Alverez was deeply in love with a young woman whose parents thought he was no good: one of those society playboys who are only interested in gambling and fast cars. In order to convince the girl's parents that he was different, he dedicated his life to helping the poor and unfortunate. When he was killed he had been delivering a vital serum, paid for with his own money, to a sick boy in Puerto Montt already at death's door. His dying words to the truck driver who had caused the accident were of forgiveness and a plea to deliver the medicine. Guilty and heartbroken, the truck driver delivered the serum and the boy lived.

As a child I was very much in love with Jaime Alverez and

I took it upon myself to care for his *animita*, to bring fresh flowers, pull out the weeds, to put new blacking on the metal fence. Something which was a great mystery to me was that Jaime Alverez also had another admirer or at least someone who brought flowers, because often I would come to the *animita* and find a fresh bouquet. I never saw who did this and could never quite decide who it was. Sometimes I thought it was his fiancée who regularly drove down a thousand kilometers from Santiago as a kind of pilgrimage. Sometimes I thought it must be the truck driver who was responsible for his death. I never felt jealous of this other admirer, probably because I was too young and love for me had no sexual meaning. Many years later when I married a man named Javier Albañez, I occasionally wondered if I had been attracted to him because his name was similar to Alverez. He too had a mustache, although it was always in need of trimming. We were married for ten difficult years and I carried him like a sack of stones. We had one child, Ruth, my treasure, and then he left. Sometimes I see my ex-husband. Each time he is passing in a taxi and each time it is with a different woman. The last time he was with a woman at least twenty years younger and both were laughing.

That, I think, is the reality. The ex-husband passing in a taxi as his former wife watches bitterly from the curb. But as a child I was full of romantic notions. Often, for instance, I would walk through the woods searching for my special prince. Perhaps I wasn't searching as much as expecting to be found. For these occasions I would wear a perfume of my great-aunt Clotilde's which had a smell so strong that it seemed I could chew it. The trees were very dense and it was hard to see more than ten feet ahead. Even so I would imagine him on horseback. I would imagine him galloping up and sweeping me into his arms. Sometimes he looked like my brother Spartaco. Sometimes he looked like Alcibiades. Sometimes he looked like

Jaime Alverez. I would walk through the woods and say my name over and over: Lucy Recabarren, Lucy Recabarren, Lucy Recabarren. I would say it faster and faster until the words blended together, becoming a hum which I wrapped around me like strong thread.

It is strange now, as a music teacher giving piano lessons to young children, to realize their heads are full of such mystery. And my daughter, Ruth, as well. We will be eating dinner and for the tenth time I will tell her to finish her milk or to sit up straight or eat her vegetables and she will be looking off through the window, dreaming, dreaming. What does she see there? Does she too see a dozen rich stories with herself at the center? And aren't those stories her weakness, her frailty? Won't they lead her some day to ride in a taxi with a man whose laughter she shouldn't trust?

One of my great fears during the time of the earthquake was that the *animita* of Jaime Alverez might be destroyed. I worried that a crack had opened in the ground and the *animita* and its metal fence had been sucked down into the depths. But I also believed I would meet Jaime Alverez very shortly and he would know how I had taken care of his shrine so carefully and I would become his dear friend. I suppose I believed my grandmother that we would all die very soon, or rather I had no doubt. I imagined us all holding hands, the whole family and maybe even the dogs Peppo and Margarita, and suddenly we would be carried away. For a moment the light would be unbearable and the whiteness would hurt my eyes and there would be a rush of wind and then, walking out of the light, would come Jaime Alverez holding out his hand and running behind him would be my uncle Gabriel, who had died as a child, while behind them both would stand my father and he too would be smiling and glad to see us.

This event lay before me as certainly as tomorrow lies beyond
sleep, and we were only awaiting the arrival of the rest of the
family for it to happen. But I also imagined a time when school
would begin again and I would see my friends. Or I would look
forward to the summer when we would go to the beach and my
mother would make little sandwiches. These contradictory future times existed side by side with others and the fact that
they were mutually exclusive didn't bother me. I would meet
Jaime Alverez in Heaven and we would marry. I would resume
school on earth and once more have to study my times tables
and work on my penmanship, which my teacher said was my
greatest weakness. I would learn that everyone had been mistaken about my father's death and he would stroll back laughing
as if it were all a joke and he would sweep me up and nuzzle
his nose into my neck, making me giggle.

My guides through these confusing futures were my two
saints who were very different and even as a child I realized
that they represented the divided sides of my nature. Both were
named St. Lucy but one was St. Lucy Filippini and the other
was St. Lucy the Virgin Martyr. St. Lucy Filippini was known
as *Maestra santa*, the holy schoolmistress, and her day was
March 25. She founded many schools and she herself predicted
the day of her death, March 25, 1732, when she succumbed
to a long illness. She was a young saint and had been canonized
when my mother was just eight years old and it was from that
time that my mother had decided to name one of her children
Lucy. St. Lucy was very good and pious but I couldn't help
thinking she was also a little dull. My grandmother was suspicious of these younger saints as if St. Lucy Filippini were
somehow a beginner and not good at her job, because of being
canonized in 1930, and it was my grandmother who told me
about St. Lucy the Virgin Martyr whose day was December

13. St. Lucy was a true saint who was persecuted by the Emperor Diocletian after her rejected suitor denounced her as a Christian. She was thrown into a brothel from which she was miraculously saved and was also saved from a raging fire. At last in Syracuse a soldier drove his sword into her throat and she died. St. Lucy had great power to cure the illnesses of people's eyes and in pictures she is often shown holding two eyes on a plate.

Really it was because of the eyes that my grandmother chose her because her own eyes had been weak for years and she swore she would have gone blind many times if it hadn't been for St. Lucy the Virgin Martyr. So even though my actual name day was March 25, my grandmother and I also celebrated December 13 as a kind of secret name day; and even though I prayed to St. Lucy Filippini on Sundays, it was St. Lucy the Virgin Martyr who was my protectress during the rest of the week. I often talked to these saints in my head but I would only bother St. Lucy Filippini for truly serious things, while St. Lucy the Virgin Martyr was a friend to whom I could confide all my daily worries and doubts. A dozen times a day I would ask her a question and although I never received a definite answer it often seemed I could see her smiling face, and on each of my school notebooks I had made a little drawing of two eyeballs on a plate, which Spartaco said looked like a pair of eggs and which led him to call St. Lucy the Virgin Martyr my breakfast saint.

When I awoke that Monday morning after the earthquake, it was raining and the drops drummed on the roof of the Opel. It was late, past nine, and everyone else was already up. The rain, as I soon discovered, was a warm rain and my grandfather said it was warm because it had passed through the hot steam of the volcanoes. The rain came as a blessing because it helped put out the fires still burning in town. Although in Puerto Montt, as we learned later, it caused a terrible mud slide and many people were killed.

There was cooking going on under the tarpaulins where my great-aunt Bibiana was supervising Anna, who was stirring a stew of mutton and vegetables in a great iron kettle. My uncles were sitting nearby wrapped in blankets and only Alcibiades gave me a smile. Walterio was eating something. Hellmuth was tilted toward Alcibiades talking passionately and striking his fist into his other palm. Every few moments the smoke from the fire would blow across the three of them and set them coughing and waving their hands in front of their faces. My grandparents had a car, a blue Citroën, and I could see Dalila sitting in the front seat with her head resting on the steering wheel even though there was no place to go. Although her face was hidden by her hair, her sadness showed itself in every line of her body. The air smelled of smoke and cooking food. Everything was gray and damp and the farmyard looked very shabby. It was the day of St. Desiderius whom Gregory the Great had once rebuked for teaching grammar: an occasion which Spartaco liked to discuss when he was tired of doing his homework and which often led my father to say he was sick of St. Desiderius.

As I got out of the car, Spartaco came running over to me through the mud. He seemed full of important information and his face was eager. Along with my father's leather coat, he wore one of my grandfather's hats tilted back on his head in a very adultlike fashion.

"Hurry," he said. "I have something to show you."

I drew my coat around me and we ran across the yard. The dogs Peppo and Margarita barely had their heads poked from their front doors and their noses looked like old leather buttons. We ran between their houses to the gate separating the farmyard from the orchard. Spartaco was saying something about dogs but I thought he meant the dogs in the farmyard. He held open the gate and I ran through it. Then I stopped so fast that I slipped and fell in the wet grass.

The bodies of three sheep dogs hung from the limbs of an apple tree. Each dangled from a short rope, their bodies elongated, their heads violently bent at a sharp angle by their individual nooses. Two black dogs with white markings and a golden one. The golden one was twisting slightly as it hung. Their tongues lolled out, black and swollen, and their eyes were fixed and startled. Around them a few red apples were still caught up in the boughs.

"They were crazy," said Spartaco. "The earthquake made them crazy. They were killing sheep."

I had fallen very close to them and as I looked up through the rain the dead dogs seemed to hover above me and water dripped from their tails. They were not dogs I knew well. They were working dogs, businesslike dogs. I tried to imagine what they had thought killing the sheep and if they believed they were doing the right thing, as if the danger of the earthquake were even greater than the danger of death itself, or if they felt that since the earthquake had brought all life to a stop, then at least this gave them the chance to take revenge on their burdensome charges.

"They killed over twenty-five sheep and injured lots more," said Spartaco. "Grandfather hung them this morning. I got to go with him."

My grandfather had gone out as soon as it was light. He had called the dogs but they hadn't come. One by one he had hunted them down. He hung them, he said, because bullets were expensive. "Why bother?" my uncle Hellmuth had said. "Why kill them when we're all going to die anyway?" And my grandfather had pretended not to hear and went about his business. Now the dead dogs hung from the apple tree and they seemed like a warning, although I didn't know whom it was for. Peppo and Margarita were certainly not going to venture off and kill sheep. Back in the farmyard Hellmuth was striking his fist into his open palm and saying "Stubborn old man." Now my grandfather had gone off again, taking the farm worker with him, trying to help the wounded sheep and round up the others. As I stared at the dogs, there was a sudden screeching of birds and the ground started to shake as another tremor overtook us. The boughs of the apple tree began to jiggle and the dogs themselves jerked on their short ropes. This was terrifying to me, as if the dogs had suddenly come to life, and they flopped on their ropes like angry angels. Frightened, I jumped to my feet and ran back into the farmyard. Alcibiades was standing by the fire and I ran to him and wrapped my arms around his waist and sobbed and sobbed, although I don't know if I was crying for the dogs or some fear of my own.

My grandmother and Great-aunt Clotilde and my mother came hurrying out of the house, followed by my little brother, Manfredo, who was holding his hands over his ears. We all stood, nervously expectant, as the shaking continued and the boards in the shed bumped and rattled together and the house creaked and the chickens bunched together into a white feathery knot. And then it stopped. For a second we held our breath, waiting to see if it had really stopped. Then my grandmother laughed. She was holding a broom and she shook it.

"The earth's just practicing," she said. Then she returned to the house with her sailor's walk. As I soon discovered she was cleaning the mess from her bedroom, which was a large long room and nearest to the farmyard. Sleeping outside was wet and cold, and my grandmother was preparing her bedroom so that we could stay there. The bedroom had two doors and four windows opening onto the farmyard and if necessary we could leave in a hurry. At first, however, Walterio was the only one of my uncles who chose to sleep inside.

During the tremor Dalila had gotten out of my grandparents' Citroën. She was disheveled and frightened and she kept her hands pressed to her face. When the trembling stopped, she gathered her coat around her and hurriedly began walking off across the yard to the driveway, splashing right through the mud puddles. Hellmuth went after her and stopped her at the corner of the house. They were arguing.

"It's gone," he said. "It's all destroyed."

She pulled herself free of him. She was a tall woman and drops of rain were caught up in her black hair. "I want to see for myself," she said. Then she turned the corner. I ran after her but she was walking quickly down the hill. In the garden I saw Ana the kitchen girl sweeping up the petals which had fallen from the flowers during the earthquake. The ground seemed carpeted with petals and fallen leaves. Ana was putting them into a reed basket. She didn't seem to notice the rain at all. To the east, a cloud of smoke hung over the town and I could hardly pick out the three red steeples of the Church of the Sacred Heart. The lake was a gray haze.

"Dalila!" I called.

She turned but made no sign of recognition. Perhaps she was a hundred meters away. Standing at the edge of the dirt driveway halfway down the hill, she looked small and separated from all the world, like a single dot on a piece of paper. Her face was very white. Her dark hair blew around that white center and was her only movement. I waved and waved. She kept her hands at her sides. After another second, she turned and continued down the hill. One of the houses at the bottom had burned and black beams stuck up from the wreckage like dark skinny fingers. Across the field to the south half a dozen vultures were busying themselves with a dead sheep.

I remembered one Saturday morning early that fall when I had gone to Dalila's house looking for my uncle Hellmuth. I had some message from my father. The house was on a hillside overlooking the town square and had a wonderful view. Hellmuth wasn't home but Dalila invited me in anyway. Many times Dalila showed no interest in us children, as if we were invisible. But on this morning she was quite friendly. It was a rare sunny morning and from her parlor windows I could see the blue of the lake with the perfect snowcapped cone of Osorno rising up in the distance. The sun made Dalila's white walls very white and sparkled off the little ceramic figurines and colored dishes with pictures of distant cities, the doilies on the chairs and tables, the bright reds of the rug, the polished wax on the floor and tables and the oak backs of the chairs. There were pictures on the walls of women in old-fashioned dresses holding parasols and walking small black dogs or laughing or looking from behind their fans at gentlemen in top hats. The curtains were light blue and almost transparent and they fluttered slightly in the breeze from the window. Dalila had two little yellow finches in an ornate black cage and the finches were twittering and singing and hopping from perch to perch.

It was a crowded room with many pretty souvenirs from faraway places, many little tables with pictures in china frames, paperweights with flowers, several music boxes, ivory elephants, china dogs and cats, little bouquets of dried flowers in delicate vases. Along the top of the walls was a red-and-blue-stenciled pattern of S shapes and doves. Against one wall was an upright piano which Dalila sometimes played. She loved the songs from Argentina, melancholy milongas and tangos, although she played them rather poorly. But I think it was from listening to her play these songs that I got my wish to play the piano as well.

The room was so full of sunlight that it made me blink.

Dalila sat me down at a little table and asked if I would like tea and toast. I was so struck by her friendliness and the rareness of the occasion that I felt shy, but I nodded and smiled and she went off to the kitchen. I sat very still and only my eyes moved. That day I was wearing a dress and as I waited I smoothed the light-colored fabric down across my knees.

We had tea in white china cups each with a border of roses around the lip. There was a blue teapot and a blue plate with toast and a jar of apricot jam. There were white cotton napkins in crystal napkin rings and the silverware was shiny and undersized, almost a doll's silverware.

"Tell me," she said, leaning toward me, "who is your favorite uncle?"

It didn't occur to me to say it was Hellmuth, her own husband. "Alcibiades," I answered.

"It's not Freddy Piwonka Gray? He's so funny."

"He tickles us and won't let us go," I said. "I can't catch my breath."

"And what do you like about Alcibiades?" My aunt that day was wearing a pale yellow dress with yellow flowers. Her black hair was loose and seemed to be swimming away from her head. Her full lips formed a little pout whenever she asked a question.

I was shy to tell her my feelings about Alcibiades. "He's very nice," I said.

"Do you think him handsome?"

"Oh, yes."

"Is he the handsomest man you know?" she asked.

"I'm not sure."

"Who do you think is handsomer?"

And so I told her about Jaime Alverez and the *animita* and that he was the handsomest man I had ever seen. I described his dark wavy hair and straight nose and mustache and that the man at the Copec station said that Jaime Alverez looked like an Englishman.

Dalila listened with a slight smile as she nibbled her toast and patted her lips with a napkin. "That's very precious. You must take me to see his picture."

"I keep wondering who else brings him flowers."

"Perhaps he had a lover."

"I would like to meet her," I said, "and ask her about him."

"She might become jealous," said Dalila.

I couldn't imagine that. I thought I would meet this unknown woman and we would talk eagerly about Jaime Alverez and become good friends.

"I was very much like you when I was small," said Dalila smiling. "I had grand passions. There was a pharmacist on the corner who was very handsome. I would go into his shop to buy some little thing and try to speak to him, then lose courage."

As Dalila spoke she twisted strands of black hair around her fingers, making ringlets. "When I was small, even younger than you, my mother liked to dress me up as a princess. She had a First Communion dress that had been her own and she sewed colored ribbons on it and lace and it had many petticoats. She would dress me in it, then hang jewelry around my neck and make a little crown of pearls and put rouge on my lips and cheeks. I had a little wand and red shoes and I would stand on a hassock and give my mother orders and she would say, 'Yes, your highness' and 'Certainly, your highness.' Sometimes I would have to stay on the hassock as a surprise for my father and he would be late. I would stand there and want to get down and my mother would become impatient with me. At last my father would come home and sometimes he would sweep me into his arms and sometimes he had been drinking and would be angry. And as I waited for him on top of the hassock,

I would always be nervous because I didn't know which he would be."

That Saturday morning in early fall Dalila told me much about when she was a little girl and what her expectations had been. I thought how Spartaco would never have permitted me to behave like a princess, not out of meanness or superiority but because it didn't fit into his games. He needed a boon companion, a henchman, not a princess. But Dalila had imagined another sort of future, a future which her mother was continually describing to her. And had she really seen my uncle Hellmuth as a prince? Perhaps at thirty-one he had been full of energy and charm. But as Dalila spoke, it hardly seemed she was speaking to me, and I felt I could have been anybody, even though I was glad to be there and glad for the tea and toast with apricot jam. Much later it occurred to me that on that particular day she saw me as a younger version of herself, as if her child self had come to call on her adult self, as if our private tea were just a game. Certainly I saw her many times after that and she never referred to that Saturday morning, nor did she look at me in any special way and it hurt me that she had seemingly forgotten our time together.

But on the day of St. Desiderius as I stood on the hill in the rain and watched Dalila disappear into town, I thought of her white house and all her nice things and how my uncle had said their house had slid down the hill and was destroyed. Everything was ugly and the mound of vultures hopping and fluttering in the distance was awful to me. I turned and made my way back up the hill to my grandmother's house. All of Dalila's pretty things were ruined and somewhere in town my father lay on a slab waiting to be buried and back in the orchard the sheep dogs were hanging from the apple tree. Really I felt we were all going to be destroyed and I hurried toward the farmyard just so I wouldn't be separated from my family, so that when we were swept up and carried off to Heaven I would be standing right there between Alcibiades and Spartaco.

There was a banging from one of the sheds which had half collapsed and looking in at the door I saw my grandfather with two workmen. They were using long thick boards as braces to prop up a wall. My grandfather grinned when he saw me and stopped his work, taking off his hat and wiping his forearm across his brow.

"No school for you!" he shouted. "It's all broken to pieces. No telling when it will start up again. You'll have to work here with me." And he laughed as if the idea tickled him immensely. "Here, I'll give you a hammer." He dug around in the debris while the two workmen waited.

All morning people had been arriving with news from town or from faraway places and all their news was of destruction. Watching my grandfather, I didn't think he was crazy so much as in error. Why bother with the shed when shortly we would be taken off to Heaven? But I was happy to have my own hammer and I joined him, swinging at nails and now and then hitting them. Sometimes it seems that one of my greatest joys as a child was driving nails into wood: those simple actions where something is forcefully accomplished.

"The tidal wave swept away Maullín," said my grandfather, speaking of a fishing village near the coast. "They say that houses were left up in the tops of trees."

"All the houses from Quenuir came sailing down the river," said a workman whom I hadn't seen before, a shabbily dressed man with a red nose. "And the tidal wave swept up the grave-yard and the coffins came sailing by like little boats. We watched from the hill. And one man saw his mother's shiny new coffin swept forward on the crest of a wave and he wept. And when we came back down to Maullín the trees were full of bodies but everyone in my own family was saved. Praise the

Lord." Here the man dropped to his knees and clasped his hands together.

"He's an evangelist," said my grandfather, somewhat apologetically. He took off his hat and slapped the man across the shoulder so that a little puff of dust rose from the brim. The evangelist slowly got to his feet, then heaved a heavy pole up against the wall and my grandfather began hammering it in place. "But he'll work all day on a cup of coffee," said my grandfather over his shoulder. "It makes me glad to see his tenaciousness."

After a while I left them and went off in search of Spartaco. I found him with my grandmother and Manfredo in her bedroom. They were arranging a half dozen cots against the wall and putting several folded blankets on each. Manfredo still wouldn't talk and Spartaco was cross with him.

"I can't get him to say anything," said Spartaco. "Sometimes I think he does it just because it makes me mad."

Manfredo stood by my grandmother staring at the floor and it seemed that his whole body was scrunched shut.

My grandmother bent over and kissed Manfredo's cheek. "Wait until we reach Heaven," she said. "He'll sing beautifully. Everybody sings beautifully in Heaven."

"What do people do there?" I asked.

"They're happy all day long," said my grandmother, sitting down on the edge of a bed and beginning to massage her knees.

"Are there games?" asked Spartaco.

"Those things don't matter in Heaven," said my grandmother. "In Heaven you can be happy just looking off at the sky."

"I like to do things," said Spartaco, with misgiving. "If I can't have games, then I like projects."

"We'll all be together," said my grandmother, putting her

arm around Manfredo. "And my parents will be there and their parents as well."

"Isn't it crowded?" I asked.

"No," said my grandmother. "In Heaven everyone is very small so there's lots of room."

My great-aunt Clotilde came in with more blankets. "In Heaven all our needs will be taken care of," she said. "We'll no longer want anything anymore. If what you wanted was a new bicycle, then once you're in Heaven, you'll forget all about it. If you wanted a new hat or a swimming suit or a puppy, in Heaven you won't want anything."

Spartaco and I exchanged a look. "I don't know," said Spartaco as politely as possible. "I just can't imagine what it'll be like. It sounds like a lot of sitting around."

"I almost married a man who died and went to Heaven," said Clotilde. "At least I think he's there. He was very handsome. Going to Heaven will mean being with him again, although when I get there I won't even care. I probably won't even look at him. He won't matter anymore."

"You mean because of the singing?" I asked.

"Because of everything," said my aunt.

"Well," I said, "I'll be glad to see my father."

"If he's there," said my grandmother darkly.

I stayed with my grandmother making the beds and helping to shift the furniture. Then, around noon, there came another tremor. At first when the ground began to shake we all stood perfectly still, but as it got worse and the noise started up, we ran from the house. Everything was banging and rattling and it drowned out our cries. Manfredo clung to my grandmother's skirt. The ground went back and forth so violently that I thought there was something wrong with my legs. Across the yard, my grandfather and the two workmen came running out of the shed.

Then there was the tearing sound of wood being ripped from wood and the shed collapsed behind them. The tarpaulins shivered and swayed and drops of water were flung from them. My mother ran to me and swept me up in her arms and squeezed me so that I could hardly breathe. Hellmuth and Alcibiades were crouched like runners and Walterio had his hands over his eyes. Falling steadily, the drops of warm rain were the only things not jiggling, then they hit the earth and bounced and hopped across the surface. My grandmother, I saw, had an expectant look, as if this was going to be the big earthquake, the one that was going to sweep us away. Then I saw a look of disappointment cross her face and moments later the tremor subsided.

Almost immediately after, Dalila walked into the yard. She was carrying two small suitcases. Her shoes were muddy and her coat drenched. Her black hair was matted across her forehead. She went over to my grandparents' Citroën and climbed into the front seat without looking at any of us. Hellmuth went over and pulled open the car door. He seemed angry but was trying not to show it.

"So what did you rescue?" he asked.

He tried to take one of the suitcases but she pulled it away. Grabbing her arm, he yanked it from her. Whatever was inside made a rattling, broken noise. He opened it.

"Junk," he said. "Can't you realize there's nothing left?" And his voice softened as if he were trying to convince a child.

Dalila snatched the suitcase from him. "And what kind of person are you?" she demanded. "You're lucky I don't tell them all."

My aunt Miriam Droppelman Schiele arrived late that afternoon from Puerto Montt with her four children. I heard the whinny of a horse and running to the farm lane I saw a pony cart being led by my cousin Hugo who was fourteen. Seated on the cart was his sister Rosvita, who was a year younger, and my aunt with a red blanket over her knees. In back were the twins, Nancy and Norma. They were five. When the twins saw me, they jumped down and ran to greet me. They were wet and spotted with mud but seemed very jolly. My aunt was holding a man's black umbrella above her and Rosvita and the drops rolled down onto their laps.

"We've been in that cart ever so long," said Nancy.

"Ever since dark," said her sister, "and we're awfully hungry."

"We're glad you aren't dead," said Nancy. "Hugo said you might be."

By then my grandmother was hurrying up, as well as my uncles. The cart was led into the farmyard. Peppo stuck his head from his little house and barked three times—ouch, ouch, ouch—then retreated again. My mother helped her sister down from the cart and wept and embraced her. The twins began weeping as well, although they had seemed perfectly happy moments before. Rosvita remained on the cart and was looking around with a certain disdain until she saw Alcibiades. Then she waved. Spartaco was helping Hugo unharness the pony. Hellmuth was trying to ask my aunt about her husband, Freddy Piwonka Gray, and my aunt was shaking her head as the tears streamed from her eyes. My grandfather was giving advice in a loud voice. The two workmen were lifting the bags down from the cart. My great-aunts Clotilde and Bibiana were hovering nearby and asking questions. Walterio was offering cookies to the twins, holding one hand above the box to protect it from the rain. Only Dalila remained apart and stayed in the front seat of my grandparents' Citroën with her broken trinkets and her grief.

My aunt Miriam Droppelman Schiele was about forty and

while it is the custom in my country for women to keep their own names when they marry, my aunt liked to refer to herself as Miriam de Piwonka to indicate that she was married to Freddy Piwonka Gray. I once heard my father explain this by saying that Freddy Piwonka had so many girlfriends that my aunt wanted to establish her legitimacy among them. As a child I thought he was serious and it made perfect sense but as an adult I wondered at her willingness to make herself the property of a faithless husband, despite his numerous charms and funny stories. And in those days Freddy was a sort of ne'er-do-well, someone who was forever borrowing money for peculiar schemes and never paying it back. It was only later that he became quite wealthy.

My aunt Miriam was thin and dark and her body was very angular. When she sat or stood she kept herself slightly bent and so had developed a hunch, although I don't believe that anything was wrong with her back. She held her body un-gracefully, as if she had never gotten used to it, as if it were a burden to her, but her face was thin and pretty and she had a tangle of dark hair, but it was not glossy like Dalila's. She had a very attentive face, as if she was expecting you to toss her a ball. As a child, I was struck by the veins on the backs of her hands, which were thick and dark and protruded like cords of heavy string. Miriam was my grandmother's older daughter and had born the brunt of her mother's pessimism. She tended to see herself in the worst possible light but did it rather humorously and was always making jokes about her inability to cope with the world. My father claimed she let herself be defeated. But certainly she suffered from all those times when her mother had told her that she couldn't do some-thing or that it was all right to fail or that it didn't matter that she wasn't as pretty as other girls. Long ago she had studied to be a nurse but she gave it up when she married.

Miriam was very quick to notice other people's successes, and although she was glad for them she also envied them and perhaps part of her even wanted them to fail, even though she was not an unkind person. Because of this attentiveness she had a great capacity to understand human behavior and was able to make sense out of the most impossible situation. She was a good listener and seemed nonjudgmental and as a result people told her everything. If they held back, she urged them forward. But guiding her questions, as well as her life, was her own sense of failure and it seemed that her failure had overwhelmed all her other characteristics. For instance, she could not abide to see anything out of place and at home she was constantly cleaning and tidying, as if to use the perfections of her house to make up for the imperfections of her life. How she kept her house, how she spoke to people, how she carried herself, all reflected her sense of failure. As a child I was struck that she was the only one of the adults who expressed no surprise about the earthquake: she had known it was coming, as if the earthquake were the gigantic catastrophe always on the horizon, and what she liked about it was its egalitarianism. It afflicted us equally and no one was to blame.

Miriam was devoted to her husband and even admired his philandering, admired that he was able to live without any interference. In fact she romanticized Freddy as a sort of outlaw and was always praising the clever new things he was doing. At the moment he was in Ancud on the large island of Chiloé trying to operate a fabric store. He had won the controlling interest in a card game and now hoped to make it pay. But all communication with Ancud had been broken except for some ham radio operators and their stories were of a tidal wave that had swept through the town. Consequently, my aunt was very upset.

Miriam and her children had left Puerto Montt early that

morning and the journey had taken most of the day. The one paved road was impassable and there were also many fissures and new streams and fallen trees. Even though their house in Puerto Montt was on the side of a hill, it had been scarcely damaged by the earthquake: only broken windows and fallen plaster. Early that morning, however, there had been a mudslide.

"It sliced off half of the house as neatly as slicing a piece of cake," said Hugo, as if speaking of a personal triumph. "It cut right through my room without even waking me up."

"Hugo will sleep through anything," said Rosvita.

"It's true, it's true!" said the twins.

Freddy Piwonka Gray had been keeping the pony cart in the backyard as collateral for a loan. The horse—really no more than a shaggy brown pony—was so frightened that they had to blindfold it until they got outside the city.

"Houses had fallen down all over," said Hugo. "And the fires were terrible. Many people were hurt and they were sleeping in the street. There were cows even downtown and rubbish everywhere. I had to lift all sorts of things that had fallen across the road."

Hugo was a rather dull-witted affable boy of great strength. Lifting heavy objects was his only skill and so he went about lifting things and betting people he could lift things. Once Spartaco bet him that he couldn't lift a box in the shed. It wasn't a very big box but earlier Spartaco had secretly nailed it to the floor and Hugo nearly killed himself trying to pick it up. He was very angry and chased Spartaco but he couldn't catch him. Spartaco could always run faster than anybody. My parents said that Freddy Piwonka Gray used to beat Hugo terribly and had turned him into a cretin. In those years I found Hugo awfully dull because he was always talking about sex and girls and what he had seen through people's windows and what went on in darkened rooms when people had their clothes off. Even Spartaco didn't like to hear it.

They had taken the back road from Puerto Montt and described many stranded trucks and cars, collapsed barns, burned houses, broken trees. Hugo spoke of the animals which were wandering as if dazed: beavers and foxes and even a puma. Many horses were running loose. And the vultures were so stuffed with carrion that they could hardly fly. Everywhere people talked about the total destruction in distant places and how lucky they were to have survived but how their own time was coming. And when they spoke of their approaching deaths, it was as if they were a joke, which didn't mean they didn't believe in their destruction but that it was amazing to them. Many creatures had come out of their holes, rats and mice and snakes, as if afraid of being crushed underground. Springs had closed up and streams had gone dry, yet other springs had suddenly appeared.

"There was a hot spring right in the middle of the road," said one of the twins.

"And the pony nearly fell into it," said the other.

Nancy and Norma were exactly alike and very emotional, with blond hair and rosy cheeks. They were big, solid five-year-olds and it seemed they were always running about and telling what everyone else was doing. Even later in life they had that strange, nearly telepathic relationship which is not uncommon in twins, as if an invisible telephone wire ran between their heads. They married brothers and some people claimed they all slept together in the same bed and that even the brothers didn't know which was which. As children they invented their own personal language made up of barks and growls and strange guttural words. They were good-humored snoops and would do anything that their sister Rosvita told them, just like little soldiers.

As for Rosvita, in those days I couldn't stand her. She had a great sense of herself as a future actress and was very pretty and always wore dresses. She had little time to waste on us younger children. Occasionally she told me about her breasts and about how big they were getting, although they were hardly noticeable. She imagined that Alcibiades was attracted to her in some way (although she was not even fourteen!) and she flirted with him terribly. It nearly drove me wild. Later she had quite a difficult life and a retarded daughter and I have long since forgiven her for the extravagances of her adolescence, but during the time of the earthquake she was a terrible nuisance and a complainer and I think it was her jealousy of Dalila that caused so many problems. Certainly no one would have known anything if it hadn't been for Rosvita. She had pretty light brown hair that was very fine and very difficult to control. Her mother kept it in braids which Rosvita found humiliating.

As we stood by the cart, my mother told her sister about my father's death and they began to weep and hug each other and I began weeping too. His death was always there, like something hovering at the corner of my eye, and I kept noticing it again and again. And each time it seemed like a surprising thing. Now the twins were crying and Walterio was crying and my great-aunt Bibiana was crying, but I noticed that my grandmother's eyes were dry and unforgiving. Her hands were on her hips and when she looked at her family she squinted. After another moment she called to the workman with big ears and told him to put my aunt's bags in her bedroom. Then she went about getting them all something to eat.

Spartaco, who was always somewhat impressed by his cousin Hugo, had told him about the dead sheep dogs and they set off across the yard to the orchard. I followed them, trying to stay out of the mud. When we passed through the gate, my brother made a disappointed noise. The three dead sheep dogs had disappeared.

"I don't believe you," said Hugo. "I don't believe they were there."

"They *were* there," I insisted. Hugo was big and lummoxy and blond and liked violent games.

"I saw all sorts of dead things in town," said Hugo. "Even dead children."

"But they weren't hung," I said. I was still crying, I don't know why. It was as if the switch to turn off my tears had broken.

"Grandfather must have cut them down," said Spartaco. "Otherwise they'd attract vultures."

"We'll see them again," I said. "When we die, we'll see all the dead things as if they were alive. They'll be as fresh as fresh. Even my father. And St. Lucy will be there as well. Both St. Lucys!"

But Hugo wasn't interested in this. He glanced through me as if I were no more than an window opening onto a better place, then he strolled back to the farmyard. Spartaco gave me a friendly shrug and followed him. Why is a child's allegiance always to an older child, no matter how stupid that older child may be? I sat down on the wet grass. I was cold and my clothes were wet through. Really, I thought, the sooner the earthquake came to carry us away, the better.

Alcibiades found me there and picked me up, so that I rode on his hip, and carried me to the fire.

"Don't you have any other clothes?" he asked.

I told him I didn't know. My mother, even at the best of times, was a distracted sort of person and what we wore or didn't wear or whether we washed or didn't wash was pretty much our own concern, unless our father happened to notice.

Alcibiades found a dry blanket and wrapped me in it. I

wanted to go to the highway and see the *animita* of Jaime Alverez, to see if it was safe, but I didn't have the strength.

"I know you're very sad about your father," said Alcibiades, sitting down beside me. "I'm very sad as well." There were beads of water caught up in his wavy blond hair. Even his mustache was wet. We were sitting near the fire and I could feel its warmth on my face. Nearby Hugo and Rosvita and the twins were eating mutton stew. Hugo kept making animal noises to make the twins laugh. Spartaco was laughing as well.

Alcibiades put his arm around me and I leaned back against him. "Your father was one of my best friends," he said. "And you know how much he loved you? He talked about how brave you are and how smart you are and how you read so many books." He was quiet for a moment and reached forward to poke the fire with a stick so that sparks flew up. "He was seven years older than me and when he began seeing your mother, I was just your cousin Hugo's age. I was suspicious of him but he went out of his way to make me like him. I remember he had a motorcycle and he took me for rides. Once we went down to Puerto Montt. We wandered around Angelmo and near the fish market I looked into some sailors' bar and got in trouble. You know how kids can be, they see something they don't understand and they smile. I smiled at some angry-looking fellow and he thought I was making fun of him and he came rushing out. Then your father showed up and told the man he would have to fight him first. It was almost funny because your father wasn't a fighter and had no wish to fight. And the fisherman, or whatever he was, didn't want to fight your father who was a lot bigger than I was. So the fisherman said he would forget it if I apologized. Your father asked what I had done and when it was explained to him, he said he was sorry but he felt it was the fisherman who should apologize. I remember there were a bunch of people around us who wanted a fight. Your father kept asking exactly what had happened and once that became clear he decided the fault lay with the fisherman. He was so persuasive that he convinced this other man and he apologized, not because he was afraid of fighting your father, but because he had been truly convinced. Then the three of us went back into the bar and your father bought the fisherman a glass of wine. As we were about to drink, your father said, 'Salud,' and the fisherman got angry again and said, 'Only drunks say Salud,' and your father laughed so hard that the fisherman began laughing as well."

I sat next to my uncle in the damp and my hand rested on the sleeve of his leather coat. It always surprised me to hear about my father's life. He seemed to belong to our family so completely that to hear about him in relation to other people gave him an almost mythic dimension, as if these were not other experiences but other incarnations. My uncle's story made my father very real to me, because I too knew his obsession with precision: to see clearly, remember clearly, speak clearly. For a moment my father stood with me again; then the realization of his death made him doubly dead and I began to weep.

Alcibiades hugged me and when my weeping subsided, he said, "Dalila, too, has suffered very much and is very unhappy. You should be nice to her and see if you can do anything for her."

"Do you really think we're all going to die in another earthquake?" I asked.

My uncle looked around the yard. It had begun to rain more heavily and the drops drummed on the tarpaulin above us. I tried to think what he was looking at and now I think he was simply trying to imagine the house and farmyard, all that he had grown up with, as not existing. "I don't know," he said at last. "It's impossible to predict anything."

Slowly my grandmother moved us all into the large bedroom.
Cots and pallets were arranged on the floor. Candles and kerosene lanterns were found. There were now seventeen of us,
plus Ana in the kitchen and the two workmen: the evangelist
and the man with big ears. My grandmother was trying to draw
us all together as if we were chickens at the moment before a
tremor, all bunched together. She had a brother out in the
country whom she worried about and of course there were
cousins and Freddy Piwonka Gray, but we seventeen were the
core of the family: her five children and their families, her two
sisters and her husband. Yet even though these people didn't
particularly believe in a future time when their lives would
return to normal, and even though they seemed willing to accept
their imminent destruction, they all believed it differently and
to different degrees. While my grandmother and her sisters
were preparing the room, which my aunt Miriam humorously
referred to as our burial chamber, there came the steady banging of my grandfather and the two workmen repairing the shed:
a shed which by evening had already fallen down several times.

And then, I think, the supposed imminence of our deaths
and the destruction of the normal world was very liberating,
and not necessarily in a good way. The house, for instance,
was full of food. This was food which had been prepared over
a number of years and was reserved for certain occasions. Not
only had the earthquake flung this food around the rooms but
it had apparently wiped out the possibility of those future
occasions. As a result, there was a lot of eating. The twins
both had jars of jam. Then there was fruit, sweet pickles,
various breads, many cakes and hundreds of cookies. Even
Manfredo, who still refused to talk, constantly had his mouth
full. The twins seemed to see it as their special task to force
him to talk and followed him around making him miserable

with their questions and teasing. He refused to speak, but he ate like a machine whose only purpose was to eat.

But it was my uncle Walterio whose eating most affected me. It was as if he had been freed from a great burden and now could turn himself completely over to food. I remember him sitting in a corner of my grandmother's room with several boxes of cookies and a jar of blackberry jam and he wasn't content simply to eat the cookies but he kept dipping them in the jam until his lips and mouth were stained dark blue and his fingers were all sticky. As I said, he was already plump and his thinning hair was fine like a baby's, and sitting in that corner with his supply of sweets he looked like a hulking caricature of a toddler. And the thing is, my grandmother encouraged him. When my uncle Hellmuth made some critical remark, my grandmother was quick to come to Walterio's defense.

"What's the harm?" she said. "Let him have his pleasure while he can."

The room where the cookies were stored was up on the second floor in a corner far away from the stairs. It was dark and the floors creaked dangerously and if there was a serious tremor one could easily be trapped up there. None of us felt comfortable going upstairs. Only Walterio was willing to risk his life in such a way and others would even ask him to bring them cookies and jam, to go on errands they were afraid to go on themselves. And again and again I remember seeing his elephant-like behind slowly ascending into the darkness as the stairs creaked ominously and bits of plaster fell around him. The twins and Hugo and my great-aunt Bibiana saw him as heroic, while Spartaco, who earnestly looked for occasions to test his heroism, saw his uncle as only foolhardy.

This sense of being freed from convention affected us all.

For the children it meant the absence of parental control. We could go to bed when we wanted and eat what we wanted, although I was too caught up in the fact of my father's death to have this change do more than convince me that my world was upside down. And Spartaco, as I say, saw in the earthquake the chance to be brave. But perhaps we were touched more deeply. There were tremors all day and night: some slight, some big enough to set everything rattling. And with each tremor came the possibility that it would build and build and the earth would open and we would be swept away. As a result, we were in a constant state of apprehension and bewilderment and our only consolation was that we were together.

The other most obvious effect of the earthquake was on my great-aunt Clotilde. In retrospect it seems that she and Walterio had the greatest potential for eccentricity. The inhibitions and restrictions of normal life had so far kept them under control. Those restrictions were like an old-fashioned corset and without them Walterio and Clotilde—who were both the youngest children of their families—sagged and collapsed and their self-control vanished.

But they were also very different. Clotilde had no interest in food, while greed, I think, was unknown to her. Of course, there were many Clotildes. There was the Clotilde I knew when I was eight years old who told stories of disappointment and sighed wonderfully. As a child, I saw her as almost two-dimensional. Perhaps for a child everything is two-dimensional. She was thin and gray-haired and dry as a nut. Her fingers with their rings and painted nails seemed frighteningly long. Her complaints could sour any party. But what did I know about her disappointments?

As I grew older and got to know her better, she became a different person: not less disappointed but sadder and fleshed out. She was a woman who felt she possessed an excess of romantic love and was convinced that if she had been loved in return, then she could have accomplished great things: that love would have allowed her to take charge of her life, would have given her the will and energy to fling herself into the world. Without this enabling power of love, she fretted and complained and nibbled her life away. She was a hypochondriac and when she died it was a surprise to everyone, since her death suddenly legitimized one of her many complaints. It was almost amusing. Everybody swore they hadn't known she was ill, while Clotilde herself had been proclaiming her illness a hundred times a day. Even her illness, uterine cancer, seemed ironic. But she was kind to the degree that her eccentricities allowed her to be kind and she loved her sisters and was loyal to her family.

When I graduated from college, she gave me a ruby ring. By then she was already sick and had not long to live. She was just seventy-one and had turned her youth into a kind of fiction. Or perhaps all memory is fiction. Every yesterday seems a mixture of strangeness and routine, and if asked to describe it five different times, one might give five different answers. But when Clotilde gave me the ring, she said it had been given to her by a young man by the name of Franz who had loved her. Then he went off to the far south, to Porvenir, to make his fortune, and he died there in a boating accident. My aunt Miriam swore that Franz had never died, that he had simply chosen not to return, and that in any case his connection to my great aunt Clotilde had been very casual. It was Miriam's idea that even the ring was an invention, that Franz had never given it to Clotilde, that she had bought it herself or only found it somewhere.

But I feel certain that when Clotilde gave me the ring, she truly believed her own story; and even if the story had begun as a lie, it was a lie no longer. Her memory had turned it into a truth: the man was dead and not, as Miriam claimed, a baker in Punta Arenas with an Indian wife and nine children.

When she gave me the ring, Clotilde described how she had met Franz at the cemetery. He was on his way to the highway where he would get a bus to Puerto Montt and then catch a boat to Porvenir.

"We sat and talked," said Clotilde. "We were very near my mother's tomb. Her family's, really. And their name, 'Grob,' was carved in big letters just a few yards away. He was in a hurry but he kissed me, first on the cheek, then on lips and neck. He urged me to lie down on the ground with him. He said he didn't care if he missed his bus, that he could walk or catch a ride later. For a moment I let him kiss and fondle me, but turning, I saw the name Grob, and the letters seemed bigger and they reminded me of who I was and I pulled away and made him stop. Truly I believe if we had been sitting anyplace else, I wouldn't have had the power to stop. I think my decision made him respect me even more. He wore this ruby ring and he pulled it from his finger and thrust it upon me. Then he grabbed up his bag and ran for his bus. He promised to write, but shortly after that I heard he had drowned. Of course, his death was awful to me and I often thought of our few moments in the cemetery, but each time I was aware of having done the right thing."

Even at twenty-two, I was conscious of Clotilde's lie, that for fifty years she had regretted not making love to this man, that thousands of times she had probably fantasized his caresses there on the ground under the name Grob. But who knows, perhaps he never even touched her? Perhaps it was all her dream. Although, as I say, when she told me the story she had no doubt as to its veracity, nor did she doubt that she bore her virginity into the grave as a kind of curse, a burden from which she had never been freed. What good was her sense of propriety and correctness at seventy-one? And the ring was a symbol of her mistake, that she should have let him have his way with her there on that grass, that she should have followed him to Porvenir.

But at twenty-two what did I know myself? The ring was evidence of a sad and romantic story, not a lesson or warning, because despite its evidence I took it and placed it on my finger and plunged into my own life, my own mistakes and bad marriage, my own missed opportunities. At thirty-eight I try to tell myself that I am lucky to have my life under my control, to have a daughter who loves me and employment that I like, to play the piano and give occasional recitals. But then, unwillingly, comes the vision of my former husband passing in a taxi with still another woman and he is smiling and I am swept up and think how much I would give to have some man smile like that at me.

My great-aunt Clotilde kept herself under the tightest supervision. That constraint was like a harness and her complaints and sighs and hypochondria were like the creaking of leather. But at the time of the earthquake, her supervision slipped, just as it did with Walterio, and her impulses made away with her.

Off my grandmother's bedroom was a little alcove, a sort of dressing room, and into it my grandmother had put a daybed which was raised at one end. That evening when I came into the house after being with Alcibiades, I found Clotilde standing in her sister's bedroom wearing the wedding gown that her sister had worn and her mother had worn and her grandmother had worn and which she, too, had hoped to wear and which she was wearing now. And the strange thing was that she was acting as if she was doing nothing out of the ordinary. She put on the gown and went into the little alcove and lay down on the daybed and stayed there with her hands folded across her breasts. It took me some time to realize that she had dressed herself for Death, as if Death were her bridegroom. She lay on that narrow bed and waited for him as if her actions were the most normal in the world. And my grandmother, too, treated her actions as normal and even encouraged her and spoke sharply to my grandfather and uncles if anyone made any criticism. We were all going to be swept away and if Clotilde meant to be swept away in a wedding gown, that was no business but her own.

It was a peculiar time and peculiar things were happening and Clotilde's eccentricity dissolved into the events of the day, becoming as natural as Walterio's gluttony and the hanging of the sheep dogs and the fact that we were all going to settle down in my grandmother's bedroom to await the destruction of the world and the only irritant was the *bang-bang-bang* of my grandfather's hammer as he tried to prop up the collapsing shed.

Not everyone chose to sleep in my grandmother's room that second night. Hellmuth and Alcibiades slept outside and Spartaco and Hugo stayed with them. But we all ate in my grandmother's room—another stew of vegetables and mutton, and at last I understood why mutton was so plentiful. But as we were eating there came a noise at the door and I turned to see Dalila. She was no longer crying and she had brushed her hair. Indeed, she looked very proud and also carried a kind of anger. I was nearest to her and I stood up and offered her my seat. She thanked me and even stroked my hair but said she wasn't hungry.

"You haven't eaten all day," said her husband.

"Is there any water?" she asked.

Although the water tank had fallen, there was a well in the yard with a hand pump and so we had plenty of water. Alcibiades poured her a glass. He was too far away to hand it to her so he stood up.

"Would you like wine?" asked Bibiana. "There's plenty of wine."

"Wine gives her a headache," said Hellmuth.

"I'll have a glass if it's no trouble," said Dalila without looking at her husband.

"Of course it's no trouble," said Bibiana. And she sent Ana to fetch a glass. Most of the adults were sitting at a round table where several candles were burning. Walterio was on his cot in the corner. Clotilde had already retreated to her alcove. My mother was seated by the window and her unhappiness was a heavy weight upon her. I went to her, leaving my chair which was next to Alcibiades. There was a brush in my mother's lap and I took it and began brushing her thick dark hair.

Dalila accepted the glass of red wine. She was standing uncertainly, then she took the seat next to Alcibiades. Her anger seemed to have disappeared. She turned to Alcibiades and toasted him. "*Salud,*" she said, then drank off the glass.

Hellmuth seemed on the verge of saying something but remained silent. Dalila spoke for him. "Dear Hellmuth has a delicate stomach and wine upsets it. We hardly ever have it in the house."

"A little bit wouldn't hurt now," said my grandmother.

"Yes," said Alcibiades, "what's the harm?"

I watched them and tried to understand their tone. Hellmuth suddenly looked very angry. My mother, caught up in her own despair and isolation, began to weep again. Was she weeping for my father's death or the fact that he had died with his mistress? Even today I cannot answer that question. I brushed and brushed, and as my mother wept, her hair crackled with electricity and tiny sparks leapt out around my hands. From far away came the rumble of thunder and one of the dogs began to moan. I thought of the *animita* of Jaime Alverez out on the highway where for once there were no cars and no trucks and I imagined the *animita* split open and rain falling onto the laughing face of this dead man whom I thought of as James. For a moment the room was silent except for the crackling of my mother's hair as I brushed it.

Then my aunt Miriam laughed loudly and said, "I'll have a glass of wine, too. Why not?"

4

ON THE NORTHWEST side of Puerto Varas is a cone-shaped hill called Calvary. A winding path corkscrews up to the top and along it are twelve statues depicting the twelve Stations of the Cross. Each statue shows the suffering Jesus and each is very plaintive. At the very top on a mound of stones is a huge cross with a life-size painted Jesus and the spikes through his hands and feet are real spikes. On either side of the cross stand the Virgin Mary and Mary Magdalene. They, too, are painted a sort of pinkish color. The Virgin's head is covered by her robe but Mary Magdalene has long brown hair and she clasps her hands across her breasts and stares up at the Savior. Around the cross is a flat area with a few benches, and around that are tall trees, mostly eucalyptus and pine, although the side facing the town and Lake Llanquihue is open. One of the most beautiful views of Puerto Varas is from this spot and one looks out across the red roofs of town and across the lake to the volcanoes Osorno and Calbuco: Osorno at 2,700 meters is a perfect cone while Calbuco at 2,000 meters is flatter on top and slopes more gently. Between them, although thirty miles farther east on the border with Argentina, stands Tronador, the Thunderer, rising to 3,500 meters.

I used to go there often as a child. Our house across from

the hospital was very close. But more than the view and the solitude of the spot, I liked the messages. Attached to the rocks supporting the cross and nailed to the surrounding trees were dozens of placards with messages such as "Thank you Jesus for the miracle that restored the hearing of my little daughter" or "Thank you for the restoration of my health" or "Thank you for relieving the pain in my legs which has been my affliction for thirty years" or simply "Thank you, Jesus." These placards came in all varieties. Many were very elaborate: delicately carved cherry or walnut with copper letters and carefully painted or stained. Later I realized that somewhere there existed a small industry of artisans to whom one could go for such placards. Others were very simple and homemade: a few words gouged or painted on a shingle. I suppose it was the nearness of the hospital that gave most of the placards the common theme of health, although I remember one that said, "Thank you, Jesus, for helping me fight off bankruptcy" and another, "Thank you for letting me discover the fire in time." Each was signed, usually with just a first initial and a name: J. Prowda or O. Gomez.

At night after everyone went home, I imagined that Jesus came down from his cross and walked from tree to tree in order to read the messages. He would be stiff after his long day and move slowly, and after reading a placard he would somberly nod his head and his long brown hair would tremble in the breeze. Sometimes I wondered how Jesus could see the placards in the darkness and I tried to imagine him with a flashlight, but then I thought that Jesus probably didn't need a flashlight. He wore only a white cloth around his waist like a towel and during the winters I felt sorry for him being up there in the rain. Every few weeks I would climb the hill and read the placards and see if there were new ones and if I recognized the names of any of the families. Sometimes in the summer I would take a book and sometimes I would just stare out across the lake.

After the earthquake the surrounding trees were covered with hundreds of new placards. Most were homemade, but quite a few also had that professional look. It seemed right somehow that in this period when all work and industry had come to a stop, the men and women who made the "Thank you, Jesus" placards were busy from morning to night. Most said something like "Thank you for sparing my family's life in the terrible earthquake." Others were more specific. One thanked Jesus for sparing his daughter, another for sparing his dog. Another thanked Jesus for giving him no more than a broken leg. Another thanked Jesus for sparing his car when others on the street were destroyed. And, as usual, many just said thank you. All the trees were covered to heights up to five meters.

Even as a child it seemed to me that people weren't simply expressing their gratitude. They were also reminding Jesus of their existence in the hope that he would continue to save them, because each day brought still more earthquakes and tremors and we still believed the worst one was coming and it only made sense to remind Jesus of one's continuing gratitude and devotion. And there were so many placards that I imagined Jesus climbing down from his cross very early in the evening, then working steadily until dawn, carefully reading each one and copying the names in a book which perhaps the Virgin Mary kept concealed in her robes. And perhaps he was helped by the other saints, even by my own St. Lucy the Virgin Martyr who was also the patron saint of light. Then, as dawn broke, Jesus would climb back onto his cross exhausted and glad to be there, while already he would hear the footsteps of new pilgrims and soon would begin the *tap-tap* of hammers as new placards were attached to the trees.

They said later in the newspaper that the earthquake that Sunday afternoon was so strong it made the whole planet vibrate. It measured 8.5 on the Richter scale. The center was located near the coast at about the latitude of Puerto Montt and at a depth of about fifty kilometers. At dawn the previous day there had occurred an earthquake near Concepción, a port city about six hundred kilometers north of Puerto Montt. About one hundred and fifty people had died and there were many fires. That earthquake measured 7.5 on the Richter scale. In the south we had felt that earthquake as a severe tremor, but many people took it as a warning and were careful with their stoves and put aside food and so when the big earthquake struck on Sunday afternoon they were not entirely unprepared. Even so, the earthquakes that week killed more than four thousand people and damaged half a million houses. About fifty thousand houses were totally destroyed. Quakes and shocks and tremors continued along this five-hundred-mile area for months. The city of Valdivia about two hundred kilometers north was also badly damaged and had to be evacuated. Much of the loss of life came not from the earthquakes themselves but from the tidal waves, or tsunamis. In 1939 a catastrophic earthquake near Concepción had killed thirty thousand people and after that quake a new building code was put into effect and most of those new buildings survived. But the tidal waves wiped out entire villages.

Their cause was not entirely clear. In one argument there was a slippage along an offshore fault paralleling the coast, a sudden rise or fall along the ocean floor. Others blamed submarine landslides and turbidity currents: fast movements of muddy water along the bottom. Others spoke of masses of light molten material bursting up from the heart of the earth which pushed toward the surface of the ocean and then sank again as they cooled. And there may have been truth to that since

in Lebu south of Concepción there was a tidal wave of hot sea
water. And, as I mentioned, the rain on Monday was a warm
rain.

The tidal waves were preceded in each case by extremely
low tides which acted as a warning. In some cases the sea
seemed to disappear completely. First there was the earthquake
and a few minutes later the sea began to disappear. Those who
knew what would happen opened all their windows and doors
and went up to the hills, so when the water returned it swept
in and out of their houses leaving only mud and dead fish. In
most places four waves returned, the third being the biggest.
Near Valdivia the wave was nearly fifteen meters tall. At Ancud, where Freddy Piwonka Gray was visiting his girlfriend
and running a fabric store, the wave was about twelve meters.

There is an island near Ancud called Isla Cochinos, or the
Island of Pigs or Dirty People, and when the water went away
people could walk from the island into town. But when the
water came back, the wave swept over the entire island and
many people were killed. Ancud is a fishing town and this was
the middle of the oyster harvesting season. More than three
hundred oyster boats each with at least five workers were in
the harbor at the time. When the water began to disappear
many of the oyster fishermen thought they would be safe if they
put out to sea. There was a very brave policeman in Ancud
named Vergara who set out after them in the police launch *La
Gloria.* He told them of the danger and took many on board
and roped their boats together and headed back to Ancud.
Then the wave came and people in town could hear all the
fishermen on the police boat—about sixty people—screaming
and crying out to be saved. When the wave struck, *La Gloria*
completely disappeared and people thought the ground under
the sea had opened up and swallowed it, although later some
of the bodies washed ashore in Corral three hundred kilometers

to the north. The only survivors were a woman and her two daughters who were found on Isla Cochinos the next day.

Seventy houses were swept out to sea in Ancud with people clinging to their roofs still crying for help. The wave swept over the center of town, destroyed the post office and bank and badly damaged the cathedral so that it had to be torn down. In the next few days about seventy bodies were found along the shore but this was only a fraction of those who were lost. When they dynamited the cathedral a few years later, they found more bodies and skeletons underneath. And just in 1987 when they were excavating for the new cathedral they found even more skeletons and some were recognized by their jewelry.

In many coastal towns, houses were carried far inland. One man found his house five kilometers from the water in the middle of a wheat field and the fire was still burning in the stove and the plates were still on the table. A bus owner in Ancud had his bus swept away twenty kilometers and he had to build a special road to get it back. Because the tidal waves continued for the rest of May, many people stayed in the hills; and one farmer near Maullín had thirty families stay with him for a month, while a cousin, who had a farm above Ancud and saw the water disappear, drove his truck down to the city and loaded people into it, then drove back to his farm, unloaded them, then drove down again, making trip after trip. People came from their houses carrying all they could carry, but the police made them leave their belongings behind. My cousin made trips for forty-five minutes before the tidal wave struck and for nearly three months he had eighty people staying in his house. Forty were children and a woman from Puerto Montt organized games. They ate chick peas everyday and had lunch in four different shifts and no one wanted to leave because it was the end of the world.

Maullín, where the evangelist was from, is also a town with many fishermen and many of these went out in their boats when the water disappeared. Maullín is on the River Maullín several kilometers from the coast and the river became just a trickle even though it is normally about two kilometers wide. Many people also went into the hills. One rich man in Maullín was fleeing up the hill when he remembered he had left his strongbox in the house. He hurried back to get it, but when he got inside his house, the wave struck, and when the water retreated again, the house and the rich man had vanished. His name was Atala, but he was called "the Turk," meaning anyone from the Middle East.

Maullín was partly protected by a pine forest which had been planted to protect the sand dunes from further erosion, but despite this protection many houses were swept upstream. The boats with the fishermen were shot upstream like rockets. Many people died. Boats and houses were left in trees or in the middle of fields. A farm worker named Sanchez who worked for my great-uncle was on horseback and his horse went crazy and dragged him for over a mile and the man lost his leg and had to be flown to Santiago. Two other men whom my great-uncle knew were on horseback when the tidal wave struck. They leapt into a tree. The wave passed over them and passed back, sweeping their horses away. Another farmer and his foreman were on horseback near the water when the wave struck. The wave washed the foreman away. The farmer lassoed his leg, breaking it but saving his life. The ferry boat that took cars and people across the river landed in a field three kilometers from Maullín. Eventually it was disassembled and brought back to the river piece by piece.

The tidal waves that struck the coast that Sunday also set out across the Pacific. The four waves moved at speeds of up to seven hundred and fifty kilometers an hour and were so far apart that they measured one hundred and sixty kilometers from crest to crest. Ships passing over these waves only noticed a certain slowing. Warnings went out and in Hawaii the city of Hilo was evacuated. In Japan, however, the people at the tsunami warning station were away at a sporting event and so no warning was given. Nearly two hundred people were drowned in Japan and four thousand homes were washed away. Sixty people died in Hilo. Australia, Okinawa, the Philippines, New Zealand, Alaska, Russia—all were battered with waves from ten to thirty feet tall. In California hundreds of small boats were torn from their moorings. In each case the waves were preceded by extremely low tides and in some cases the water seemed to disappear completely.

It has always seemed strange that the earthquake which sent the piece of brick flying through the air that killed my father on a street in Puerto Varas also killed so many people so far away. I would imagine the grief in those distant places and know it was also my grief. In Hilo and Onagawa and Kushiro and Shiogama were children who had also lost their fathers and who, as the years slid by, saw that time in May as the time when their childhoods changed irrevocably. My life has been many things both wonderful and sad but I have always felt it began on that Sunday afternoon with the news that my father was killed.

On Monday, May 23, there was another severe earthquake in Valdivia, as well as hundreds of tremors. An avalanche on Osorno overswept half a dozen houses and about fifteen people were killed. In the fierce seas off the coast near Valdivia, two freighters, *El Canelo* and the *Santiago*, sank with all hands. Osorno had been smoking all that day as had other volcanoes and that night they erupted. Osorno, Caulle, Corral, Casablanca, Puyehue—all sent up explosions of molten rock. Two new volcanoes were formed as well, one of which had been a lake. The lake rose and rose, shoving itself into the sky, then erupted in fire. Two other mountains disappeared. They just fell down and became valleys. The cities of Osorno and Llan-quihue were ordered evacuated. Araucanian Indian settlements high in the mountains were destroyed and hundreds of Indians died. Molten lava poured down into the lakes. The heat from the volcanoes caused high winds and there was also thunder and lightning and strange colors in the sky. New islands appeared offshore. New lakes appeared, others vanished. Many lakes and rivers and tidal inlets changed their positions and much of the land became covered with water. The train tracks were submerged and their beds had to be rebuilt. Fence posts would lead off across the new lakes and can be seen even today sticking out of the water like sad thumbs. Houses were flooded and sometimes only chimneys or roofs would rise up from the water. In memory of those who had died, people planted water lilies in this new water so that for years during certain seasons the water would be covered with flowers. Then slowly, the junquillos, reeds which are used for making baskets, overgrew the flowers.

During those first days the volcanoes were almost as frightening as the earthquakes. We couldn't quite see them because of the rain but everything became dark and it seemed that the sun was going out. The darkness was caused by the volcanic ash and over thirty centimeters fell onto the fields. If winter wheat had been planted, it killed the wheat. The ash got into everything. My grandmother and aunts hung wet sheets and towels in the windows but despite their efforts the room where we slept grew full of ash and everything was filthy. People wore wet bandannas over their mouths. The darkness, the rain, the constant trembling, the smell of sulphur, the thunder and lightning and high winds—our family was not the only one that imagined the end of the world. The men would sit and discuss fault lines and volcanoes and tidal waves until I expected to see a wall of water sweep over the remains of the shed. People would come from town or nearby farms and all the stories were of families waiting for the end.

Everywhere there was strangeness. The volcanoes drove all sorts of animals out of the mountains—pumas, mountain goats, deer—and we would see them in the fields. And cows wandered through from far away and people caught them and ate them. People waited and slept outdoors and tried to stay warm, but they made no attempt to clean up or to resume their lives. At one point on Tuesday the firemen came around and said that the earthquakes were over but no one believed them and shortly after they left there came another earthquake and everything shook and shook and the birds screamed and we ran from the house and crouched down in the rain and once more the shed collapsed and grandfather was so furious that he beat at the boards with his stick and I could see that my grandmother thought he was crazy.

In town even more houses collapsed, as well as part of the hospital, and the firemen must have been very depressed. Many times a day airplanes would pass overhead and we felt we were being inspected by officials from the capital and we wondered what they saw: dirty, ragged people picking over sheep bones in the fallen-down doorways of collapsed buildings. But some of the airplanes were also delivering aid from all over the world and on Tuesday the Explorer Scouts came through passing out blankets and my grandmother was angry and said we already had lots and lots of blankets, that of course we had blankets. But in the schools of Santiago all studying stopped and each classroom made a blanket with each student knitting a square and the teacher sewing them together. And these blankets were very colorful. And years later people sold them and collected them and displayed them and they became very valuable.

We buried my father that Tuesday. Because many people had died and so many more were hurt, the priest was very busy and the service was held outdoors because no one wanted to go into the church. The priest seemed angry the whole time and when he spoke he bit off the ends of his words. I thought it was the rain that made him angry but much later I decided it was the circumstances of my father's death. The priest's name was Father Opilio and he was an eccentric man. He was famous for his interest in young girls, as well as his ability to say mass in five minutes, which made him very popular with young people. Years before, he had lost the index and middle fingers of his right hand in an airplane accident. But every day since the accident he had taken splints and new bandages and made a long protuberance that resembled two bandaged fingers. In this way it looked as if he had not lost his two fingers but simply wounded them. These actually were the fingers he used to bless the congregation at the end of mass and many people were upset that they weren't being blessed by a pair of fingers but by a bandage. But other people said if it was a priest's bandage, then it, too, was holy and must be respected. Spartaco had a fierce desire to see under the bandage and often talked about it. Once he managed to shake the priest's hand and truly he intended to give the bandages a strong tug, but he was afraid of embarrassing Father Opilio and so he lost his nerve.

Father Opilio was a short dark man whose mustache and eyebrows and graying hair were very bristly. The individual hairs would never lie flat but stuck out in all directions. My father once said he looked like an oversized cleaning tool, and even though my mother was angry that he had spoken irreverently before us children, I saw her smile. And when my mother wasn't listening Spartaco would refer to Father Opilio as "God's dear pot brush."

My grandmother didn't come to the funeral, nor did her sisters, nor Walterio, nor my aunt Miriam and her children. My grandfather was there, as well as Hellmuth and Dalila and Alcibiades. Manfredo wanted to stay with our grandmother but our mother wanted him with us and Spartaco said he would pinch him if he wasn't good. The service was very short. Father Opilio had a way of speaking very quickly so that you didn't know where one sentence ended and the next began. I concentrated very hard because this was my father's funeral and I wanted to remember every word, but then suddenly we were already at the Pater Noster and it was over. Afterward the coffin was put on the back of a horse-drawn wagon and we followed it through the rain to the cemetery. The day was very dark because of the volcanic ash and the drops of rain had a greasy feel and made gray smudges on the umbrellas. Father Opilio and my mother rode on the wagon. Father Opilio had a special black glove that fitted over his bandage but it was very bulky and Spartaco said it looked like he was holding a pistol. Alcibiades and Hellmuth walked behind the wagon with Dalila between them. Then Spartaco, Manfredo and I followed with my grandfather. My father was quite well liked and about twenty other people came as well. Many had bandannas or handkerchiefs over their faces and Spartaco said they looked like a band of outlaws. Some people I knew, some I didn't, but it touched my heart to see how sad they all were.

My mother, for all her sorrow, kept peering around suspiciously. I would say, "Who are you looking for, Mother?"

"No one," she replied, with a mixture of anger and grief.

At the time I thought she was hoping that my grandmother would change her mind and come after all, but later I decided she was looking for Elisa Anabalon Schwabe, my father's mistress.

There was a tremor before we reached the cemetery and the

horse lay down right in the middle of the road. My mother and Father Opilio jumped from the wagon. Everyone stood with their heads cocked as if waiting for important news. Dalila threw her arms around Hellmuth and he looked irritated with her. The trees shook and flung their rain drops in all directions. As the tremor got worse, the wagon began creaking, then the coffin began banging in the back. It made a dull thudding noise almost as if someone was trying to get out. Then the coffin began jumping in the wagon. It seemed to want to bounce right out onto the road. Alcibiades put his hand on it as if to quiet it, to reassure it. Manfredo stared at the coffin in absolute horror. He still refused to speak, still felt full of guilt, and as the wagon shook and the coffin banged about in the back I am sure he felt that our father was going to leap out and ask him about the pistol and why he had fired it. Manfredo's breathing got all strange and after another moment he tore himself away from us and ran up over the field toward my grandmother's house. Spartaco called after him but he refused to stop. We saw him cutting through the high grass as fast as he could run and I knew that his only wish was to bury himself in my grandmother's skirts. After another few moments the tremor subsided and the horse got to his feet again. Father Opilio was very angry with the horse and shook his finger at it, but Spartaco said that the horse understood that although the human beings would go to Heaven, he, the horse, probably wouldn't be allowed within Heaven's gates and this is what made animals more frightened than people.

The cemetery was on a hillside on the southwest side of town. The farther up the hill, the poorer were the graves, as if to be buried at an angle reflected one's financial condition, and at the very top were just Indians and friendless people, although, as Spartaco said, the view was best from the top. The Droppelmans and Grobs and Schieles and Gebaurs all had their tombs at the bottom: substantial stone houses with carved cherubs and weeping dryads in which whole families were buried. The Recabarrens, my father's family, were a little higher up and didn't have a tomb but a series of granite slabs. Father Opilio said a short prayer, snapping out the words like spitting pebbles from his mouth. The four workmen lowered the coffin into the grave and we all lined up to throw a handful of dirt on top.

When it was my turn, I looked down with great sadness. My father's coffin was shiny dark brown with a copper cross on the lid. I wished I had something of his, even one of his little fingers which I could keep with me in a little box with white cotton and which I could touch to my lips in order to calm me. Although I expected to see him again quite soon, I hated this separation and I asked both my St. Lucys to look out for him. Everything was confused and my mother was too distracted to pay attention to us. My mind was full of things that I wanted to tell my father, to climb into his lap and be glad for his deep seriousness, but all I could do was to toss bits of dirt and pebbles into the grave. They made a hollow sound on the wood and for a moment I waited for some responding noise, a rapping or distant call, but there was nothing.

I stood there not wanting to move away and after a moment Hellmuth knelt down beside me and put one of his large hands on my shoulder. "It's very hard," he said, "but you have to let him go now."

"I'll see him in Heaven," I said.

Hellmuth looked down at the ground and I could feel his shyness and uncertainty. "That's right," he said, "you'll see him in Heaven."

My mother was still glancing around in a nervous way, peering over the shoulders of the people who had come to the cemetery. The earthquake had toppled many of the crosses and monuments and some of the tombs were cracked right open. Father Opilio kept shaking his head and making clucking noises.

"Excuse me," I asked him, "if we all die together, who will be left to bury us?"

He gave me a look as if I had stuck a pin in him. "Don't be fresh," he said.

My mother paused in her weeping to give my arm a shake, then Father Opilio took her aside to console her. She wore a black pillbox hat with a veil and it made her whole face look gray.

"They say the American soldiers are coming to Puerto Montt," said Spartaco. "Perhaps they'll bury us."

"If some American tries to bury me," said my grandfather in a gruff whisper, "I'll whack him with a stick, because I don't plan on dying."

"Me neither," said Spartaco with sudden resolve. "I'll stay with you."

Hellmuth and Alcibiades had found a Droppelman tombstone which had fallen over and were trying to lift it back in place. Dalila stood nearby with her umbrella. She had borrowed a black coat and black fur hat belonging to my great-aunt Clotilde and looked very pretty.

After the service, Father Opilio returned to town on the wagon, urging the driver to hurry so that the wagon bounced and rattled. Father Opilio was a man who always had lots to do and was always late, and even when he was talking to you, he seemed to be thinking of the next thing down the line. He didn't live in the present but a few moments into the future and consequently he never paid attention.

People walked back to town. My grandfather and Spartaco

set off across the fields to the farm but Dalila and my mother didn't want to get their skirts wet and so they took the road. Hellmuth and Alcibiades went with them.

My mother embraced me. Despite her umbrella, her dark coat was quite wet as if thick with tears. "Now you're almost an orphan," she said, still crying, "and I'm a widow."

Hellmuth and Alcibiades went first down the road. They were great friends and always talking and Hellmuth had his hand on Alcibiades's shoulder. Sometimes they discussed the price of cattle. Sometimes they discussed the price of men's hats. Sometimes they talked about fishing. There were salmon in the River Maullín which had been brought from Alaska in 1930 and five or six times a year Hellmuth and Alcibiades would go fishing. Then my grandmother would smoke the salmon and serve it on special occasions. Once Alcibiades took me fishing as well. The River Maullín goes right through the forest and the trees press so thick that the river is like a tunnel. There are many swans on the river, shy, black-necked swans that always swim ahead so that you only see them when you round a bend. Even when fishing Hellmuth would talk about the price of cattle and clothing and where to get the best price on a car. But Alcibiades, I knew, loved the beauty of the river and although he heard his brother, he was letting the green water and distant swans fill his heart.

Dalila walked after the two brothers, then I followed with my mother. Dalila was uncomfortable with my mother's grief and she had no interest in me and consequently she was bored. She began to sing something, then looked at my mother and stopped. She kicked at some stones. She looked around at the murky day. When she turned, her black hair swirled around her shoulders. The mountains were invisible and the lake was just a smudge.

"I miss my perfume," she said to no one in particular. She

was wearing high-heeled black boots that buttoned up to her calves. Her feet were very small and when I put my own feet in her tracks I saw that mine were nearly the same size. "I found some jewelry," she said, "but no perfume. Why is it so dark? It's only one o'clock. Oh, this whole thing is so boring." Here she looked at my mother again, as if afraid of having offended her, but my mother was blowing her nose into a white cotton handkerchief.

After another moment, Dalila picked up a pebble and threw it at Alcibiades's back. He was wearing a short brown leather jacket and the pebble made a slight thump as it bounced off. Alcibiades turned and looked at her in surprise. She looked away, pretending she hadn't thrown it, although really, who else could have done it? My mother was weeping and I was too far away. And of course I wouldn't have dreamed of throwing a stone at Alcibiades.

A minute later Dalila picked up another pebble and threw it as well. Again Alcibiades turned. This time he glanced at me but I made no sign. Hellmuth was still discussing money and hadn't noticed. He was leading the way and had turned up the lane to my grandmother's farm. Hellmuth had a bearlike way of walking as if he were uncomfortable on two legs and he splashed in the puddles as if he didn't care one way or the other.

After another minute Dalila threw a third stone which hit Alcibiades in the middle of his back. This time when he turned he was grinning. I found myself wondering what Dalila's face looked like, whether she was grinning or looking serious. As we continued up the hill, Dalila tossed several more pebbles at her brother-in-law, mostly hitting him, and he would grin or duck. Hellmuth continued to talk and was apparently unaware of the pebbles. Then Dalila missed Alcibiades and hit Hellmuth's hat. He turned violently and looked very angry.

"Can't you stop this foolishness?" he said.

I was surprised at how angry he was and even my mother stopped crying and looked up to see what was wrong.

"I'm so bored," said Dalila, stamping her foot in the mud so it splashed.

"Then help my mother," said Hellmuth, "or knit something or do something useful." He turned back again, as if flicking a switch on his attention so that Dalila no longer existed. Alcibiades, however, had stepped aside. He ducked down and grabbed a pebble which he tossed back at Dalila. She shielded herself with her umbrella and the pebble bounced away. Alcibiades winked. Then, when he noticed I was watching, he blushed and turned back to his brother.

Early Wednesday afternoon, I decided to walk out to the highway to visit the *animita* of Jaime Alverez. I had the worst fantasies of its being split apart and Jaime Alverez's photograph lying face up in the rain. I took a rake. Spartaco came with me and brought a shovel. Our cousin Hugo came as well because he was restless and the farm was gloomy. He also liked to imagine that he was a conquistador and that Spartaco and I were his Indian slaves and he would give us small tasks, such as bringing him a piece of cheese or a sweater. In return, he would tell us about the world and the strange things he had seen there. Most of these things concerned women and how some of them wanted *"It"* so badly that it had driven them crazy. And he liked to describe a poor beggar woman in Puerto Montt with one eye and a twitch who used to be a schoolteacher until her sexual hunger drove her into the abyss.

"And when I walk by her," Hugo said, "she hisses at me and even though she is ugly and has only one eye, I can tell she still wants it. Oh, there are women driven mad by it all the time." He said this with a satisfaction which suggested that he, too, had fierce inclinations in that direction but that he also had the moral fortitude to fight them off.

Through all this talk he treated me—his eight-year-old female cousin—with a sort of sympathy: the sympathy one has for a calf before it becomes veal. I, too, would some day become the slave of my desires. That was my fate. I didn't argue with this but I remember feeling relief that the imminent destruction of our family would save me from future peril. Hugo's mother had been drinking all day, constantly sipping at a glass of wine, and it affected her behavior. Her speech was slurred and she would suddenly laugh at nothing in particular. Sometimes she would bury her face in her skirts and weep. For a child, adults tend to be mysterious. It is unclear why they do what they do. And I found myself wondering if my aunt Miriam wasn't drinking because of being driven mad by sexual hunger. After all, Freddy Piwonka Gray was in Ancud. Hugo, too, was disturbed by his mother's drinking, although he joked about it, and that was one of the reasons he came with us out to the highway: to get away from her. The twins came as well, or rather they tailed behind, watching us and hoping to observe deviant behavior which they could later report to the world at large.

We cut through the orchard, then over the fence and across the fields. Because of the volcanic ash, we wore handkerchiefs over our mouths which Spartaco happily said made us look like thieves on a devilish errand. The fields were filthy with ash and we were soon covered with it. The ash clung to our hands and had a greasy feel. Several times we came upon the bones of sheep which had been picked clean. Hugo found a sheep's skull in very good condition and he carried it for a while and even tried wearing it as a hat. It was still drizzling and his blond hair was matted to his head. Hugo crouched over with the skull on his head and made an animal face and wanted to chase me, but I didn't want to run and Spartaco told him to leave me alone. For a few moments he hopped up and down and grunted and glanced around uselessly for someone to be bad to. He flapped his arms and his feet splashed in the mud. I have known Hugo for many years and he is now middle-aged and fat and has high blood pressure, but every time I see him, maybe once a year, I still picture that skull on his head, as if that is an emblem of what he is: a bullyish and lummoxy boy clowning with a sheep's skull in the rain.

The highway had been completely destroyed by the earth-quake, its panels of concrete all twisted and tilted and col-lapsed. The highway had been paved for just a few years and it seemed a shame that it was destroyed already. Apart from roads in town, it was the only paved road anyplace and to see it in ruins was very sobering. It was, after all, our single link with the north. Two great trucks were lying on their sides and a few other cars and trucks were stranded or stuck in the mud where they had tried to drive off through the fields. The Copec station was also destroyed and the huge underground gasoline tanks had been pushed right out of the earth like a dog spitting out a pill. The only person around was a soldier on guard and he waved us away.

Spartaco called to him, asking about his friend who worked at the station, but the soldier pointed his gun at us and we ran. I thought that perhaps the soldier had been confused by the handkerchiefs over our faces, but Hugo said no. He had told us about looting in Puerto Montt and how people had been shot. We assumed the looting was over by that time, or at least under control, but actually it had only begun, because as we moved further into winter, people grew more desperate.

The *animita* of Jaime Alverez was damaged but still intact. The surrounding metal fence had been badly bent and the cross had tumbled down, as well as one of the flower boxes. Inside the *animita*, Jaime's photograph had fallen over. I took it out and inspected it and wiped it off. At least the glass had not broken. Jaime Alverez's handsome face looked as cheerful as ever. He had a square chin with a dimple and his lips were not too thin and not too full. Some weeks earlier I had made a bouquet of dried flowers and had put it inside the *animita* along with a poem and a photograph of myself so that Jaime Alverez would have some company. Hugo was surprised that I had given my photograph to the *animita*.

"What if someone finds it and gets angry?" he asked, leaning over my shoulder to look at it.

"Why should they get angry?"

"Because it's like trespassing. And with a picture it would be easy to find out who you are and where you live. Then your father might have gotten angry and punished you."

"Why would he have gotten angry?" I asked.

"He just might have, that's all," said Hugo. He had been working hard to bend back the metal fence, while Spartaco and I were raking the gravel and trying to put back the cross. In the distance, Nancy and Norma watched us like a pair of blond crows.

"What is the poem?" asked Spartaco.

It was a stanza from a poem by Gabriela Mistral and I read it to him.

> Heavy are our eyes with weeping,
> but a brook can make us smile,
> and as the lark lifts up its song,
> we forget we will die for a while.

"That's about sex," said Hugo.

"Don't be silly," I said.

"Well," said Hugo, "it could be."

"How could it be?" asked Spartaco.

"The weeping part," said Hugo. "I hear my mother crying sometimes when Freddy is with her. Sometimes it hurts them."

"What hurts them?" I asked.

"The man's pecker," said Hugo. He was leaning against the fence with his arms folded. Drops of rain rolled down his face but he made no attempt to wipe them away. "I heard Dalila and Hellmuth last night. They were going at it and she was moaning something awful and Hellmuth told her to shut up. Alcibiades heard it, too. Hellmuth told her to be quiet and pushed her away and she was crying, just like in the poem."

"I didn't hear anything," I said.

Hugo laughed. "That's because you were snoring all night long."

"How do you know Alcibiades heard anything?" asked Spartaco.

"He was sleeping right next to me," said Hugo. "His breathing changed and I knew he was paying attention. Dalila was moaning and I got a boner just from listening."

"What's a boner?" I asked.

Spartaco made a face. "Don't talk like that in front of Lucy," he said.

"She's the one asking the questions," said Hugo. "Anyway she should know what it is just so it doesn't catch her by surprise later on."

I felt mystified but curious. "Why do you always talk about sex?" I asked.

"Freddy says . . ." Hugo always referred to his father by his first name. "Freddy says that before men are born God comes around and gives each one a choice: either he can be born a man and walk on two legs, or he can be born an animal like a dog and lick his balls. And the reason why some men are so sad is that they realize they've made the wrong choice."

I found myself thinking about Peppo and his strange bark.

"That's a stupid thing," said Spartaco.

"Freddy never says stupid things," said Hugo.

"Well, that sounds like a stupid thing," said Spartaco.

"Let's talk about something else," I said, brushing the ash from the roof of the *animita*. "Do you think we could get some fresh flowers for Jaime Alverez?"

Hugo had grown tired of working on the fence. "Who cares about a dead man anyway?" he said.

"Our father is a dead man," I said, "and I think about him all the time. And we'll be dead ourselves pretty soon."

"Not me," said Hugo, "there's lots of girls right now who need someone to look out for them."

"I'm going to stay with grandfather," said Spartaco. "If the earth opens up, I'm going to be standing right next to him."

"He makes you work too hard," said Hugo. "Bang, bang, bang, why's he bother with that old shed anyway?"

After another few minutes we finished with the *animita*. I wondered if I really would see Jaime Alverez very soon and the thought made my skin all prickly. Then we gathered up the rake and shovel and headed off across the field. Nancy and Norma went to inspect the *animita*, then followed us. The sky was dark and had a yellowish cast. At the edge of the field was a tall brown animal. I had no idea what it was. When it noticed us, it seemed to disappear. Hugo kept wanting to talk about people having sex and how he sometimes watched his parents through a hole in the wall. But Spartaco was bored with that subject and wanted to talk about the Americans instead. He had heard they were giving away food and blankets and they laughed a lot and were big and blond.

"I'm big and blond, too," said Hugo.

"Not like an American," said Spartaco.

When we got back to the orchard, we found our grandfather going from tree to tree and shaking them. The branches and remaining leaves were covered with a wet layer of volcanic ash.

"They can't breathe," said my grandfather. "They're just sitting out here suffocating."

Spartaco hurried over to him. "I'll help. I can climb into the high branches."

"I was hoping you would do that," said my grandfather, patting Spartaco's shoulder. "I can't climb like I used to."

In my grandmother's bedroom, my family appeared to be waiting for someone of consequence, like waiting for a doctor; they looked bored and alert at the same time. It was very dim and half a dozen candles were burning. Hellmuth and Alcibiades were playing chess and talking quietly. Hellmuth's hands were so big that the white chess pieces seemed lost within them. In her alcove, Clotilde was with my cousin Rosvita. Clotilde was still wearing the wedding dress and had a string of pearls around her neck. Her cheeks and lips had been rouged and her gray hair was covered by a veil. If you squinted, she looked quite young. Rosvita had found a stack of Paris fashion magazines from the 1920s and she and Clotilde sat side by side on the daybed studying them intently with the aid of a kerosene lantern. The drawings showed skinny shorthaired girls dressed as flappers and skinny long-haired girls dressed as society women. Rosvita and Clotilde were picking out clothes for themselves and asking each other's advice.

"I think you would look quite pretty in that pleated ball sleeve," said Rosvita.

"They tend to drag in the soup," said Clotilde, "but they look nice when you dance."

Rosvita's fine hair was loose and she kept playing with it and wrapping it around her fingers in a way that reminded me of Dalila. It worried me that in five years I might behave in a similar manner and again I felt relieved by the thought of the impending earthquake, that death would save me from future humiliations.

"Come and help pick out clothes," said Clotilde. "We'll find you a pretty dress."

"She doesn't like dresses," said Rosvita, who was not eager to have me join them. "She's a tomboy."

"I wear dresses sometimes," I said.

"You always need to look your best," said Clotilde, "so the men will pay attention. A pretty dress is like a promise."

"What kind of promise?" I asked.

"Of things to come," said Rosvita and she giggled.

In the larger room my great-aunt Bibiana was fanning herself, although it was quite cool. My grandmother sat across from her at the round table, reading out loud from the Old Testament, and she had to use a magnifying glass in order to see the words.

" 'There were giants on the earth in those days, and also after that, when the sons of God used to cohabit with the daughters of men and bore children to them and they became mighty men of old, men of renown. And God saw that human wickedness was great on the earth; that the intention of all human thought made nothing but evil all day. Then the Lord repented ever having created man, and He felt grieved in his heart. . . .' "

My aunt Dalila and my mother were sitting on a bed and Dalila was doing my mother's nails. My mother was staring out the window and seemed a thousand miles away. Miriam had just had her nails done and Walterio was waiting. He wore a bulky brown jacket like a loose bag and the side pockets were bulging with hard little silver cookies. The front of his sweater was spotted with crumbs.

"I've never, you know, had my nails done," he said.

"In the city," said Dalila, meaning Puerto Montt, "people always judge each other by their nails. I often look at a person's nails before I look at their face. If a person's nails are in good condition, it shows they like themselves and have self-respect. Ugly nails show a lazy mind."

"I must have a lazy mind," said Miriam cheerfully. "My nails are always breaking." She sipped a little of her wine, then held up her nails to the candle. They were painted bright red and sparkled.

Dalila finished with my mother. "If you blow on them, they'll be dry right away," she said.

My mother glanced at her nails. They, too, were bright red and sparkled. "It doesn't matter," she said.

I got the brush and began brushing my mother's hair. It was the only thing that seemed to make her happy. She patted my hand and sighed.

"I don't want any of that red stuff on my fingernails," said Walterio.

Dalila took one of his hands and began to inspect it. His hands looked like fat white potatoes and his fingers like little swollen sausages. "Colorless polish," said Dalila. "It will make them hard. Why, you have crumbs under your nails."

"That tickles," said Walterio.

My mother's hair was thick and dark and I liked how it felt when I filled my hand with it and squeezed it. "Can I make you one long braid?" I asked.

"Do what you wish," she said.

"Can you try to be happy?"

"I am happy."

"What are you doing to those things, the cuticles?" asked Walterio.

"Pushing them down," said Dalila. "It doesn't look nice if they show."

"I never look at a person's cuticles," said Walterio.

"Everything you need to know about human nature is right there in a person's hands," said Dalila.

"My hands are a wreck," said Miriam. "But Freddy always has his hands done. Even when we have no money he manages to get them done."

"Are you sure that polish won't show?" asked Walterio.

"No, it's clear," said Dalila, "but if you keep eating cookies while its wet, you'll get crumbs stuck to it."

"It's funny, you know," said Walterio, "what I mean is, having my nails look so nice with no one to show them to."

"There's us," I said.

"Oh, well, you're family," he answered.

And in the background I kept hearing my grandmother's voice. " 'And the flood was forty days upon the earth; and the waters increased and lifted the ark so that it rose from the ground and still the waters kept mounting and overran the earth, while the ark floated on top of the waters. And still the waters kept rising and covered all the high hills under the heavens to a depth of eight meters and more, and all the mountains were covered. . . .' " My grandmother held the magnifying glass in her right hand and every now and then she glanced up and her eye through the round magnifying glass was huge and attentive.

"Now it's Alcibiades's turn," said Dalila.

"Maybe I could have just my little finger," said Walterio, getting to his feet, "maybe just have that one painted red."

"People would stare," said Dalila disapprovingly.

"But if it's just us . . ."

"I don't want my fingernails done," said Alcibiades. He was still playing chess but I couldn't tell who was winning. Hellmuth didn't look at his wife.

"I've done everyone else's," said Dalila. "It's your turn now."

"You didn't do mine," I said.

Dalila didn't hear me. "It's unfair not to do it. Even Walterio had it done."

"Even I did it," said Walterio. "You should see them."

"You didn't do Hellmuth's," said Miriam. "Do you ever do his nails?"

"Never. They smell of cattle."

"My father's hands smelled of cinnamon water," I said. I kept brushing my mother's hair and she kept looking out the window. It was nearly dark outside. From the yard I could hear the twins shouting strange words: "Bjork, bjork, ribbit!" I wondered if my grandfather was still shaking the trees.

"Please, Alcibiades," said Dalila, teasingly, "let me fix up your nails. I'll feel bad if I don't."

"Leave him alone," said Hellmuth without looking up.

Alcibiades looked at Dalila, then looked away. I realized he felt shy.

"Please, Alcibiades. Really, I can see from here that they look a sight."

"Maybe after this game," said Alcibiades.

"But you can play anytime and I'm all ready." She sat on the bed and her tools were laid out in a row beside her.

"Leave him alone," repeated Hellmuth. His voice was flat and without energy as if his words bored him.

"I'm tired of your telling me what to do," said Dalila. Then she laughed. "Really, being married to you is like being in the army."

"Freddy says that being married to me is like being married

to a loaf of bread," said Miriam, and she laughed so hard that she spilled her wine.

"I don't mind your telling me what to do," said Dalila to her husband, "but I think it's a shame when you won't let your own brother have his nails done." She stood up and took a few steps toward them. "Look at them. They're all cracked. What if they were like that in the store?"

"The store's destroyed," said Alcibiades with a smile.

"I don't care if you do his nails," said Hellmuth, with more energy. "It's the infernal chatter while I'm trying to think."

Dalila looked around at us in a triumphant way as if Hellmuth had just exposed himself. "Maybe you'd like us all to go out and sit in the rain until you're done," she said. "Maybe you'd like us to get drenched and cold. We'd all catch some dreadful flu, I'm sure. You know the doctor said I had to be careful about bronchitis. It's bad enough that my house is ruined. I have no clothes, no perfume." She stood slightly to the side of Alcibiades with her hands on her hips and her chest pushed out. Alcibiades looked up at her. Hellmuth stared at the chess board. "I'm not just doing people's nails because it's amusing," continued Dalila. "It gives them self-respect."

"You can do my nails," I said.

Again she didn't hear me. "Come along, Alcibiades. I simply insist." She stamped her foot and again he looked up.

"Paint his nails, I mean, why not paint them red?" said Walterio.

"They do looked cracked," said Miriam, standing up.

"I'm waiting," said Dalila. She folded her arms across her breasts and stared straight ahead.

Alcibiades tugged at his mustache. He looked embarrassed.

"Just let me make this move," he said. He moved his knight, then stood up slowly. Dalila took his hand and led him over to the bed. She reminded me of an impatient schoolteacher.

"Really," she said, "if you don't take care of these problems right away, they get worse."

They sat down facing each other. Dalila put his left hand in her lap and began poking at the thumbnail with the file. "You have very pretty hands. You must learn to take care of them. Once you ignore even a piece of yourself, all the rest begins to slide."

"They're just hands," said Alcibiades. He saw me watching him and he shrugged. Even though he seemed uncomfortable I could tell he was enjoying himself.

Hellmuth looked at his wife in a speculative sort of way. He, too, was a shy man apart from business, the sort of man who let other people instigate the action, who let other people telephone him or come to his house, who had few friends outside of my father and Alcibiades. My father was often suggesting that they go out for coffee or to the Club Alemán or up to the casino and play roulette. Hellmuth would go and even have a good time, but they wouldn't go out again until my father called again.

Hellmuth moved his bishop, then stood up. "I'll be outside. I need a smoke." He walked across the room so heavily that the candles shook and the light flickered.

Alcibiades began to seem more relaxed. "You're a real professional," he said.

"Sometimes I think of giving lessons," said Dalila. "It's a shame to have a gift and not share it. If I taught the high school girls, then everyone in town would have beautiful nails."

"The high school fell down," I said.

"Why not paint, you know, just one of his little nails red," said Walterio. "Or even blue."

And from the alcove I heard Clotilde say, "I used to have Charleston beads but your grandmother took them away from me."

And my grandmother kept reading. " 'Then the Lord came down to see the city and the tower which the sons of men were building. The Lord said, "Behold! One people and all with one language! The way they are starting to behave, there is nothing they can think of that they won't be able to do. Come, let us go down and confuse their language so that they cannot make out each other's words. . . .' "

That night there was another severe earthquake. Its center was off the coast near Maullín about sixty kilometers away and it measured eight points on the Richter scale. In Maullín it caused another tidal wave and one hundred and fifty people perished when the wave overswept one of the islands off Chiloé. This was Wednesday night and we were all sleeping in my grandmother's room either on cots or on mattresses on the floor. I had a nest of blankets and suddenly it seemed that the blankets were fighting and I was bounced out of them. One kerosene lantern was burning on the table and Alcibiades had the presence of mind to grab it; otherwise it might have fallen and started a fire. This earthquake overtook us with great speed and abruptly we were in the midst of noise and violence. The twins and Rosvita were screaming, others as well. We scrambled for the windows and doors. A board fell from the ceiling and nearly hit my great-aunt Bibiana. The floor shook so fiercely that walking was like one of those dreams when you run and keep being thrown back. All the pictures of Jesus, Mary and the saints were flung from the walls and crashed around us. My grandfather helped my grandmother to the door. Similarly dressed in white pajamas, they shuffled side by side and their shoulders were hunched. Clotilde in her wedding gown jumped from the window.

Not only were people running, the tables and chairs and beds were running, too. Even the blankets jumped and fluttered as if spirits were hiding beneath them. I tried to help my mother. People called to each other but the noise of the shaking was so loud that our words were lost. I saw Manfredo clinging to my grandmother's nightgown as my grandfather urged them out the door. Walterio sat in the corner with his hands over his ears. Around him on the floor dozens of little white cookies were jumping up and down, as if they were dancing, as if Walterio were their god and they were praising him. Alcibiades dragged him to his feet. Hugo was trying to help his mother. A bottle of red wine had spilled and the wine rushed across the floor like a red snake. I got my mother to the window and Spartaco helped me push her through. She was as ungainly as a mattress and didn't care what happened to her. Dalila was very frightened and kept stumbling and falling. Her nightgown was open and I could see one of her breasts and even the breast seemed to be jumping. Hellmuth was trying to help her out of the room but she was so frightened that it seemed she was trying to climb up on top of him as if he were a boat in rough water. Then I fell through the window right on top of Spartaco who said, "Ooof."

Outside the noise was worse and it was raining. The sheds and what was left of the barn all banged together. The cooking fire and stove tumbled down and the red coals hopped across the yard until the rain put them out. There were several flashlights and the kerosene lantern and all the lights were shaking. I helped my mother into the backseat of my uncle's Opel. Shingles were flung from the roof of the house and they banged on top of the car. We hugged each other in the backseat. The car felt like it was going very fast down a bumpy hill and it did actually bounce part way across the yard. I was thrown up and my head banged against the roof. In the mixed light I could see my grandmother standing by herself in the middle of the yard. Her face was raised to the sky and she appeared to be shouting, although nothing could be heard. She looked very happy and when I stared up into the darkness it seemed I could see my father waiting for us and he looked happy, too, and I was sure that St. Lucy the Virgin Martyr was waiting as well. "We're going!" I called to my mother. "We're being swept away!" My mother stared into my face, not understanding. And just as I began to repeat that we were being swept away, it all came to an end. The earth stopped moving and everything was quiet except for the crying of the twins and the fearful beating of my heart.

There was a great deal of damage but in the darkness it was impossible to tell how bad it was. I thought that at least all the trees in the orchard had gotten a good shaking and not one bit of volcanic ash could remain clinging to a single leaf. I think we all felt light-headed. After a severe quake one is almost in a state of shock. Perhaps it is the rush of adrenaline or the body's terror. My legs were shaking so much that I could hardly walk. The tarpaulins had fallen down and Hellmuth and Alcibiades were trying to put them up again. Someone brought out more lights. My grandfather was stamping on the ground and shouting, "What a bruiser, what a big bruiser!" He seemed quite happy. My grandmother had already gone back into the house with Manfredo. It was cold and wet and I didn't know what to do. Spartaco and Hugo were helping Alcibiades. Dalila was sitting in the front seat of the Citroën smoking a cigarette. Its red glow moved back and forth from her mouth to the steering wheel.

After a while I went back inside. My uncles, except for Walterio, chose to sleep outside for the rest of the night, as did my aunt Miriam. My mother didn't care where she slept. Bibiana slept in one of the cars and Clotilde returned to her bed. We all felt confused, as if we had been slapped. I crawled back to my nest on the floor and pulled the covers over me and shivered. Then I must have gone to sleep. I awoke sometime later to find my grandmother sitting on the floor next to me and stroking my hair.

"You were crying," she said.

And it's true, my cheeks were wet with tears. I had been crying in my sleep but on waking I had no memory.

"Come," said my grandmother.

She took me into her bed on the side away from my grandfather who was snoring. Their bed smelled of dust and sweat and lavender soap. My grandmother put her arms around me and pulled me into her pillowy bosom.

"It's frightening to be a child," she said.

I wanted to disagree but then I started weeping again. I was embarrassed and didn't know what was wrong with me. My grandmother's arms were bare and soft and I pressed my face against them.

"Your uncle Gabriel was often frightened," said my grandmother, speaking quietly so as not to disturb her husband. "That's why God took him up into Heaven. Because it's safe there. He used to weep and weep and he had pains in his back. When he went away he was just four years old and he must still be four years old because in Heaven people get neither older nor younger. He's four years old but he must be very wise. When we get there, he will be your special friend. Did I show you his picture? I will tomorrow, if there's time before we're taken off. I thought it almost happened tonight. It seemed so close. I could feel Gabriel waiting for us. When he was here on earth, he loved the baby lambs and it occurred to me that the dogs killed the sheep just for Gabriel, just so the sheep could go to Heaven, too. Does that seem foolish? He had the softest hair. Even after he died I sat next to him and stroked it and stroked it until they took him away. I try to picture him in Heaven. Father Opilio says that in Heaven we won't have our bodies as we now know them, that we'll be like light or bright and shiny air, but in the illustrated religious books all the angels have bodies and they wear robes like the Greeks and Romans and I imagine Gabriel wearing a robe and looking just like a little Julius Caesar, but I don't think he has wings. I think only the angels have wings, unless they made him an angel, which they might have because he was so precious."

I went to sleep again with my grandmother talking to me and the rest of the night passed in sweet-smelling darkness and I had no dreams. When I awoke in the morning, my grandparents had already gotten up and I was alone in the bed. It was a sunny day, although because of the volcanic ash the air seemed yellow. My great-aunt Bibiana was instructing Ana to put the wet sheets over the windows where the glass was broken. When she noticed me, Bibiana said, "Wasn't that a busy shaking in the night? I was so frightened that I nearly wet myself." Then she laughed and laughed and unpinned the handkerchief from her breast and wiped her eyes.

That Thursday morning a letter arrived from Freddy Piwonka Gray in Ancud. A man on horseback brought it and he said the waves between the mainland and Chiloé were very dangerous. And he also said that people had seen wolves, but my grandfather laughed and said there were no wolves. He was building the shed again and it made my grandmother angry to watch him. Freddy's letter was as follows:

> Dear Wife: I am fine and in good spirits. ["*When was he anything else?*" *said my grandmother.*] The fabric store was swept away but I was saved. As you know it was in a small building in front of the house where I am staying. When the wave came, it carried off the store and left the yard full of different colored candles. Yesterday and today I saw the fabric floating out on the sea. There is red and blue and orange, long trails of

cloth. Tomorrow if it's there I will row out and get it. I have gathered up all the candles. There is no electricity and I have been doing a brisk business. Did you worry about your Freddy? The shaking was very bad and many houses fell down. The tidal waves were even worse. But the shaking freed some coins from people's pockets and I have been doing lots of collecting. On the beach yesterday were boxes and boxes of dishes as well as many mattresses. The mattresses were ruined, but I have collected many of the dishes and only a few were broken. Everyday there are new things on the beach. It is like Christmas. Just this morning I found ten crates of bananas and I have already sold two. People are looting and stealing from stores which I can hardly understand because there is so much to be found on the beach. But they like small things: watches and jewelry because they think they are easy to carry. I must tell you that ten boxes of bananas are very heavy. And the dishes, whew! The police have called a curfew and several people have been shot. One of them was Eduardo Cuperman who owed me money and I don't think I can get his wife to pay.

Many houses have disappeared and the priests are full of complaints about the cathedral and say it will fall down. The great clock on the tower stopped exactly at three o'clock. The police have taken charge of the school so people can have a roof over their heads. The police feed more than two hundred people a day and school has been canceled for the rest of the year. People are very depressed but I do not let it get me down. Every occasion offers its own prosperity. You will be surprised when I tell you that I have become a photographer. People are very eager to have photographs of their houses, or, in some cases, just the empty lots where their houses once stood. You take a picture of a house and it doesn't need to smile and you don't have to tell it to stand still. Already I have sold nearly a hundred pictures and I am busy all day and all night. When people don't have money, they give me other things and I sell those, too. I have even hired a girl to run the store. Don't worry, she is very ugly and she has a hump on her back.

The trouble is I will soon have done all the business in Ancud that I can do, so I am writing to say that I plan to return to Puerto Montt. Surely in a city so big I can take many pictures and there must be many things to sell. And the Americans are coming. Already they have been giving away blankets in Ancud. I have gotten several boxes and they are also in my store: good wool blankets. I sell them cheap because people are cold.

Pray for me and wish me good fortune. I will write to you again soon. Are Hellmuth and Alcibiades working hard? Love to you and the children.

Your dear husband, Freddy

My aunt Miriam read the letter out loud as we stood in the yard. She read it in almost a sustained shout so that my grandfather could hear as well. My uncles Hellmuth and Alcibiades were very struck by what Freddy had said.

"He's taking photographs," said Alcibiades.

Hellmuth looked as surprised as if someone had thrown water over him. "He's going to become rich," he said. "What did he mean about my working hard?"

"He thinks you're making money," said Hugo, who for once got something right. "He thinks you're going to become rich, too."

5

OFTEN I AM struck by the difference that time brings to our perceptions, how each new experience changes our understanding of the old. It seems that every day the confusing jumble of images that we call our past appears in a different aspect, while events which had long been unclear suddenly spring into clarity years later. We move from light to shade to light again while time thickens our waists and constantly adjusts and perhaps distorts the lens through which we see the world. Such thoughts sometimes lead me to reflect upon the two recordings that Glenn Gould made of Bach's "Goldberg Variations": the first recorded when Gould was hardly more than a child in 1955 and the other done not long before his death from a stroke (was he only fifty when he died?) in 1981.

The first recording is impetuous and bold and meant to shock. Even the aria at the beginning is played all in a rush and not with the "aloof carriage" that Gould himself said it required. The entire piece is packed with wonderful episodes but remains almost anecdotal, the individual parts being more important than the whole. Despite the expertise and brilliant execution, the aria and thirty short variations are played without a sense of past and future, as if they existed outside of time. Listening to him play this first version is like listening to the self-absorbed chatter of any young egoist. In fact, the final variation before the concluding reprise resembles a triumphant march. But what has been conquered?

The 1955 recording is a triumph of fingers, while the recording made twenty-six years later is a triumph of the whole man. It has the weight of Gould's entire life behind it, the weight of his mortality. It, too, is bold. It, too, looks forward. But it is not brash. It lacks impetuosity. Although it contains sadness and melancholy, it is not melancholic. The first variation, which on the 1955 recording is played only a little faster than the aria and with little shift in tone, here in the second comes as an explosion: the contemplative life overthrown. The past, the future and all the changes in between, all the vicissitudes that mark us—these take on actual mass. The whole piece has what Gould called that "unity through intuitive perception, unity born of craft and scrutiny" which the earlier version lacked.

Gould always hummed as he played. One can hear him on any recording. But on the first version of the "Goldberg Variations" the humming is subdued, a sort of cheerful accompaniment. In the second, the voice becomes a second sonorous instrument and with it one hears the fullness of a man's life, a life quickly approaching its end. It is not wisdom that one hears in the second version (would that it were!); it is simply time. Years have gone by and to look at any object or person or event is to look through those years. I don't like the man of the first version. His brashness, his gall and self-absorption form a barrier. But with the man in the second I feel I could sit down and converse. He would tell something of his life and I would tell something of mine, and who knows, perhaps these stories might even contain some truth.

Isn't it accurate to say that once a word is uttered, once an event has occurred, then it is gone, that it rushes away like something falling into outer space? We make lunges after it, lunges of understanding and remembering. We say it was this or that, but in truth all our remembering is a fiction. What we have from the past are a series of physical images, sensations, the smell of our grandmother's kitchen, a perfume, the smell of something burning, the vague memory of a lover's body. A mood remains, a taste in the air. We try to rebuild these events. We try to summon back the touch of another's flesh. How did it feel to have his hand pressed against my cheek? We catch glimpses of some dead face. We hear a snatch of music or the rushing of the wind. We look at the events of the past and we are constantly saying what this meant, what that meant, but other people who lived through the same events would give different stories, different interpretations. We live at the edge of two mysteries: what lies ahead and what falls away behind. But even if we inadvertently turn our pasts into fictions, they still color us. We see the world through what we imagine these past events to be. If we believe we have suffered a great affliction, then everything around us, day after day, becomes afflicted. Yet might not that affliction be false, something we invented out of spite or hurt pride or rejection?

My husband used to reproach me for using intimacy as an occasion for complaint. We would come together in an evening. Perhaps he had been late the night before and had missed dinner the night before that. And as we sat trying to be close to each other, my grievances would begin to rise to the surface. Where had he been? Why hadn't he called? When was he going to fix the bathroom? The faucet in the sink had been dripping for two months. I would be angry or hurt and once we were seated together all this imagined past would overflow into the space between us. He hated this and became suspicious. He even came to distrust my wish for intimacy. But couldn't he see that I, too, wanted intimacy without complaint? I wanted nothing more than to hold him and be held in return.

Couldn't he help me to reach some place beyond that complaint instead of seeking out other women with whom he had no past, where each moment was a discovery instead of a supposed repetition? What is this memory, this palpable interference that intrudes itself on present events, this fiction that we call truth? I would yearn for the simple response, to act as I had acted as a child, to touch and converse, but the weight of memory would press me down: that fiction, those grievances.

It was not with other women that my husband betrayed me; it was by not giving me time, not helping me move past griev-ance to occasions when we could be together on an equal footing. Instead he turned away. Who are these women that I see him with? I'll be standing on a corner waiting for the light to change and one of those black Peugeot taxi cabs will come rushing past and there in the backseat will be my husband with some woman. She will be young and they will be laughing. Does he see them more than once or twice? I remember reading long ago how the Cardinal Richelieu loved kittens but disliked cats and how he would surround himself with kittens, yet when they grew to a certain size he had the servant take them away. How unfair that is and how I grieved for those adult cats that, in my imagination, I saw being thrown into the Seine. And wasn't my husband the same?

We first met in the house of a friend and began going out together almost immediately. Within a year we were married and six years later our daughter, Ruth, was born. My husband worked in insurance and real estate and is the sort of man who has many projects and deals advancing at once. Perhaps it would have been easier if we hadn't had a child. She cried at night. She took much of my time and my husband resented that, while I resented his resentment. We were two lines that came together and ran parallel for a while and then began veering off. I began teaching school and giving piano lessons.

I would go to concerts by myself. I had my own friends. And then one day he was gone. I look at my daughter and see my husband's face in her face. How is it possible to protect anyone else? Even now, somewhere in the city, lives a child who will someday break her heart. During those winter months of 1960, when I was expecting to die and was grieving for the death of my father, my future husband was a schoolboy in Santiago working on a square of cloth which would form part of a blanket which would be sent to the south. My grandmother was very proud and would let none of those blankets into the house. She had her own blankets. But it might have happened that I received the blanket with the square fashioned by my future husband. One of the schemes of Freddy Piwonka Gray was to sell these blankets. He became a wealthy man and when my husband and I were married Freddy Piwonka Gray sent a case of champagne. He was too busy to come himself.

Certainly, this is the weight of time, its burden. This is what makes the second version of the "Goldberg Variations" so different from the first. This is what resonates beneath Beethoven's late quartets. I love my daughter. I love my work. Perhaps I will even marry again. Perhaps the day will come when I can see my husband passing in a cab and it will be like seeing a stranger. But when I was eight years old each action was fresh. Is that what it means to be virginal? Each morning, the world was a new world and I hurried out to greet it. But then came the earthquake and the death of my father, and when I hurried out to greet the morning, not only did I greet it but I again greeted the fact of the earthquake, the fact of my father's death. And as I grew older, as any of us grows older, the renewed consciousness of each day meant the reawakening of memory. There is a man with a brow like my husband's. There is a woman who laughs like my aunt Dalila. Here is another man as oxlike and stubborn as my uncle Hellmuth. Here is a bright young face as wonderful as poor Spartaco's. And so I carry this bag of stones into the future.

When the first earthquake overthrew our lives, we all came together to my grandmother's house in order to die. Obviously we survived, much to my grandmother's disappointment. But certain things happened to change us. Never again did we come together as a family. My uncles Hellmuth and Alcibiades had been the best of friends, each had been the great comfort of the other's life. All that was changed. Walterio with his cookies, my aunt Miriam with her drinking, Great-aunt Clotilde in her wedding dress—all changed. My grandmother with her expectations, my great-aunt Bibiana with her laziness, Dalila with her beauty—all changed. My little brother Manfredo with his fearful memory of firing his father's revolver at his own dear brother and the entire earth revolting against his action and casting him out. How could he be the same again? My mother with her weight and her dreaminess drifting through her life until it collided against the stone wall of her husband's death; my father lying dead in the street in his underwear, his head cradled in the lap of his mistress. Every perception which came to my mother afterward was seen through that event which she considered her great humiliation.

During those days I truly expected to die. I expected the world to end. It was not simply my grandmother who made me think this. It was the constant tremors and quakes, the darkness of a sky tainted with volcanic ash, the total disruption of our lives, the death of my father and the sense of his waiting just a little beyond. I felt I was standing at the very doorway of oblivion, that I could see through to the other side and the place I saw was far more real than the place I was watching from. It had color and mass and there were people there who loved us and St. Lucy the Virgin Martyr was beckoning me forward. Once we crossed over all our problems would be solved. It was like looking into a rainbow. My father would be waiting. He would lift me up and embrace me and I would nuzzle my nose into his collar.

My brother Spartaco was perhaps the only one among us who actively wanted no part of this dream. Even my grandfather who continued his daily chores and kept rebuilding the shed had little doubt that some much greater earthquake was coming. Even Rosvita with her hunger for Paris fashions and womanhood felt that these things would be denied her, that she would be swept off to a Heaven she wanted no part of. But for Spartaco this sense of an end was the enemy and he fought it. He was passionately on the side of life and perhaps this is why he had such admiration for the American soldiers for they, too, represented survival.

It was Thursday afternoon when we first saw them. Spartaco and I were sitting in the grass on the hill in front of my grandmother's house and looking out over the town. The sky was clear although full of ash, which leached it of its blue, making it a yellowish-tan color. Across the lake the volcano Osorno was belching great clouds of steam. There had been many tremors that day but now we hardly noticed them unless the noise began, the noise of everything that was not tied down smacking and banging against everything else. Even so, I could stare across the field and imagine how the earth would suddenly divide, how a great muddy valley would rush toward us up the hill, the earth splitting and sinking as the roots of trees and buried things and the coffins of the dead were shoved up into the openness, and how we would tumble down within it and how it would snap shut. Sometimes I saw this so clearly it was as if it were already taking place.

Spartaco was talking about his friends.

"And Jaime Gebaur, what do you think happened to him?"

Spartaco had taken a blade of grass and was trying to blow through it to make it whistle. Occasionally it squeaked.

"His parents had a brick house," I said.

"Do you think that protected him?"

"Only a rubber house would be completely safe."

Spartaco grew indignant. "Nobody lives in a rubber house."

"Maybe they will after this," I said.

"I want to go into town," said Spartaco. "There's Jaime and Samuel Yunge and Ottocar Horn. I want to know if they're safe."

"What about the big earthquake?" I asked. "Maybe we should stay together."

Spartaco threw away the blade of grass and stood up. "Even if you were swallowed up here and I was swallowed up in town, what would it matter? We'd both be going to the same place. We'd meet sooner or later."

"I expect there would be a big crowd," I said. "You might get lost." And I tried to imagine the great crowds of Heaven.

Spartaco kicked at a stone. "I don't want any part of it," he said. "I'll tie myself to a tree. They'll have to take the tree as well. I'll bet there aren't even any trees in Heaven, nor rocks, nor mountains, nor anything." Then he paused and looked down toward the cemetery. "What's that?" he said.

Moving along the road toward town was a great olive-drab vehicle that looked half like a truck and half like a tank, although it had no guns. It made a low roar and a clanking noise.

Spartaco stared, then abruptly leapt forward. "Come on!" he shouted and began galloping down through the high grass.

I scrambled to my feet and ran after him.

"It's the Americans!" shouted Spartaco.

He ran ahead and I can still see the sheen of his black hair as it bounced and blew back in the breeze and how his arms flew out from his sides for balance as he leapt forward down the hill. Although the strange vehicle was moving fairly quickly, the road passed right in front of us and Spartaco meant to intercept it. As I got closer I saw about half a dozen young men perched on the sides. It wasn't so much their cleanness that surprised me as their rosiness. Two were black men, the first I had ever seen, and even these had a sort of rosy exuberance. All wore camouflage fatigues and field jackets and when they saw Spartaco they waved. Attached to the back of the vehicle an American flag fluttered in the breeze.

What did the soldiers say? I have no idea and in memory I have confused the scene with scenes from old movies showing Americans entering recently liberated French and Italian towns. They were friendly and called something to Spartaco which we didn't understand. They had the cheerful expressions of young men who like to be liked, who couldn't imagine not being liked. The vehicle drew to a stop right where Spartaco was waiting. One of the black men tossed him two blankets and something else. Then it started up again, rattling and clanking and roaring. By the time I reached Spartaco, it was already entering town, leaving behind it a trail of dark exhaust. One man in the back was still waving.

"Weren't they great?" said Spartaco happily. "Look, blankets."

He carefully held two olive-drab blankets folded in squares. In the center of the square was a large Hershey bar.

"They weren't blond," I said. Actually, I think his fascination made me a little jealous.

"Not all of them are blond," said Spartaco with some exasperation. "And look, they gave me a chocolate bar."

"We have lots of blankets," I said.

Spartaco stared off down the road where the strange vehicle had disappeared. "Not American ones," he said.

We hurried back up the hill to my grandmother's house. From somewhere I heard the *bang bang* of my grandfather's hammer. Ana was in the garden sweeping up the leaves and petals which had fallen from the flowers. She was shaded by the tall palm in the center of the garden and its fronds swayed slightly in the breeze.

"These are good blankets," said Spartaco. "They smell a little bit like sheep."

Hellmuth and Alcibiades were sitting outside by the fire playing chess.

"I got American blankets," called Spartaco.

Hellmuth didn't look up and seemed hunched behind his heavy glasses. Alcibiades smiled and said something like "Good for you," but he, too, was concentrating mostly on the game.

We found our grandmother in the bedroom which was dim because of the wet sheets hanging over the windows. Several kerosene lanterns were burning. She was not pleased to see the blankets.

"We already have lots of blankets," she said. "You should take them back." She reached out and felt the edge of one. "They're thin," she said. Manfredo stood beside her. He, too, felt the blanket but did not speak.

"I'll use them on my own bed," said Spartaco.

"You already have blankets," said my grandmother.

"But I'll use these instead. They're American blankets."

Walterio lumbered over to us. Each day he seemed fatter and his mouth was always full and there were always crumbs on his clothes. His skin was the color of bread dough just before it is put in the oven.

He gestured to the chocolate bar. "What's that?" he asked.

"The Americans gave me chocolate. It's a Hershey bar," Spartaco said, pronouncing it without the initial *H*.

"Are you going to, you know, eat it?" asked Walterio.

I don't think the idea had occurred to Spartaco until that moment. He had no passion for sweets and we had around us in the house a veritable mountain of sweets. But, of course, we had no Hershey bars.

"I might," said Spartaco.

"I've never had a Hershey bar," said Walterio, speaking not to Spartaco but to the Hershey bar itself.

I expect it was Walterio's desire that led Spartaco to define the Hershey bar's importance to himself more specifically. The candy was a souvenir of the United States, a token from these rosy-cheeked men who had come to rescue us. To eat it would be a sacrilege. And what would he have left? Just the brown paper with a name on it. It wouldn't be the same.

"I think I'll save it," said Spartaco, stepping back from his uncle.

Dalila was sitting at the table and the twins were standing beside her. She had a jar of brandied peaches and one of the twins, Norma or Nancy, was feeding Dalila bits of peach with a little silver fork. The other twin stood slightly behind Dalila kissing her bare shoulder, which was pink in the light of the kerosene lamp.

"I had a Hershey bar in Puerto Montt," said Dalila. "It's not as good as Dutch chocolate." She pursed her lips and sucked a slice of peach off the fork.

"It would be nice to see," said Walterio.

Spartaco had retreated to his mattress which lay on the floor next to mine. He began stripping off our grandmother's blankets and replacing them with the American ones. Our grandmother watched him, peering through her weak eyes with her arms folded across her bosom. Manfredo stood pressed against her long dark skirt as if it were a curtain he could draw around him.

"I want to save it," said Spartaco.

"You could give us just half," said Dalila.

Spartaco pretended not to hear and continued to make his bed. All of our beds were just a jumble of multicolored blankets. Gradually Spartaco's became neat and perfectly smooth and that single olive-drab color. It looked very different from the others. I watched my grandmother absorb that fact, then went to make my own bed so Spartaco's wouldn't seem so unusual.

"You'll be cold with those blankets," said my grandmother.

Spartaco patted them. "They seem pretty warm."

My grandmother shook her head. "No, they're thin. You'll be cold in the night and you'll want one of your old blankets but they'll all be put away."

"He can have one of mine," I said.

"I won't need any other blankets than these two American ones," said Spartaco.

Walterio had followed him to his bed. "How much, I mean, could I buy the Hershey bar from you?" he asked.

Spartaco pretended not to hear.

"I want to buy the Hershey bar," said Walterio.

"It's not for sale," said Spartaco firmly.

The Hershey bar lay on the bed and Walterio stared at it. And it seemed in that moment that the house became completely empty of sweets, as if all the cookies and preserves and jam and cake and hard candies had disappeared, had only been dreamed of, and here at last was this one small representative from the sweet world, a veritable apotheosis of sweetness, and Walterio couldn't get his hands on it.

Spartaco noticed Walterio's expression and slipped the Hershey bar under his pillow. He was not a selfish boy and he often shared, but he also knew that the house was full of candy. Besides, it wasn't a matter of candy. If the Americans had given him a stone, it would have been just as important.

"We could raffle the Hershey bar," said Dalila. "I love raffles. I once won a hat in a raffle. It had a green ribbon."

Spartaco didn't even look at her.

"I think," said my grandmother in a low voice, "that somebody I know is having too many ideas and is thinking too much about himself." As she spoke she reached down and stroked Manfredo's hair.

"I'm going outside to help my grandfather," said Spartaco and he left the room without looking at anyone.

Walterio continued to stare at Spartaco's pillow. It wouldn't have occurred to Spartaco that Walterio might try to steal his chocolate bar. After all, Walterio was his uncle.

Walterio stared at the pillow for another minute, then tore himself away and sat down with Dalila. He pointed a thick finger at the brandied peaches. "Are there any more of those?" he asked petulantly.

"Jars and jars," said Dalila. The twin behind her, perhaps it was Norma, was still kissing her bare shoulder, but her lips and fingers were sticky with syrup and Dalila's smooth pink skin shone with it.

My grandmother bent down and kissed Manfredo's cheek. "You're the sweetest boy in the world," she said.

My mother was in her bed on the far side of the room with a blanket pulled half over her head. Seeing her, it occurred to me that I hadn't thought of my father all afternoon. It made me feel guilty and I went to her. I sat on the edge of her bed and stroked her hair. She turned slowly and gave me a weak smile that was like diluted milk.

"Can I do anything for you?" I asked.

She took my hand. "How long will this go on?" she asked.

I wasn't sure what she meant. "We saw some American soldiers in some kind of big truck," I said. "There were even two Negroes. They went into town. Spartaco says they're going to make everything all right."

My mother gave me a smile that adults give children when they say something amusing but basically stupid. "Can they bring your father back?" she asked.

And suddenly it seemed I could see my father standing in the room dressed as I had last seen him on Sunday afternoon with his tweed jacket and tan pants and he was smiling so sweetly that for a moment I couldn't breathe. Then he disappeared. I threw myself down over my mother and lay there for a long time and all sorts of pictures came back to me: of the days my father had walked with me to school, of his sitting with me when I was sick, of his taking me to a cousin's farm and letting me ride a horse. And on warm summer days he would sometimes take us to the beach at Puerto Chico. He had a great fear that we would be sunburned and scarred for life and he would rub us not with lotion but with real cream which he had brought from the dairy, heavy whipping cream which he smeared thickly over our backs and arms and faces and which, in the hot sun, soon turned rancid and spoiled and smelled terribly until we ran into the cold water just to wash it from our bodies.

My great-aunt Clotilde and Rosvita were in my aunt's alcove. The wedding dress seemed to sparkle in the dim light and whenever my aunt moved the stiff fabric would creak and rustle. Clotilde was brushing Rosvita's hair and teaching her French.

"Nightgown," said my aunt, *"une chemise de nuit."*

"Une chemise de nuit," said Rosvita.

"A brassiere, *un soutien-gorge.*"

"*Un soutien-gorge*," said Rosvita.

"Eye shadow, *un crayon à paupières*."

"*Un crayon à paupières*," said Rosvita.

That night after another dinner of mutton and vegetables my great-uncle, Teodoro Schiele Grob, arrived from the country. He had broken his leg and was seated on a horse led by his wife, Olivia Azocar Quintas. Great-uncle Teodoro was my grandmother's brother and two years younger than she. He was a pessimistic and somewhat bitter man and his conversations were full of warnings, for the future for him was full of tricks and deviance and plans come to naught. He was heavyset and black-haired and had little puffs of black hair sprouting from his ears. My great-uncle seemed to carry a lot of anger deep within him, or perhaps it was just a general impatience with the world. He often imagined conspiracies and people getting away with things and doing what they shouldn't. When he spoke, his anger began to bubble up and burst forth across his lips in little barks which he tried to disguise as rhetorical stress or soften with abrupt smiles which lacked humor and exposed his poor teeth. It gave his face a lot of movement, a lot of jumps and twitches, and consequently his face was heavily lined.

His wife had set his broken leg with two sticks and a lot of rope which held in place a poultice made from special leaves and grease. She was a strange woman who told cards and read palms and claimed to be related to the Gypsies. Originally Uncle Teodoro had found this eccentricity romantic but he had long since tired of it and he tended to ignore his wife. Her face was thin and somewhat hooked and she had a lot of gold in her teeth, mostly in the crevices. Her hair was black and stringy and she was forever brushing it from her face with the back of her hand. We children were often afraid of her but not, I think, for any good reason. But she was one of those people with whom it was impossible to be relaxed. When we visited her house she was always hovering slightly outside the circle and if we were having tea she seemed too eager to clean up and would linger nearby ready to snatch up the plates and begin tidying. She made everyone eat quickly and when we at last left their farm we all felt exhausted without really knowing why.

My uncles Hellmuth and Alcibiades carried Teodoro into my grandmother's bedroom while his wife, Olivia, circled around them, urging them to be careful. My cousin Hugo was trying to carry him as well, but Hellmuth kept pushing him away. I could see this hurt Hugo's feelings. Carrying was one of the things he did nearly as well as lifting. Bibiana and Miriam began moving the beds to make more room. My aunt Miriam had been sipping wine all day long and was unsteady on her feet. Everyone was asking questions. Great-uncle Teodoro and his wife had four sons but they were all grown up. One usually lived on the farm but he was away in Castro on the island of Chiloé and they had had no word. Of course, they were very worried. My great-uncle, I came to see, was a rather mediocre farmer and often counted on my grandfather to lend him machinery or extra seed or tools, which he would return only after having been asked several times. Consequently, my grandfather was not pleased to see him.

"Did that old house of yours fall down?" shouted my grandfather.

"The barn's gone," said Teodoro, snapping out his words, "and the sheds and granary. The cows have all run off."

"The house twisted half around on its foundation," said Olivia.

Teodoro had broken his leg as he tried to flee his house

when the earthquake struck. He had been taking a nap and as he ran from his house, he had stumbled and a large cupboard had fallen on top of him.

"What were you taking a nap in the middle of the day for?" shouted my grandfather, but no one paid any attention what with the commotion of moving the beds and getting Teodoro and his wife bowls of stew.

"There'll be no farming this spring," said Teodoro. "The fields are a mess. There's nowhere to begin and nothing to begin with. Even the oxen have run off."

"I read the cards," said his wife, "and each time the future comes up blank, like a blank sheet of paper."

Great-uncle Teodoro lay on a bed under the window and his wife sat on the edge of it. My uncles Hellmuth and Alcibiades sat at the table with my grandfather. Hellmuth had his pocket knife and was carving something out of a small block of wood. He would stare at it and wrinkle his brow so that his glasses would slide down his nose, then start carving again. Walterio was on his bed in the corner and appeared to be eating. In the entry of the alcove my grandmother stood flanked by her sisters: Bibiana short and round, Clotilde tall and thin. Dalila was braiding the twins' hair. I sat on my mattress next to Spartaco who held the Hershey bar, turning it over and over, holding it lightly so it wouldn't melt. Sometimes I saw Walterio glance at him. My mother appeared to be already asleep.

"So what made you leave your house?" asked my grandfather.

Uncle Teodoro looked at us darkly. "Marauders," he said.

"People from Puerto Montt," said my aunt. "They have nothing to eat and they've been raiding the farms."

We were all quiet for a moment as this news sunk in. Teodoro was staring at his sister Clotilde in the wedding dress. He seemed on the verge of remarking about it, then decided to remain silent.

"What about the army?" asked Hellmuth.

"Several people have been shot," said Great-uncle Teodoro. "But mostly they stay in the woods along the river. They loot the farms, then go back to the woods. You remember Hellwig Berner? He and all his family were killed, all except the little one. Someone will go to Hell for that, I promise you." Teodoro's words seemed full of nails and sharp stones.

"Luis Demangel stopped by their farm," said my aunt Olivia in a whisper. "He found the five adults in the living room all dead. Their throats had been slashed. There was blood everywhere. And the baby, Josefa, maybe she is three, she was sitting in the middle of the blood completely covered with it. She was cooing and cooing and her hair had turned completely white."

Spartaco and I looked at each other and I drew my blankets up to my neck.

"And another child, José Ferran, was out in the fields by himself and he was attacked by a puma," said Olivia. "He had the sweetest face and the puma spared his face, but it ate his stomach completely."

"Do you remember Jorge Carcamo?" said my great-uncle. "He had a farm near Los Maitenes. Everyone said how his barn was so neat that you could eat off the floor. A fissure opened up and swallowed his house and barn and everything. And when the earth closed again, there was no sign that it had ever been there. And then a lake came."

My great-aunt Olivia made a hissing noise. "They said he knew the devil and at night people saw hopping creatures and a strange green light around his house and now he has been punished. And Elisa Veliz told me that if there are fish in that lake, they will all have the face of Jorge Carcamo and people will leave them alone."

These stories seemed to go on and on, stories of death and destruction throughout the countryside, until it seemed amazing that we had survived. Sometimes Hellmuth or Alcibiades or my grandfather would ask a question but mostly they listened. A condor had been seen carrying away a sheep dog, and another man had the ground rise up under his farm until it became a hill and his house rolled down it and burned, and another man's wife went mad and ran into the River Maullín where they said she was pecked to death by swans.

I grew drowsier and drowsier and shortly I drifted off down a corridor built from the voices of Teodoro and his wife and all the colors were bright and violent. When I awoke later in the night the room was dark. My aunt Miriam's bed was close to mine and she was singing a song about a white horse. It had many verses. I awoke frightened about the possibility of marauders and my aunt's song calmed me. Now I realize she must have been drunk, but at the time I only thought she was sad and missed her husband, Freddy Piwonka Gray. I don't know how long she sang. Then my uncle Hellmuth told her roughly to be quiet and the singing stopped.

On Friday morning the air was full of the roar of airplanes. Spartaco, Hugo and I ran out to the field to watch but the sky was too gray and we could see nothing. But some of these were the great C-124 Globemaster transports that the Americans sent down and which we all came to call Los Globis. The Seventh and the Fifteenth United States Army Field Hospitals, each with up to one hundred and fifty beds, were sent to Puerto Montt and Valdivia. More than five hundred doctors, nurses and medical corpsmen were divided between the two cities. Each hospital unit had operating rooms, X-ray machines, ambulances, power and water supplies, laundries and tents. The control tower instruments at the Puerto Montt airport had been damaged in the earthquake and even a month later the planes had to land by sight, even Los Globis. These planes were so huge that when they came to a stop the back doors would open up and ambulances and trucks and Jeeps would just drive out.

In the central plaza in Puerto Montt along the Avenida Diego Portales and right by the bay the Americans erected a desalinization plant and thousands of people came down from the hills to line up for fresh water since the city pipes had burst. The Americans also had giant washing machines and great lines of people waited patiently to have their clothes washed. And some people who didn't need to have their clothes washed stood in line anyway just so they could say that they had their clothes washed by the Americans. During this time there was a lot of complaint about our own soldiers who stood by in their white gloves and did nothing, unless it was to enforce the curfew and shoot looters. But the Americans were very eager to help and President Eisenhower said he was going to send his own brother to Puerto Montt to see exactly what was going on. And some people hoped that President Eisenhower's brother would notice our own soldiers standing around in their white gloves.

The Americans also set up great tent cities and gave out clothes and blankets and flashlights and food and they were very popular. One soldier fell in love with the daughter of one of my second cousins and when he got out of the army he came back to Puerto Montt and married her and they still live on Avenida de Puerto Williams and he has an engine repair shop and also sells vacuum cleaners. All this time the police were going around saying the earthquakes were over, but no one believed them. The police urged people to return to their regular lives but people just laughed because their regular lives were finished. And on Friday there were two new earthquakes and more buildings fell and there was another landslide in Puerto Montt; and the mountain village of Rupanco, less than one hundred kilometers to the north, was buried under tons of rock and one hundred and thirteen people were killed. And it was during these days that in an Araucanian village high in the mountains, the Indians sacrificed a child to the spirit or god that was making the volcanoes erupt. They killed the child but it didn't do any good and later they got into a lot of trouble.

Only the firemen and Explorer Scouts kept working, as well as many people in the church, but most people were too terrified or paralyzed to work. The Caritas distribution center also gave out powdered milk and food and clothing and firewood and there were again long lines, although many poor people complained they didn't get anything and there were complaints about thieving as well. It was cold and rained every day and as the week continued people grew more desperate and there was more looting and people were shot. And my best friend in school, Claudia Hochreiter, her uncle Ramón was shot and killed in Puerto Montt for stealing a ham. And the police even had to shoot over the heads of a crowd of people waiting for food because they had refused to wait in line and tried to push forward. And there were many accusations about people stealing food. Father Opilio stopped by to see my grandmother and he said terrible things were being done but he was in too much of a hurry to say exactly what except that it was a judgment and that the Lord was keeping a list. Then he looked at my uncle Teodoro's leg and asked about the poultice of leaves and grease. Then he called my aunt Olivia a dangerous woman, and, although Father Opilio had meant it as criticism, my aunt was quite pleased.

Many people came by and brought news and none of it was good and the adults all shook their heads, but Spartaco had great faith in the Americans. Like him, they wanted to be heroes. They all seemed cheerful and when their trucks rolled by on the road below us, they would wave, but they didn't give us any more chocolate. Hugo told Walterio that perhaps they would give him chocolate if he stood by the road and waited and I think Walterio was tempted, but Hellmuth told Hugo not to be impertinent. But Hugo waited and an American gave him a flashlight. And another American pulled him onto the truck and took him into Puerto Varas. Hugo was gone for most of the afternoon. When he came back, he was filthy and said he had spent the whole day digging and lifting, and Spartaco was extremely jealous.

Despite the rain, I went out to the highway to visit the *animita* of Jaime Alvarez, because I felt it gave me strength to see it. No one wanted to come with me and I didn't want to stay in the house. Uncle Teodoro seemed to fill my grand-mother's bedroom with complaint and few people chose to remain inside. Out under the tarpaulin my uncles Hellmuth and Walterio were arguing about Ana, the kitchen girl, and why each morning she swept up the leaves and flower petals which had fallen in the tremors during the night. Didn't she know the world was going to end? Why did she bother? They sat at a small table arguing back and forth while between them sat a box of cookies. I wondered if they argued the same way about my grandfather who was still occupied with the shed.

Spartaco and Hugo were waiting on the hill for more Amer-icans. The twins were employed on private errands. The others were scattered about. I set off through the orchard and across the fields with fresh flowers and water in a tin can. The wind blew against me and it was very cold and the fields were muddy. The falling rain and curtain of volcanic dust made it seem as if I were surrounded by a gray wall and once out in the fields I could see nothing but the muddy field itself and sometimes the shadow of a large bird. There was the sense that I could be anywhere and if it weren't for the mud gripping my rubber boots, I could fall right off the face of the planet. Another tremor started up as I was making my way across the field and I stopped and watched the water jiggle in the muddy puddles.

The hill near the *animita* was very close to where my wild cousin Otto and his brothers had played a dangerous game when the highway was paved just a few years before and I couldn't see the spot without thinking that their wildness was due to their father's death, and I thought deeply about myself and tried to discover if any wildness had taken hold there. When the highway was first paved there wasn't much traffic. Otto and his brothers would gallop their horses up and over the hill and they couldn't see if any cars or trucks were coming and when they reached the highway it was too late to stop. If a truck had been coming, one of them might have been killed. So they galloped as fast as they could and held their breaths and then suddenly they were at the highway and they had several close calls. My family was very upset when they learned about this game and Hellmuth took it upon himself to beat them. And I think my cousins felt glad for that, because they, too, had become frightened. But do you see how it was? Even looking at a muddy hill would remind me of incidents that made me think of my father. Once more I would think of him and once more he would be dead.

The *animita* of Jaime Alverez had not been further disturbed although the roof was stained with ash. I cleaned it as best I could and arranged the new flowers. They were blue laurestinos and very pretty. Then I sat down by the door and looked in at the picture and took comfort from Jaime Alverez's cheerful expression. And it seemed that from somewhere Jaime Alverez must be looking back and I thought of the silence of the dead and how they must grieve for the loss of their tongues, as if

we were always surrounded by their invisible presences—my
father, Uncle Gabriel, Jaime Alverez—and they kept signaling
with their arms, waving their hands to catch our attention,
uselessly opening and closing their mouths, their words—what
would they be?—disappearing in the cold air of their dead
world.

Those thoughts have stayed with me. In Santiago there are
many beggars: the crippled, the homeless, the blind. One can't
give to them all, but without thinking I have always given to
the deaf and dumb, and perhaps it is because of my memories
of those years when I believed myself surrounded by the un-
heard voices of the dead. It strikes me now that childhood is
a time of limitless possibility. To think something means it
could happen. And I remember as a very small child watching
the clouds around Osorno and Calbuco and believing one could
climb the mountain and step out upon the clouds and how soft
it would be to walk there. And isn't aging just the slipping
away of possibility: the world we inhabit becoming a city which
becomes a house which becomes a room which becomes a box
which becomes a door leading to my grandmother's Heaven or
the nothingness which I have come to believe is our only
prospect? To hope means to recapture that world of possibility,
to take on something of the child again. But is it really possible
that I can find another man to love me? I try to resign myself
to my daughter and work, my piano lessons and a few friends
but my whole spirit balks and I find myself reading the travel
sections of the paper about European tours and weekends in
Rio. And when a friend says she has a man she wants me to
meet, my heart speeds up even though such men always turn
out to be fat and in love with their mothers.

Looking backward, it seems I can see myself sitting by the
animita of Jaime Alverez as if I were looking down a chute or
the wrong end of a telescope: a small girl wearing a dark

oversized raincoat which once belonged to one of her uncles. I think of that child imagining herself surrounded by the voiceless spirits of the dead, but the only person who is watching her is this older version of herself. What would I say to her if I could? To be brave? To be patient? Wouldn't my words only frighten her? Better to let her believe in her friendly spirits and the kindness of the world and the cataclysm which she thought would shortly sweep her into Heaven. The truth in most instances is only a nuisance.

I don't know how long I sat next to the *animita* but when I at last stood up I was so chilled and stiff that I could hardly walk. I made my way back to town, skirting the Copec station where I could see soldiers. I wanted to visit Calvary Hill and read the new placards and see if I recognized any names. The rain dripped from the pine trees and the path up past the Stations of the Cross was slippery with mud. At the top of the hill the sky was so gray that only the town's first buildings were visible and the red-roofed house of a man named Demangel which had collapsed completely. Had he been a bad man or just unlucky? Was it possible for the unlucky to be also virtuous? And what had we done that had caused us to lose our father?

There were many new placards on the trees, some so high that I could hardly read them. Many of the names were familiar to me: Retamal and Schwetter and Bucarey and Nancy Risco Risco who was grateful that her mother had been spared. The rain dripped down across Jesus' face, rolled across his chest and the open wound where the soldier had stabbed him with a spear, rolled down his legs and dripped from his toes. I picked up several eucalyptus nuts and put them in my pockets because I liked their smell and wanted to keep it with me. Both the Virgin Mary and Mary Magdalene looked very de-

pressed and I wondered if they looked forward to the summer
and if it was always sunny in Heaven.

When I turned around, I saw someone coming up the steps
to the entrance of the grove. The light was poor but after a
moment I realized it was my cousin Rosvita. I doubted that
she had come to read the placards. She showed little interest
in anything apart from herself and when she recognized me,
she showed no curiosity as to why I was there. She wore a tan
raincoat and carried a small blue umbrella, more like a parasol.

"Have you seen Dalila and Alcibiades?" she asked.

I was surprised. "Up here?"

"They went for a walk."

I was struck by how agitated Rosvita appeared and how there
was nothing to explain it.

"Is there something wrong at the house?" I asked.

"Of course not," she said. "Don't be silly."

She came into the grove and looked around the pile of stones
supporting the cross as if someone might be hiding there. She
was a pretty girl but her face was thin and suspicion made it
seem pinched.

"Are you sure you haven't seen them?" she asked.

"No," I repeated. "Have you seen Spartaco?"

"Oh, he and Hugo are off being boys," said Rosvita in
exasperation. Then she turned and made her way back down
the hill.

I glanced around, almost expecting to see Alcibiades and
Dalila. It struck me that they might have come up the hill to
attach a placard to one of the trees. I hadn't recognized either
of their names on the ones I had read. I spent a few minutes
reading several more, then gave it up. I wanted to visit my
house and perhaps rescue some of my things. Or perhaps I
only wanted to see it, to remind myself of it.

Most of the houses near the hospital stood empty and I hardly saw anyone. Many tents had been put up in the park and people had moved there. In the subsequent tremors and aftershocks more houses had fallen and the north wing of the hospital had collapsed completely. Our own house stood as we had left it, although the piano had fallen and lay on its back in the yard. I touched several of the keys and they made a depressed noise, not musical at all. There was no sign of old Mrs. Moedinger. I sat on a stool and looked up at our apartment like looking up at a stage set. There was my father's room and I could see one of his tweed jackets hanging from a hook on the door. There was our living room, the chairs all wet with rain. There was my room with books scattered across the floor and a new yellow sweater I had gotten at Christmas. I decided to go up there. The stairs were open and I only had to pick my way across the broken façade of the house which covered much of the front lawn.

But as I began to make my way to the stairs, someone called to me.

"Don't go inside! It's not safe."

It was Alcibiades.

I waited for him as he came hurrying up. He was alone.

"I want to get my sweater and some books," I said. "I want to get my father's hat."

"The floor's not safe," said Alcibiades. His brown leather jacket seemed wet all the way through and water dripped from his blond mustache. Despite the wetness, he looked quite cheerful and he bent over to kiss my cheek.

"There's an umbrella up there as well," I said. "I know just where it is."

Alcibiades looked at the house more closely, then glanced up and down the street. "They've been shooting looters," he said.

"We're not looters. This is my house."

"It's still against the law," he said. He glanced around again, then jumped over a broken window frame lying on the ground and hopped onto the front step. "Wait here," he said. "Whistle if you see anyone coming."

He gingerly climbed the stairs and I could hear them creak. Briefly I saw his head appear in my father's room, then he appeared in my room as well. I watched him reach out and snag my sweater with the tip of an umbrella. Then he disappeared again. A minute or so later he made his way back down the stairs carrying an armload of books and clothes.

"Some of these books are pretty wet," he said, "but they'll dry off." I took the books and he opened the umbrella. Several were the novels of A. J. Cronin which I had read many times and which I loved. Then I put on my father's hat. It was a black, wide-brimmed hat and much too big for me but it kept the rain off my face and I was glad to have it.

"I brought you this as well," said Alcibiades. He handed me a framed photograph of my father. It had been taken at the beach and my father, bare-chested, was grinning at the camera. A lock of hair had fallen across his left eye and he looked very handsome. I tried to thank Alcibiades but couldn't speak and I pressed my face against the wetness of his coat.

"We should be getting back," he said after a moment.

I wrapped the books in my sweater and we walked out to the road. A dog barked at us.

"Were you putting up a placard for Jesus to read?" I asked.

Alcibiades stopped. "Why on earth should I do that?"

"People do it because they feel grateful," I said. "I thought maybe you had put one up or maybe you had done it for Dalila. I was just up on the hill."

Alcibiades began walking again. At first I thought he wasn't going to speak, but then he said, "Too much is changing. Things aren't safe anymore."

"Do you mean the earthquakes?"

He laughed but not in a humorous way. "I mean myself," he said.

I didn't know what he meant but he said it very strangely and, as the days went by, I couldn't get it out of my mind.

When we got back to the house, Hellmuth and Dalila were quarreling, or rather Hellmuth was talking in a low angry voice and Dalila was standing with her back to him. I put my books on my bed to dry out and put my father's picture under my pillow. Spartaco was sitting on his bed covered with the American army blankets. He looked furious.

"Walterio tried to steal my chocolate bar."

I glanced across to where Walterio was sitting on his bed watching Dalila. "Did he get it?"

"No, but I had to hide it. Do you think I should give it to him?"

"Do you want to?"

"Never."

"Then don't."

Spartaco leaned back against the wall. "That's what I thought myself but I was afraid I was being selfish. He's even been offering money for it."

I took out our father's photograph and showed it to him and he looked at it for a long time. "I've been afraid I was forgetting what he looked like," he said.

Hellmuth sat down at the table with his back to us. Near him was his pocket knife and several chunks of wood which he had been carving. They were small and square and looked like little figures. Dalila sat down on the edge of my grandmother's bed and began painting her nails. I've always liked that smell. It makes me think of preparedness and getting oneself ready and it has always reminded me of her. Alcibiades had remained outdoors.

"You use people," Hellmuth was saying. "You don't care who they are. If they have something you want or if they flatter your vanity, then you use them."

"I do nothing of the kind," said Dalila without looking up. She wore a dark dress and her hair fell forward to obscure her face. "You leave me alone and go off. What am I supposed to do, stand in a corner until you get back? You'd like it if I had a switch and you could turn me off and on when you wanted. Everybody knows how you treat me."

"Why do you flirt with everyone?" asked Hellmuth, and although he spoke crossly, his voice was also full of disappointment.

"I don't flirt. Can I help it if I'm friendly? I like people and I like people to like me." She paused and her voice became lower and angrier. "I'm just an object to you. You talk about using people, what about you? What do you call what you do to me? You don't even ask."

"I don't want to discuss that," said Hellmuth, glancing at Walterio, who was looking through a magazine and sometimes looking at Spartaco. Great-uncle Teodoro was asleep and Clotilde was back in her alcove.

"You never want to talk about it. But what about me? You have no more sensitivity than an animal. You don't like me, you don't respect me. I could be anybody. I could be a whore."

"Be quiet," said Hellmuth. "You've said enough." And again I heard the disappointment.

"People like to be liked," said Dalila.

Hellmuth slapped his hand on the table and the knife and pieces of wood bounced up and fell back. We all looked up. "I said you've said enough!"

"Pooh," said Dalila.

The room was silent for a moment. Then Clotilde coughed and put her head around the corner. She still wore the wedding dress but now also wore a blue apron in an effort to keep the dress clean until the final earthquake took us away. "Dalila, dear, will you do my nails as well? I want them to look as nice as possible."

Now I assume that Clotilde's interruption was intentional. My own sense of what Dalila and Hellmuth had been saying was that it was adult talk, like listening to French when you only know half the language: only certain parts made sense. What took my attention was the intensity of their speech, how Hellmuth had come to the very edge of losing his temper and how Dalila had mocked him.

Dalila got up and went into the alcove. Hellmuth lit a cigarette, then picked up his knife and a piece of wood and went back to his carving. A minute later the bedroom door opened and my grandmother came in with her sister Bibiana and Manfredo.

"Well, come along," said my grandmother to someone behind her.

After a moment my mother entered the room as well. Her hair was wet from the rain and hung around her face in damp strings.

"We've moved all the unbroken jars and canned food out to the yard," said my grandmother. "We've even been upstairs. What a mess."

Uncle Teodoro woke up. "I've been dreaming of black horses," he said.

More people came in. Aunt Olivia carried a bucket of water to her husband's bed. "I've got to wash you," she told him.

Teodoro made a face. "Do you have to do it now?" He pulled the blanket up to his chin.

Hellmuth got up and walked out, slamming the door behind him. When I turned away from looking at him, I found Walterio standing at the foot of Spartaco's bed.

"One last offer," he said, trying to stand as tall as possible. "Real money. I have a gold piece. What do you say?"

Spartaco refused to look at him. "It's not for sale," he said. Spartaco could be very stubborn especially when he thought a principle was involved.

Walterio narrowed his eyes, then walked back to his bed and lay down with his back to the rest of us. I went to the table to see what Hellmuth had been carving. They were chess pieces but very rudimentary. He had about a dozen of them. The pawns all had little faces and the knight looked more like a dog.

"Who's ready for lunch?" said my grandmother, peering around at us. "And this afternoon we're going to make bread. That is, unless there's an earthquake." She laughed and Bibiana laughed so hard that the tears came to her eyes. Manfredo, however, looked scared and he folded his arms and hugged himself. I went to my mother and began drying her hair with a towel. She patted my hand. The twins came in and hurried to their bed where they began talking to each other in their strange language. One of them looked around at Dalila and giggled.

Throughout the afternoon I was aware of some kind of tension. People came and went. Dalila and my aunt Miriam were having a long conversation in the corner. I had not thought of them as close, but Miriam was a good listener. She sipped her wine and now and then held Dalila's hand. My mother sat on her bed and I brushed her hair. Rosvita looked in, then hurried out again. The twins appeared to have a dozen secret errands which they would occasionally interrupt in order to tease Manfredo. They were deeply amused by his refusal to talk.

"Which one of us are you going to marry?" Norma would say. "Is it going to be me or Nancy?"

"If you don't say anything, then that means it's me," said Nancy.

Manfredo stood with his hands in his pockets and looked at the floor. He had a way of hunching his shoulders that made it seem as if he had no neck. The twins stood on either side of him and their blond hair was very shiny.

"Please say something," said Norma. "If you don't, then you'll have to marry Nancy."

"If you marry me, then you're going to have to kiss me," said Nancy. "You're going to have to kiss me right away."

"Manfredo says he wants to kiss Nancy," Norma told the room at large. "And he wants to marry her, too."

After a few minutes of this, Manfredo fled back to my grandmother and buried himself in her skirts. She smiled and her face grew wrinkled and she peered around with her weak eyes, then patted his head and called him the sweetest boy in the world. I don't think she knew his terror. Late in the afternoon I showed Manfredo the picture of our father. I didn't do it to upset him but he ran away and the twins ran after him.

The twins were also involved in some plot with Walterio. The fact that Spartaco had hidden the Hershey bar someplace in the house changed the nature of the conflict. It turned the chocolate bar into hidden treasure, which meant, according to the twins, that it belonged to whoever found it. Consequently, they would run off to look somewhere, then come back to consult with Walterio, then run off again. Spartaco pretended not to pay attention but I could tell he was angry and hurt by the behavior of his uncle. I expect he had also stopped caring about the Hershey bar but he didn't want to give in. The twins were also involved in something with Rosvita and the three of them kept whispering together and giggling. Their constant rushing in and out disturbed my great-aunt Olivia and she snapped at them. Walterio said she should let them have their fun and she glared at him with her dark Gypsy eyes and made him blush.

My own attention was distracted by my own concerns. I kept thinking of my father and Jaime Alverez and little Uncle Gabriel who were waiting for us in Heaven. And there were many other people as well, who my grandmother said were in Heaven and who would be glad to see us, and I kept discussing these matters in my head with St. Lucy the Virgin Martyr. This attention on the other world cast the living world into a kind of fog. It's the same when one leaves on a journey. The place where one is going, be it ever so far away, seems far more real than the place one inhabits; the imagined chair has greater palpability than the chair on which one is sitting.

In the evening another earthquake sent us running into the yard. It wasn't quite as strong as the others and this time the shed didn't fall down. My grandfather was very proud and he stamped his foot on the ground and shouted, "Ha!" Hellmuth and Alcibiades had carried out Uncle Teodoro's bed and he got rained on and complained. After a while we went back inside. My grandmother had made bread that afternoon and we ate it with the stew: thick white slabs of bread that smelled of butter and yeast. My uncles and grandfather sat at the table and talked until late, sharing the stories they had heard during the day. An island had appeared in the lake and then had sunk again. A man named Sanchez had hung himself. A gang of children had been found living in the ruins of the school. They talked and my uncle Hellmuth kept carving his little blocks of wood. Bibiana knitted. My grandmother read her Old Testament. My great-aunt Olivia read the cards for Clotilde and told her that she had no future, that none of us had a future. My aunt Miriam sang. Hugo and Spartaco sat on Spartaco's bed and discussed the Americans and they said what their favorite food was and favorite sports and favorite cars and favorite music and favorite movies. I went to sleep with their voices in my ears.

Late Saturday morning there came another letter from Freddy Piwonka Gray.

Dear Wife: Events have been moving so rapidly that I have hardly had time to sit down and write. I arrived in Puerto Montt on Wednesday. What destruction! Along with the quakes there have been terrible fires and much of Angelmo was burned. And the mud slides have destroyed whole neighborhoods around Muñóz and Villa Reloncavi. Needless to say I have been taking many pictures and have hired two boys to help.

I have also opened a store on San Martín right near the plaza where the Americans are giving out water. I have been doing a brisk trade in flashlights and blankets and powdered milk. And also firewood. Of course, there is little money, but people give me things and I give them what they need. Then I trade those things for bigger things. For instance, I already have six cars. People laugh at me. They say what can I do with cars when every road is smashed? I simply put the cars in two garages I am renting. Will the roads stay smashed forever? Of course not. And when the roads are fixed people will need cars and I will have them. And electrical things as well. People have given me record players and vacuum cleaners and toasters and radios and I give them blankets and candles and flashlights and powdered milk. They think how foolish I am to take these vacuum cleaners when there is no electricity. But will there always be no electricity? Of course not. So you see I am very busy and I have six people working for me and Thursday night I worked all night long. Some people are angry and say I am no better than a looter, but I say that I have traded nothing that I have not paid for, and as for the American aid, why should it not help me as well as others? Don't I also have a family? And, of course, I am not the only person selling things.

Give all my girls a kiss and tell Hugo he is often in my thoughts. There is much work here if he wants it. How are Hellmuth and Alcibiades? Send me news.

My aunt Miriam read the letter while standing by the table in the bedroom. Her voice was slurred and sometimes my uncle Hellmuth asked her to repeat something. I could see that he was very struck by his brother-in-law's words.

"I want to go there," said Hugo.

My grandmother grew angry. "What is he going to do with all those cars when the whole city is swallowed up?" she said. "And will the Lord Jesus be happy that he has those cars? No, he will not. And those vacuum cleaners. Does he think they will need vacuum cleaners in Heaven?"

"I need you here," Aunt Miriam told her son, putting her arm around his shoulder. "I need you to help me."

But Hugo made no answer and I could tell he felt torn. Uncle Teodoro was very skeptical. "He will certainly be shot," he said, "and we will be arrested because we are related to him. He doesn't think of us at all."

Later in the afternoon I was with my grandfather in the shed. He had propped up the walls and was now securing the roof. He was very cheerful and kept whistling and singing snatches of a song about the dead dancing under the ground in Chillán. The workman with the big ears was helping him. I had a hammer and every now and then my grandfather would let me hammer a nail.

"Perhaps you will grow up to be a carpenter," said my grandfather. "Long ago there was a woman carpenter in Puerto Montt and she was very famous. Maybe it is time for another."

"I don't think I will grow up," I said.

My grandfather looked at me and raised his eyebrows. "You mean the earthquake? Well, who knows."

"Grandmother says it is getting ready right this moment," I said. "She told me it is like a spring and it is getting wound tighter and tighter."

"Maybe she is right," said my grandfather. "But what can we do, just wait for it? That would make my body soft and my mind, too. Does Jesus want us to grow lazy? Certainly not. He liked carpenters. He'll expect us to keep hammering to the end."

He gave me another board. Through the gaps in the wall of the shed I saw the twins running across the yard to the house. Shortly they ran back across the yard with Rosvita who held up her skirts so she wouldn't spatter them with mud. Their faces bore such expressions of eagerness that I felt curious. Moments later Rosvita came running back across the yard to the house by herself. I went out to the yard and noticed the twins standing near the gate to the orchard. Joining them, I looked through the gate and saw Alcibiades walking with Dalila. She was laughing and Alcibiades looked pleased with himself. It was not raining but the sky was gray and the grass was very wet. Dalila carried the blue umbrella that Rosvita had had several days before but it was rolled up. Alcibiades was waving a hand and speaking with great animation. I heard a noise and saw Hellmuth walking toward me. His face was set as if he were lifting something very heavy. His glasses had slid down his nose and he pushed them back. He passed me without looking at me and strode into the orchard. Alcibiades and Dalila moved apart.

"What are you doing?" said Hellmuth angrily. "Just what do you think you're doing?"

6

YEARS LATER, while I was still married, my aunt Miriam used to come to Santiago about every six months to go shopping. Afterward she would sometimes invite me for dinner. There was a Basque restaurant that she liked near the two large department stores Falabella and Almacenes Paris. By that time Freddy Piwonka Gray was quite wealthy and had retired, although he still owned a lot of property which his son, Hugo, more or less supervised. My aunt Miriam didn't drink in those days. She would laugh and say that if she drank, Freddy would leave her. Freddy, of course, drank and did all sorts of things. But they had a large house that was a kind of showpiece in Puerto Montt, and my aunt Miriam was meant to be a showpiece as well. Her shoulders were covered with expensive cloth and fur coats and she wore expensive hats even though the stoop in her shoulders was so severe that she had to have a brace.

Besides loving my aunt as a member of my family, I liked her because she could make me laugh. Her view of life was that everything worked well except for herself and so her stories took her from one calamity to another as she chuckled and shook her head over her failings. She was always losing things and breaking things and even boiling eggs could end in disaster. But she was very perceptive about other people. I don't know if she observed them closely to see what they were doing right that she wasn't or if her attention was spurred on by envy. But she seemed sincerely to admire their successes and didn't gloat over their failures or suggest that the wreckage of their lives might have been foretold, as my great-aunt Olivia would have done.

Often we would discuss Hellmuth and Alcibiades because their falling out was one of the small tragedies of our family. By then (I must have been nearly thirty) both Hellmuth and Dalila were dead and Alcibiades was living in the north. It was Miriam's contention that Hellmuth had realized what was happening even before Alcibiades, not from jealousy or suspicion or because he was so perceptive, but simply because he and Alcibiades were so much alike. Hellmuth had been attracted to Dalila for exactly the same reason. He was shy and Dalila had swept aside his shyness. He had assumed she had done this because she saw something special in him. But she had seen nothing, not even his shyness. The world for her was something she imagined. She had seen him and chatted to him and had not known that his silence was due to terror. To her way of thinking Hellmuth was merely giving her the opportunity to talk. And so she talked and this created a sense of intimacy which did not in fact exist. With Hellmuth, of course, she was very young, and when she at last became aware of his infatuation she realized it could save her from her father's barbershop. Even though she took pride in her knowledge of fingernails, she hadn't wished to spend her life as a manicurist. And too, once past his shyness, Hellmuth seemed forceful and sure of himself and destined for success, which he was, finally, thanks to the help of Freddy Piwonka Gray.

But there was also the sexual dimension. In freeing Hellmuth from his shyness, she was also freeing his sexual desire and in the struggle between her solipsism and his desire, her solipsism lost. Actually her solipsism was little more than a dream. His desire was hard and demanding. Not that Hellmuth's desires were in any way out of the ordinary. They simply existed. Dalila, according to my aunt Miriam, had little interest in sex despite her flirtatiousness. She saw it as an intrusion, some dangerous force that threatened her ego. Hellmuth would often leave her to go on trips and there was no evidence that Dalila was ever unfaithful. She had her house and her clothes and her piano and these were her playthings.

According to my aunt, Hellmuth soon came to understand his wife, or at least to understand her limitations. It was a great burden to him that she didn't love him, that she was simply submissive. He also had no patience with her solipsism and childlike qualities and came to think her a fool. I don't believe he ever tried to help her or change her or educate her. Like a bull he simply butted himself against her. This owed something to his own fatalism and insecurity. Things didn't change, they existed. And so he accepted the frustration and tried to live with it. He was a passionate man and to be in love with her was like being in love with confetti. But he still loved her and yearned for her. Her physical presence dominated his thoughts but her personality, her indisputable nature, was something else again. She appeared beautiful and flirtatious and high-spirited, but actually she was as sour and inedible as one of those cardboard cakes in a baker's window.

Alcibiades didn't realize this. He saw her exactly as his brother had done. Dalila's charm swept aside his shyness and it seemed she recognized Alcibiades's hidden qualities and was drawn to them. Indeed, she couldn't keep away. And even though she was his brother's wife, Alcibiades let himself be attracted. Did Hellmuth seem to appreciate her or love her? No, he was rude and appeared to ignore her. Dalila's house was destroyed and he seemed to mock her. Besides, it was the end of the world, and who could tell what was true or false anymore?

"There wasn't any intimacy between Hellmuth and Dalila," my aunt Miriam told me. "There was only sex. He wouldn't have known how to tell her how sorry he was that all her pretty things were ruined. And in any case, that house was his enemy. It was the wall she put between them."

We were sitting in the Basque restaurant which was called Pimpilinpausha. On the walls hung colorful posters from the north coast of Spain. Dinner was over and we were smoking cigarettes and drinking coffee. Each table had a red-and-white-checked tablecloth and a candle in a red bowl.

"Why do you think she flirted with Alcibiades?" I asked.

"I don't think she meant anything by it at first," said Miriam. "It was just her natural manner. But she was very upset by the destruction of her house. She was perhaps the only person who took the earthquake personally: that it happened specifically to hurt her. And she knew Hellmuth hated the house and now it was destroyed. He wasn't sorry. He didn't console her. It was almost as if he had destroyed it. Remember, he had had his entire business wiped out. Even if he could buy cattle, how could he transport them? I doubt that Dalila ever thought of this. She hated his business because it made his hands smell."

"So you think Dalila did it on purpose?" I asked.

Miriam lit another cigarette. She was in her early sixties at this time and dyed her hair black, but it seemed too shiny somehow. She had been to a hairdresser that afternoon and her hair looked like a shiny black helmet. It looked expensive rather than nice.

"Not at the beginning. She wasn't cruel. Basically, she was a good person. But she was thoughtless. She flirted with Alcibiades because that was her manner. And when he responded and was friendly, she was grateful because he was the only person who seemed to care about the destruction of her house. Then, when she saw how Alcibiades's attention irritated Hellmuth, she encouraged it just to get even with her husband. But she didn't imagine it going anyplace or consider any of the consequences. I don't believe Dalila was capable of imagining even two minutes into the future. And when it got out of hand, she was as surprised as anyone."

"But Hellmuth was jealous."

"Partly. Flirtatiousness can look like intimacy and Hellmuth envied that apparent intimacy. But whenever he was close to his wife, her talk irritated him. If she had been deaf and dumb, they probably might have been happy. But even her behavior irritated him. When they had been younger, Hellmuth had let himself play dress-up games with Dalila. The memory always embarrassed him."

"Its hard to imagine Hellmuth dressing up as anything," I said.

"They would wear old clothes from the late nineteenth century. He had a top hat and a swallowtail coat and a cravat. She had long gowns and petticoats and a corset and little black shoes that buttoned up along her ankle. They would dress up like this and have tea. Afterward, if Hellmuth was nice, Dalila would let him make love to her. It humiliated him and after some years he put a stop to it."

"It sounds harmless."

"Yes, but it forced Hellmuth to behave in a way that he wasn't, to act falsely. Even as a child he had no sense of play."

"So if it wasn't just jealousy that made him angry, what was it?"

Miriam put a little more sugar into her coffee and stirred it slowly. "Well, of course, he was jealous and he disliked anyone touching what he thought of as his, but I think he was also trying to protect Alcibiades. They were both attracted to Dalila by thinking she was something that she wasn't. Hellmuth had already discovered the sham even though he loved her and remained passionate about her. He also knew that Alcibiades would eventually make the same discovery, but only after their lives were ruined, when he would find himself stuck with Dalila in some awful life. Certainly he was jealous, but Hellmuth also fought with his brother to keep him from making a terrible mistake, to drive him away. He found it better to ruin their friendship than have Alcibiades end up with Dalila."

My aunt and I probably spent half a dozen evenings like this one with the waiters hovering around our table hoping we would leave so they could get home. I would also tell her of my life and my difficulties with my husband. She set great store by submission. "He's the man," she would say. I never found this useful and it clearly said more about her than it was helpful to me. Would my life have been better if I had submitted, if I had always tried to be the person my husband wanted me to be? Of course, when we were first married we imagined ourselves moving forward through life as two equals. But nothing is ever equal; people's needs are never the same. When something irritated my husband, he would pretend it didn't exist. When something irritated me, I had to talk about it. These things are like drops of water falling on a stone year after year. After a while they make a little hole.

I was twenty-four when I was married and Alcibiades came to my wedding. Manfredo had begun medical school in the States, thanks to Freddy Piwonka Gray's generosity, and couldn't come. Of course, my mother was there and I was very glad to see her even though she obviously thought I was making a mistake.

But Alcibiades was sincerely glad for me. At that time he was working in Antofagasta, almost fourteen hundred kilometers north of Santiago with the desert on one side and the ocean on the other. He was fifty-one and his blond hair had gone all gray, although he still had his little mustache. He stood very tall and his face had hundreds of tiny wrinkles from the sun. He had some job with a fishing fleet and was often out on the tuna boats. But I was struck by what a creature of habit he had become. He was still single, of course.

He stayed two nights in a hotel in Santiago but was unable to sleep because of the noises and because the bed was different from his bed at home. And the food was different and the coffee was different and the wine was different. All his daily patterns were disarranged. The buses confused him; the taxi drivers were rude. He didn't complain about these things but they disturbed him and made him ill at ease. By the time he left, I truly appreciated the sacrifice he had made in coming.

The day after my wedding I went with him to the train station. I hated being away from my new husband, but I didn't want Alcibiades to leave by himself and my mother would have been no company, what with her humors and sighs and sad looks. As it turned out the train was late in leaving and we had to wait over an hour. We sat in a little coffee shop and he drank an Orange Crush, which, he said, tasted a little different from the identical soft drink in Antofagasta. He was also very fastidious about the silverware and wiped off the knife, fork and spoon with his napkin, even though he never used them. And he was also concerned about drafts and asked if I would mind changing places with him. And of course he was shy. He would have made a wonderful father and husband but all this remained locked up inside him. I don't believe he had any women friends, or if he did, they were extremely casual.

I asked him if he still fished, but he explained there were no rivers near Antofagasta. Sometimes he went fishing in the ocean but it wasn't the same. He and Hellmuth had fished for salmon and trout and part of the pleasure came from the beauty of the River Maullín and the wild swans one saw at every bend.

"How old were you when you first went fishing?" I asked.

"I have no idea. I must have been very young. My earliest memories are of fishing. It's as if it always existed."

"Did you ever go with your father?"

"No, it was always Hellmuth."

"You must have felt very close to him."

"He was my best friend." He said this as if stating a plain fact.

When the train finally left, he stuck his head out the window and kissed me. It didn't occur to me that he saw me as a fully grown woman and so was uncomfortable with me. He was my dear uncle Alcibiades. His reticence I blamed on his nervousness about the city and his anxiety about the train.

"Come back again soon," I called.

He smiled his kind smile. "I will, I will!"

But it was ten years before I saw him again and by that time my marriage was over.

During that period when we were all staying in my grandmother's bedroom and the earthquakes made us think we had not long to live, I was struck by how the adults talked and talked. My life was bounded by fear, grief and boredom, but the adults escaped to another life which I came to see was simply their past. It was rare that the whole family was together in such an intensive way. Weddings and funerals also give rise to such conversations: who we were long ago and who we knew and what has happened to them and what might have happened to us if things had been different. Hellmuth and Alcibiades and Miriam and even my mother would talk about their childhood and growing up, the friends they had had and trips they had made. Even Walterio would join in these conversations, although he was the baby of the family and most of his memories dealt with either food or complaint. One saw in these stories how certain plans had not succeeded, how certain expectations had come to nothing. And, of course, there had been many good times and much laughter.

And the others—Clotilde and Bibiana and Great-uncle Teodoro and Great-aunt Olivia and my grandparents—they did exactly the same. I could not understand how Teodoro could talk so passionately about a horse he had almost bought fifty years before or how Clotilde would go on and on about how some man had once looked at her in church long before my parents had even been born. They, too, had stories of their lives as children which were not very different from my uncles' or Aunt Miriam's, except there were no cars or radios and life seemed harder. But they still had school and holidays and summers and swimming. There were birthday parties and name-day parties and ox roasts out in the country. And they, too, had had plans that had come to nothing amidst all the good times.

In the wreckage of the parlor many pictures had fallen to the floor. One day I went in there and found the photographs of my great-grandparents and then the pictures—probably lithographs—of my great-great-grandparents who had come over from Germany. I cleaned them off and put them on the couch, then put cushions on the floor in case they fell again. My forebears had stern unsmiling faces and their clothes were buttoned up to their necks. But it occurred to me that they, too, had had stories. They, too, had had plans which had come to nothing and much laughter and ox roasts in the country.

As I grew older I came to recognize certain idiosyncrasies among the children of my generation, which owed something to their parents, as my parents' generation had idiosyncrasies that owed something to their own parents. Why had my grandmother convinced her children they would fail? Why did my grandfather so separate himself from the raising of his children? And I would remember the pictures in my grandmother's living room and want to see them again and say, Did you start it or did you? Were you the first? Were you responsible? But then they had had parents and there were many parents before them and certainly no parent is wholly responsible. I look at my daughter, Ruth. She loves music, she loves to laugh, but I wonder how I am also setting my dark mark on her. What burden am I putting upon her which she will carry through adulthood?

It occurs to me now that the adults in their stories were looking back to an ideal world. No, not ideal. Simply whole. In the evenings the candles would be lit and they would talk and talk, but even during the day they would talk. And the world they described seemed complete and comprehensible and under their control, while what came later was just increasing fragmentation, getting worse and worse until we arrived at the time of the earthquake. Their stories were about change and often looked back to a time when change seemed impossible. As a child I understood, of course, that things would be different as I got older, but if one only knows one's home and love and security, then how can anything that does not include these elements be imagined? It is not only bad things that happened: all sorts of things happened. I mustn't suggest it was only bad things. The enemy, if there was one, was simply change. But certainly change is the medium of life itself. It is the vehicle that carries us into the future.

Before the earthquake I had no sense that my world would ever be very different. Somehow I would find a prince deep in the woods and I would grow up and have a family but all the changes would fall within the boundaries of my childhood world: the only changes that a child is capable of imagining.

The earthquake, of course, had not been imagined, nor had the death of my father, and when those events occurred then my world began to fragment. The earthquake and my father's death didn't cause that fragmentation; they only made me conscious of it and made me conscious of how much I didn't want my world to change. Death and the entrance into my grandmother's Heaven seemed a way of keeping everything the same.

As very small children we feel self-contained and self-sufficient and our parents are just extensions of ourselves. They are our arms and legs. Then we begin to see them moving away from us and we develop language to call them back. But, of course, nothing calls them back, and so we imagine the world is small and they can't go very far away, but of course they do. So we imagine that we can pursue them and stay with them, but, of course, we can't stay with them. So we imagine this is as it should be and nothing can happen that we cannot imagine, and then perhaps an earthquake takes our world and throws it to the ground and one's father is hit on the head with a piece of flying stone and dies in the street in his underwear, and for a while it seems we have no world at all.

But I hate looking back to the far distant past as if things were better then. The time of the earthquake was when I became aware of my life and I have loved my life and I hope much more of it lies ahead. I am still young. I have my daughter and my career. I still might meet someone who will love me and whom I will love in return. My husband in those taxi cabs with those young laughing women: those images weave a rope that binds me to the past, binds me to complaint, but I must sever that rope. I must grow beyond it. The past is neither bad nor good, it is simply gone.

I woke on Sunday morning to find Spartaco sitting on my bed. It seemed early but it was just the darkness of the air. Spartaco looked very depressed and was staring at the floor.

"What's wrong?" I asked, feeling it must be something terrible.

His words were scarcely audible. "The twins found my Hershey bar."

It is hard for me now to divorce his confession from its humor. Had his life really been violated? No, the event was basically trivial. His piece of candy had been stolen. But really it had nothing to do with candy. I looked over at Walterio's bed and there he was sitting with Nancy and Norma. They were all eating and grinning. The torn wrapper of the Hershey bar lay among them. The occasion seemed cheap and ugly and I was very indignant.

"But it was yours," I said.

Spartaco shrugged.

"How did they find it?"

Spartaco pushed back his hair which fell across his forehead. "I don't know. I hid it under a cushion in a chair in the parlor. Then maybe when I checked to see if it was still there, maybe one of the twins saw me. They were always watching me. I should have just left it alone. I wish I could kick them all."

"They're being awful," I said. The chocolate bar had not been particularly large and Walterio and the twins seemed to be taking a very long time to eat it. The twins were chatting happily and Walterio was smiling.

"You know, it doesn't even matter," said Spartaco with more energy. "I mean I don't even care that they have it. But I hate sneaks."

I put my arm around him and he continued to look at the floor. It was late. I had overslept and my head felt funny. Only a few people were left in the room: Great-uncle Teodoro, of course, because of his broken leg and Clotilde because she was afraid of going outside and getting mud on the wedding dress. Ana was carrying out the chamber pots. The room seemed very far away somehow and a buzzing filled my ears. It didn't occur to me that I was getting ill.

Spartaco's grief for his Hershey bar was not excessive. He was hurt more by the betrayal than the theft of the candy. He had liked his uncle and while the twins could be a nuisance they were still his cousins. And, of course, he still liked them, sort of, but he didn't quite trust them and he began to turn away from them and from the idea of our being together.

The theft of the candy undoubtedly influenced the conversation he had with our cousin Hugo later that morning. It was about going away and the theft had made other places appear a little more desirable. The two boys sat on Spartaco's bed which was neatly made with his American blankets and which were still a source of irritation to our grandmother. I was lying down and reading one of the books that Alcibiades had helped me to rescue. Wet sheets hung in the windows. The air was damp and the room had the sour smell of too many people.

Hugo wanted to go to Puerto Montt to join his father, but he was torn. It was a long way and he would have to walk.

"Teodoro says there are looters on the road," said Hugo.

"Do you have a knife?" asked Spartaco.

Hugo looked depressed. "I can't fight anybody. That's just make-believe."

Spartaco nodded. He knew he had a tendency to impose childlike solutions on adult problems and he struggled against it. "I guess you're right," he said. "But you can run."

"You know," said Hugo, "some times Freddy beats me. He just gets mad and beats me. I don't know why he does it. He calls me stupid."

Spartaco thought about that. "But you still want to be there?"

"Sure. It sounds exciting and there's lots to do, not just sitting around like here."

"I wish I could go," said Spartaco.

Hugo cheered up. "We could go together."

"I have to stay here. My mother needs me."

"My mother doesn't need anyone," said Hugo, "except maybe Freddy."

"Then go," said Spartaco. "You can start tomorrow morning and get there before dark. You can take food. I'll even give you my survival kit. You can catch fish and cook them on a fire. It'll be great."

"What if Freddy doesn't want me there?"

"Sure he'll want you. You'll be a big help. Think of all the things you can lift."

Hugo seemed increasingly doubtful. His big blond face looked soft and he glanced uncertainly around the room. "What about the earthquake? I mean the big one."

"It'll be more interesting there. You'll be doing things and seeing things and at least you'll be with your father. You're lucky."

"I'll think about it," said Hugo. "After all, I've got a flashlight."

"You'll have real adventures," said Spartaco.

I thought about adventures and doing lots of things and the idea seemed very heavy and I wanted to put it down. I wanted to shut my eyes and then wake up and find it was summer and find everyone preparing to go to the beach, find my grandmother packing baskets of cold chicken and hard-boiled eggs and lemonade, but then the thought of food made my stomach queasy and I thought instead of flying over the land with my arms outstretched and seeing all the new rivers and lakes and brand-new islands where no one had ever set foot.

There appeared to be much coming and going that morning. The door would open and Alcibiades would look into the room, then go out again. Then the door would open and it would be

Hellmuth and he would look and go out again. My mother had been to mass with my grandmother and Bibiana. She came in and saw me reading and sighed. "What's my little girl going to do without a father?" she said. Then she went and lay down and pulled the blanket over her head. My grandmother came in with Manfredo and she was very jolly and walked her sailor walk and said they were going to cook a calf that had wandered into the yard, but Manfredo refused to look at me and he kept my grandmother's skirts between us. And Bibiana came in and said, Oh, what a mess there was in the yard and, Oh, what a mess there was in the town and, Oh, how could it ever be made better, and then she laughed and laughed, bending over and hardly able to catch her breath. And the door opened again and Dalila looked in and her black hair was bright with drops of water. She wore lipstick and a clean blue dress and I was struck that while the rest of us were beginning to look shabby, Dalila looked as nice as ever. She glanced around and pouted and then went out again, leaving the door open so that my grandmother asked Spartaco to shut it.

Then Rosvita came in. She was obviously full of some thought that was trying to burst from her insides and she seemed swollen with it just as if she had eaten lots of strawberries or cake and it was all pressing against her stomach. Clotilde and my mother were sleeping, while Teodoro was telling Walterio how you couldn't trust a dog not to turn on you if you messed with its food.

Rosvita came and sat on the edge of my bed. "Some people are too much," she said.

"What do you mean?" I felt somewhat honored to be singled out to receive Rosvita's communication. Although she exasperated and even frightened me, the five years' difference between us gave her a power that not even the adults had.

"Dalila," she said, "she thinks I don't know what she's up to but I know all about it. I know why women wear lipstick and pretty clothes. *Quelle jolie robe*, indeed!"

I felt mystified. I also felt there was something wrong with me. I felt very far away, as if there were layers of cotton between the two of us, or as if Rosvita were in a distant room, even though I could still see her. And over her words it seemed I could hear the roar of the ocean, great waves crashing against the rocks.

Rosvita bent toward me. Her light brown hair hung around her face and was puffed out with static electricity. It made her head seem big and her eyes were very large. "The truth is that Alcibiades doesn't like her at all. He couldn't be bothered with a silly thing like her. But she's trying to entrance him. She's always trying to make him look at her. He doesn't want to, of course. He only looks because she's making such a display of herself. I feel sorry for her, I really do."

As Rosvita spoke and I stared into her eyes, I found my mouth filling with saliva and the noise in my ears increased. The room tilted and it seemed that another earthquake was beginning, one that would spin and spin and send us tumbling down through its center.

"I think I'm going to be sick," I said.

Rosvita had the presence of mind to hand me a chamber pot and as I lowered my head toward its white porcelain rim the last thing I noticed was her look of surprise.

Illness in childhood is a dreamy time and the world seems slippery and insubstantial. I remember once when I had measles all I could think about was the icewater which was served with the ice cream at the Café Central. It seemed so cold and clean that I truly believed if I could only have a glass of this icewater, then I would be made well. My mother refused to take me seriously but my father went out and returned with a glass of water in one of the café's own tulip-shaped glasses with *Café Central* printed on the side. He lifted me up and I drank it and after that I knew I would get better.

That Sunday at the end of May 1960, when I got sick, it felt as if I were being swept away, as if some hot wind had gotten inside my head and was busily roaring between my ears. Despite this, I was not uncomfortable. Lying in bed, I felt as if I were high in the air and if I moved at all the room would tilt dangerously and it worried me because I knew if the room tilted, then all the beds would slide into one corner and it would be my fault. I lay on my back and my grandmother and Bibiana and Aunt Miriam, who had once studied to be a nurse, stood around me and looking up at them was like looking up at the trunks of tall trees: trees with human heads at the top, kindly and concerned heads.

"She can't stay here," said my grandmother.

"But we can't put her off in another room," said Bibiana.

They discussed this. The nearest bedroom was on the other side of the dining room which was on the other side of the hall. No one would hear me and if there was an earthquake, I would be all alone.

"She has to stay close to us," said Miriam. She had put a wet washcloth on my forehead and now she replaced it with another. A drop of water ran down the side of my face and into my ear.

"There's only one place to put her," said my grandmother.

And so I was put into my great-aunt Clotilde's alcove and Clotilde was moved into the larger part of the room. She was not pleased. She sighed and heaved herself around. She had many little bottles of scent, many little baskets of pins and ribbons and she needed more space. Besides, how could she continue to look her nicest if she were crowded in with the rest? The wedding dress would be soiled. Already there were spots and she had to wear an apron. Her self-chosen burden—and this may have been simply my fever—was to be the fiancée of Death and when he came to take us all to Heaven, he would take her as his bride and they would ride off on his black horse with Clotilde sitting sidesaddle behind him in her wedding dress, clinging to his black robes. I felt guilty and unwilling to displease her. Didn't she need a little room by herself? How else could she make herself ready?

"You can have the bedroom on the other side of the dining room," my grandmother told her.

But that was too far away and Death might not be able to find her. It would be terrible if he came and took the rest of us and left her behind. Instead, she would take a bed in the corner but more space had to be made. And so all the beds were moved and pushed a little closer together and a chamber pot was knocked over and broke. Then a blanket was hung from a string and Clotilde was given a new alcove and when the blanket was drawn shut and Clotilde was hidden behind it, one could still hear her sigh and mutter about and how she deserved better.

Sometimes I slept, sometimes I half slept, sometimes I felt better for a half hour or so and sat up. My aunt Miriam gave me aspirin and my great-aunt Olivia gave me a tea made from some leaves she had gathered. Miriam was indignant and called them "any old leaves," but my grandmother asked, "And what's the harm?" But in truth I don't believe that either made me any better. The tea was sweet and tasted like the wind in the orchard when the trees are all blossoming, and at least it was hot. Olivia bent over me and I knew she was a witch but she was a very kind witch and she couldn't help being impatient and having features as sharp as if they had been cut from a block of wood with a knife, and it seemed that all the gold in her teeth was there because she had no smile, as if the gold took the place of a smile, because even if she couldn't smile, she could glisten.

And Hellmuth looked in and frowned and said it was a bad business; and Alcibiades looked in and said he would get me anything in the world that I wanted, I only had to ask; and Walterio looked in and asked if there was anything I would like to eat and offered me a cookie, but I wanted nothing, or rather I only wanted to know they were nearby and that they cared for me.

Night came and the lights were extinguished and the air was full of invisible things that whispered and cooed to each other and there were tremors but nobody moved me and after a very long time the windows began to lighten again and I heard my grandmother wake and groan and rise from her bed and say, "Stupid old bones, foolish old bones," then she went into the yard to stir up the fire. Then my grandfather went off to the outhouse and somebody else began to brush his teeth and spit and Walterio said, "All night I dreamed of ice cream" and Rosvita said, "Some people know nothing about perfume," and Alcibiades said, "There'll be no sun today," and Olivia said, "Dark clouds, more dark clouds," and Hugo said, "I want to go find Freddy," and Dalila said, "Everything is so boring," and Manfredo said nothing, but he peeked around the corner at me, then he disappeared.

My mother asked if I wanted anything but I didn't, I couldn't imagine wanting anything, and my grandmother said I should eat something but I wasn't hungry, but Olivia gave me more of her sweet-smelling tea and I drank what I could. I lay on my back and heard Hellmuth talking to Great-uncle Teodoro and his voice had a thickness that was like a hungry man talking about food.

"Freddy must be stealing those blankets," said Hellmuth.

Teodoro cleared his throat and made a spitting noise. "If he gets caught, it will mean bad talk for the whole family."

"But it must, I mean, be more, you know," said Walterio, "more than blankets . . ."

"He's got food and flashlights and clothing," said Hellmuth. "Where can he be getting it all?"

"He's, well, sly," said Walterio.

"Somebody's stealing it from the airport," said Hellmuth.

"It's smart about the cars, though," said Teodoro. "I'm going to be needing a car myself when this is over."

"Who says, you know, I mean," said Walterio, "who says . . ."

"It's never going to be over," said Hellmuth.

I drifted off to someplace like sleep, not really sleep because it was like taking a trip someplace and I could see the colors and objects fly past me and there went a loaf of bread and there went a big shoe missing its laces and beneath me I could see my feet and beneath them were the tops of trees rushing past in a blur of green and then St. Lucy the Virgin Martyr went rushing past on a purple cloud and her smile was like soft blankets and when I came back to the alcove and opened my eyes the doctor was sitting with me and he looked very tired.

"Cough," he said and Miriam held me up and the doctor put a stethoscope to my chest and it was cold. I coughed.

The doctor was probably in his sixties and his gray hair lay all over his head as if it, too, were very tired. He wore a three-piece blue suit and there were cigarette ashes up and down the front, and the ends of his fingers were yellow with nicotine. As he listened to my lungs and heart, he sucked on a cigarette and the ash grew longer and longer until it began to tremble and bend. And I thought now it's going to fall and now it's going to fall, but at the last moment he tapped the ash into his hand and put it into the side pocket of his suit coat. The doctor wore glasses with metal frames and his eyes looked shiny. His name was Doctor Luttecke and he was the same doctor who had visited me when I had measles.

"Earthquakes and sickness," he said in a gruff sort of voice. "Life's not very nice to some people is it, girlie? Cough again." His breath smelled of cigarettes and his clothes smelled of cigarettes and even his teeth were yellow.

He looked down my throat and shone a light in my eyes and looked in my ears and checked for swelling in my groin and took my temperature and again the ash of his cigarette got longer and longer and again I thought, Now it's going to fall, and again he caught it at the last moment and put it in his pocket. And when this cigarette was done, he used the burning tip to light another, squinting all the while to keep the smoke from his eyes. Miriam and my mother and grandmother stood at the foot of my bed and watched, and my grandmother leaned forward and she squinted, too, although not from the smoke but to see better.

The doctor removed the thermometer from my mouth and held it toward the window. "Forty degrees," he said. "You're a sick little girl."

He said it in such a way that I didn't know whether I should feel guilty or proud.

"And how is your *wata?*" he asked, using the Indian word for stomach. "How is your *watita?*"

I tried to tell him that it felt all right.

"I can't hear you," he said, bending toward me and I repeated what I had said, but the words were difficult to put in a row. They wouldn't stay next to each other. They were greasy and slipped from my intention.

The doctor stood up and began putting away his stethoscope. He had a tall black leather bag that was wrinkled like an elephant's skin. "She's sick," he said. "I don't know what it is. Some virus. Keep her in here and keep her warm. Aspirin every four hours. If the temperature goes up, she'll have to have a cold bath. Try to get her to eat something and don't let her get dehydrated." He picked up the cup containing my aunt Olivia's tea and sniffed it. "What's this awful stuff?"

"Herb tea," said my grandmother.

"I don't suppose it can do any harm," said the doctor in a voice which suggested just the opposite. "Is this your nonsense, Olivia?" he called into the other room. "You'll make someone sick someday." Then he turned back to my grandmother. "Don't let her put poultices all over the poor child."

"What about the hospital?" said my mother. "Could they help her there?"

"What hospital? Do you mean those tents in the park? Do you mean the Americans in Puerto Montt? Do you know how many people are broken and banged up and sick? I get no sleep at all." He paused to light another cigarette.

"Are things very bad in town?" asked Miriam.

Doctor Luttecke scowled at her. "Winter's coming. Half the houses are uninhabitable and the other half people don't want to go into. They think the earthquakes are just waiting for them to go to sleep and then the ceilings will come crashing down. And, of course, the tents all leak and people's feet are wet all the time. And food, how're they going to get enough food? Let me see Teo's leg." The doctor pushed past Miriam and the others into the bedroom. After a moment I heard him say, "What's this stuff, what's this nasty stuff? Doesn't the room smell bad enough?"

"My wife put it on," said Uncle Teodoro apologetically.

"Well, the next time, you stop her. I'm not going to change your dressing if I have to fight my way through a swamp."

Olivia had stayed in the alcove and she peered around the

corner at the doctor, then she looked back at me and put a finger to her lips and the gold in her teeth flickered in the light.

Was that Monday or Tuesday? I think it was Monday because that was the day of Joan of Arc and it seemed I could see her up in the air clad head to foot in white armor and she looked very brave. But perhaps that, too, was a dream, because dream and waking were like twin villages and I traveled back and forth between them never knowing which was which. And once when I opened my eyes, I saw Manfredo with his chin resting on the horizontal brass railing at the end of the bed. His eyes were open very wide and he looked at me sadly. And another time I woke to find Dalila standing beside me with a steaming cup of something that smelled like lemons.

"I know I'll get sick just being here," she said. "I always catch other people's colds. Sometimes I think people get sick just so they can make me sick as well."

She sat down beside me. "When I was a little girl and when I got sick, my mother would make me hot lemon juice and water and honey. It always made my throat feel better."

I tried to tell her there was nothing wrong with my throat but my words were all mixed together in a great pile of other words and the effort needed to extract them was so tiring that I remained silent, but I tried to smile and Dalila smiled back and patted my hand.

"You have pretty hands," she said, "and when you grow up they'll look beautiful: long and slender. My hands, I'm afraid, are a little boxy, that's why I have to take such good care of them. If people see how pretty my nails are, then they won't notice that boxy quality. Of course, I could just keep my hands in my pockets but that looks so slouchy. Miriam always keeps her hands in the pockets of her sweater and it's quite ruined, the sweater. Alcibiades, I think, has the nicest hands of all, so white and smooth, yet strong. Hellmuth's hands are like hooves with fingers. Looking at them used to make me weep, but now I don't care anymore. They should have special exercises for hands so you could change their shape just like you can change your waistline. If there *were* special exercises, I would make my hands just like yours, long and thin. They must have classes like that someplace. Buenos Aires or Paris. Perhaps I can find out once we get out of here. But, oh, I'm so bored and the days are so long and I've done everybody's nails already, at least everybody who will let me."

As she talked she held my hand and turned it back and forth, looking at one side, then the other, and her hands felt very cool. I wanted to ask her what it meant to entrance somebody else and if entrance was the same as bewitch and if to bewitch a person was to put them under a spell. And was Dalila trying to put Alcibiades under a spell and what would she do with him? I remembered in stories that when one person put another person under a spell, then the bewitched person would have to wash all the dishes day after day or sweep up the house and do endless cleaning. And in another story a whole castleful of people were put to sleep and a prince was turned into a fox and in another story a man under a spell could see none of the dangers around him and he walked right over the side of a cliff.

I tried to ask Dalila about spells and enchantment and bewitchment but the words slid away like soap bubbles. Still, I was glad to have her stroke my hand and after a while I slipped off to dream again.

Later Spartaco came and read to me from *The Black Arrow* and when he read how Master Richard Shelton rode into Tunstall hamlet, I could see his leather jacket with the black velvet collar and green hood over his head and the sound of Spartaco's voice wove smoky patterns in the air. He read and read and when he paused I wanted to ask him to take fresh flowers to the *animita* of Jaime Alverez but again the words wouldn't come to me. I knew where I was and I knew where the words were, but I couldn't pick them up. It wasn't heaviness that was the problem but slipperiness.

After a long while Spartaco finished the chapter and he looked at me and he looked at the floor, then he said, "Hellmuth and Alcibiades aren't talking anymore and they don't play chess either. I asked Alcibiades if he wanted to play chess with me but he didn't. Hellmuth stays right by the house, but Alcibiades has gone into town. And they say there was a sea monster in the lake but I don't believe them. Poor Hugo is too stupid to play chess or at least he doesn't want to learn. You know, I think even school would be better than this. But this morning one of the workers said he saw a puma out in the fields and if the sky clears I'm going to get up on the roof with binoculars and look for it. It would be neat to catch it. What if you had six pumas and you tied them to a cart and painted the wheels golden? They would pull you through town and you could snap your whip above their heads. Even four pumas would probably be enough."

Spartaco continued to talk but I drifted off again and in my dreams I kept seeing great golden doorways with light shining through them and sometimes there was music. Other times my mind would embroider upon something someone had been telling me and in one dream there were many puma carts and we all had one, even my father, and we rode across the fields to the beach where my father smeared us all with heavy cream and the pumas carefully licked it from our bodies. Another time I awoke and found Alcibiades sitting beside me. His blond mustache was drooping and his blond hair was drooping and his sadness and concern made it seem that his whole face was drooping.

"Can I do anything to make you better?" he asked.

I tried to smile at him and he took my hand. His hands were cool like Dalila's but not as soft.

"Once when I was a child," said Alcibiades, "I had pneumonia and all day long I would tell myself, 'I have to get better, I have to get better.' And when I finally got better, I thought I had caused it."

I was struck by this, because until then I hadn't thought of getting better, as if my sickness were a necessary stop in my journey to Heaven.

Alcibiades kept stroking my hand. "Everything's turned upside down," he said. "I hardly know what I'm doing all day long. Are we waiting or just passing the time? And why should we do anything in particular? If this is the end, then why not do just what we want? Like Walterio, we can all eat ourselves to death or something." He looked serious for a moment, then he laughed. "Can you see us all grown fat? How would we get through the door if there was another earthquake?

He paused, then reached for the mug of tea. "Here, you should drink some of this." He held me up and I drank a little. From the other room I could hear Uncle Teodoro say, "No farming, no work, no school ever again."

"The important thing is for you to get better," said Alcibiades. "We have cousins in Santiago and you and the other children should be sent there. But they're not even going to fix the railway tracks as long as these quakes continue. Your grandmother thinks even Santiago's going to be destroyed in the next earthquake. But that's impossible, why should everything get destroyed? But who knows? At least while we're here I don't have to worry about getting another job." He paused again. "It's terrible. I keep thinking, 'Why not do what I want? Why does anything else matter?' You know, I'd never understood how rude Hellmuth was to Dalila. He's not a mean man but it's as if he hates her. Maybe it's because she teases him. Of course, she shouldn't do it but she's upset just like everybody else. I try to talk to him about it but he refuses to listen. Absolutely everything is upside down." He patted my hand a little more roughly. "You have to get better, Lucy. It's no good just lying here."

But it seemed I was entirely without a will. If I was sick, then presumably I was meant to be sick. And if I got better or worse, that, too, was predetermined. Sometimes I knew I was lying in bed in Clotilde's little alcove. Other times it seemed that I was traveling all over. Once I was with my father at my cousins' farm in the country and he was showing me how to ride a horse. It seemed I could never keep my feet in the stirrups and I slid from one side of the saddle to the other. Then my father would stop the horse and adjust the stirrups again. "We've got to stretch your legs," he kept saying. "They're just too short."

Another time when I woke up—because certainly these other journeys were no more than a dream—Father Opilio was sitting beside me.

"How are you going to sing in the choir if you don't get better?" he demanded.

I was surprised because this was the first I had heard about singing.

"Lots of people are in bed with broken bones," said Father Opilio. "It's your duty to get well as soon as possible." His two pretend fingers in their white bandage extended hugely from his hand and he blessed me with them.

Hellmuth and my mother and grandmother stood behind him. Spartaco and Manfredo were there as well.

"Do you hear any news?" asked Hellmuth.

Father Opilio stood up. He had shaved only part of his face and he looked all bristly and whiskery and his eyebrows seemed quite ferocious.

"All the news is bad news," said Father Opilio, preparing to leave. "If it weren't for the church, there'd be nothing but chaos."

"What about the army?" asked Hellmuth.

"Scoundrels every one," said Father Opilio. He drew a glove over his bandaged hand that had a special, extra large finger, like a club.

"What about the Americans?" asked Spartaco.

Father Opilio answered in a sort of stage whisper. "They're all Protestants." Then he grinned an ironic grin. "Naturally they're doing what they can. We've sent some people down to their hospital." He began making his way out of the alcove.

Hellmuth touched Father Opilio's arm. "But isn't aid being flown in?" he asked.

Father Opilio paused and his whole face reddened. "Of course it is and it sits at the airport and people go hungry. Last night my housekeeper served ham for dinner, a Virginia canned ham that had been flown all the way from the United States to feed the poor people of Puerto Montt. And how did my housekeeper get it? She bought it, that's how. She said you can buy anything, even Jeeps."

Father Opilio passed into the other room. There was a pause, followed by an indignant snorting noise. "Olivia, what is this nonsense you've slopped all over your husband's leg? I warn you, you're putting your immortal soul in jeopardy."

Olivia said something and then I heard Miriam and Walterio and all the voices seemed to blend together. I told myself that I should get up, that I would feel better if I walked around, but my legs paid no attention and even my eyes wouldn't look at what I wanted. Perhaps that was Tuesday, I'm not sure.

And perhaps it was sometime later that I discovered my grandfather sitting down on the edge of my bed and the springs squeaking under him. He touched my forehead.

"So what do you think's wrong with you?" he asked.

I couldn't think of what to say. It occurred to me that I was lonely and I was cold. I wanted it to be summer and I wanted everything to be put back together again.

"Don't bother speaking," said my grandfather. "I probably couldn't hear you anyway." He removed his hat and wiped his forehead with a handkerchief, then he replaced his hat again. "Anyway, I know how it is. I've been sick myself. Your whole head's a confusion. You're floating out there someplace and you feel that you could come back here or go someplace else. But you've got to come back. This is where you belong. We love you. We need you here."

It was night when my grandfather visited me and only a single candle was burning in the alcove. From the other room I could hear people talking but I couldn't make out their words. There was one chair in the alcove set against the wall and it seemed that someone was sitting in it. I tried to turn my head but it was too heavy. Then I realized it was my father sitting in the chair, that he had come to visit me. My grandfather kept talking but I no longer heard him. Instead all my attention was focused on my father who was dressed as I had last seen him in his tan trousers and tweed jacket. He held his hat in his hands, turning it round and round as I had seen him do many times before. And I wanted to call to him but the words had leaked out of my head like air from a balloon. And soon I realized that my grandfather had gone but my father was still there. He sat in the straight chair set against the wall and he kept moving his lips. At first I didn't know what he was trying to tell me. Then I realized he was saying that he loved me. "I love you," he kept saying, over and over. And his eyes were all sparkly and he had a wonderful smile.

I went to sleep with my father sitting near me and all night I dreamed of being with him, of walking and talking or just sitting with him, and several times I awoke in the night and was afraid that my father might have gone away, but he was still there. Did I think he was a ghost? I don't believe the question occurred to me. He was simply there. And when I awoke in the morning he was still there, although much faded and I had to look very hard and I could see the wall through his body.

Then Spartaco came in and he looked very excited and I wanted to tell him about our father, but Spartaco said, "Hugo's left for Puerto Montt. He took off this morning. Isn't that great, isn't that really great?"

7

WHO LIVES in that house in Puerto Varas now? Cousins, people I hardly know. Originally they were from Ancud and Alcibiades wrote to them at the time of my grandmother's death. They had been willing to take over the farm and not break it up, as had been Freddy's plan. They have dairy cattle and grow fodder. I met them at Bibiana's funeral, hers being the last funeral I've gone to, and she had lived with these cousins until she went into the hospital. They seemed perfectly nice. My aunt Miriam is now seventy and Freddy is seventy-eight, and presumably one of them will be the next to die, although Freddy seems stronger than ever and I recently heard that he had taken a new mistress. Miriam has developed diabetes.

It's sad to see them slip away, like people at a party who have to leave early. When I was a child, I was quite drawn to my grandmother's idea of having us all die together but when I grew up I began to think of it as barbaric and cruel, another example of an older generation imposing its will upon the younger. But now, as I see these generations disappear into oblivion, their members one by one passing through that dark door, I come around again to my grandmother's thought of how wonderful if we could all die together: all of us setting off in a group as if on a bus. I'm not entirely serious. But if we could have started together and lived long lives together, then perhaps we could have died together. I think of my daughter and how beautiful she is and how much she needs me and how she will have to live on this planet for years and years without me. How can I not worry?

My grandmother had a great desire for certainty, a great belief in control. She belonged to a world where these elements were viewed as necessary qualities, not impossible to attain, and which were needed for survival. After all, she was born in 1891 in what was basically a frontier community. What was valued was self-sufficiency and this was achieved through rigorous discipline: not entirely self-discipline but a discipline also guided by the church and society. But even in my grandmother's youth there had developed a split between the town and the countryside, the beginnings of a rivalry. My grandmother saw herself as belonging to the town and so to marry a farmer and live on a farm, even an extremely successful farm, was something of a disappointment, a sacrifice, a slight affront to her dignity and she felt, to some small degree, superior to her environment.

She dealt with her disappointment and perhaps her temptations by exerting an even greater control, by aspiring to certainty in all things. How frustrating it must have been to receive from her husband no more than a benevolent recognition as he proceeded calmly along his own paths. But her younger sisters felt her control and her children as well. And I believe that what at last broke the last remnants of her control was the earthquake itself: the event which was to sweep us into Heaven. Although, of course, the earthquake didn't cause it; people caused it. But the earthquake created the environment in which her control was swept away. Or perhaps the control was not swept away but we were swept away, swept away from her and into other lives. And, sadly, she had become increasingly anxious about this control, because of her failing vision, and so the breakup—the disintegration—of her family must have been dreadful for her. Afterward, of course, her sisters remained in the house, but although she loved them, she didn't value them and so their continuing surrender meant little.

But I remember sitting with Bibiana after my grandmother's funeral. My great-aunt wept and wept, then she would laugh as she remembered some story, then she would weep again. It was October and we were at the kitchen table drinking tea and eating some sort of *küchen* made with strawberries. Clotilde and my grandfather were long dead, and my grandmother and Bibiana had been living in the house alone, despite my grandmother's complete blindness, which she tried to conceal. Of course, Ana was still there and Ana's children worked in the kitchen as well.

"She was so good to me!" Bibiana kept saying. "She was so good to me!" Despite the fact that she was seventy-seven, Bibiana looked very much like a child, a roly-poly sort of child with red balloon cheeks and bright little eyes. And her manner, too, was childlike. She was quite plump and her black dress appeared stretched. In the few years left to her she began to lose weight and her body seemed almost to drip from her bones as she got thinner and thinner. The cousins who took over the farm were kind to her and found her amusing but without my grandmother she was directionless and vacant and her only desire was to follow her sister as soon as possible into the Heaven which was at the center of all her thoughts.

"She made me so happy," Bibiana told me, and then she recounted some occasion more than fifty years before when her sister had left a little bouquet of primroses on her night table, which Bibiana had discovered when she awoke in the morning, and how the only pair of shoes which had ever properly fit had been a pair that her sister had brought her from Santiago.

"Didn't you ever want to get married?" I asked her. I myself had been married only a few months and it seemed to me that marriage was the necessary center of each person's life. My husband hadn't been able to come to the funeral and claimed he had to work and that, too, I found perfectly reasonable.

"She made my life rich," said Bibiana. "What would I have been without her? What could anyone else have given me?"

At the time I felt that Bibiana had been so influenced, so controlled by my grandmother that she could see nothing except through my grandmother's point of view. But now I don't know. Or rather, even though she was bent by my grandmother, much in the way a gardener bends a tree, what did that bending matter if in the end she believed she had had a happy life? And certainly it was happy. Without my grandmother she might have had ten beautiful children or become a doctor or climbed Mt. Everest, but she wouldn't have been any happier.

My grandmother had had a stroke upstairs in one of the storage rooms: shelf after shelf of hard little cookies and brandy-soaked puddings. She lay on the floor all day just as if she had been put in storage as well. Then Bibiana remembered her and sent Ana to find her. Two workmen carried my grandmother down to her bed and the doctor was sent for. My grandmother lay unconscious for a week as Bibiana sat beside her. Toward the end my grandmother opened her eyes and looked around.

"And she knew right where she was," said Bibiana, "and right what had happened and she said perfectly clearly, 'Do you remember little Gabriel? I believe he's waiting for me.'"

Then my grandmother went to sleep again and the next day she was dead and the relatives were notified, although I've always been sorry that Bibiana didn't let me know right when the stroke first occurred, because I would have come immediately.

"And you know what?" said Bibiana, resuming her story. "I had forgotten all about Gabriel. I didn't know who she was talking about, that it was her own dead baby." And here Bibiana laughed and also started to cry and the tears popped and sprang from her eyes and she quickly unpinned her handkerchief and patted her eyes as if punishing them.

But then we had to deal with Freddy's scheme of subdividing the farm into building plots, which probably, in the long run, would have made us a lot of money considering how Puerto Varas has become popular with tourists and is crowded in the summer. At that time, however, it seemed wrong to break up the farm and it was Miriam who suggested the cousins in Ancud, even though she hid it from Freddy. Alcibiades came down from the north and, of course, there was Walterio and we could all smell his perfume even over the flowers, and instead of a white shirt he wore a cream-colored one made of silk. Great-uncle Teodoro was long dead, but his wife, Olivia, was healthy and vigorous and seemed to fill the room with her angular presence. She looked more like a witch than ever and the priest, a new one, suggested that perhaps there was something good to be said for those smelly teas of hers. And she winked and pressed one finger to the side of her nose. In all of this activity Bibiana drifted into the background and seemed comfortable there and I never really spoke to her again.

We are such divided creatures. There is what one wants for oneself, reaching toward life as if toward a platterful of cake or simply wanting happiness or some sort of justification for being. Then there is what one wants within one's family and that slightly larger society of friends: we want them to love us and respect us. We want to help them, which often means making them follow the paths we believe they should follow, paths which may not be helpful at all. Thirdly, there is what one wants within the greater society at large: wealth or fame or respect or security, those vague things whose absence wakes us in the early hours of the morning and sets us gnawing at ourselves. And, of course, these different desires can conflict with each other and with the desires of the people around us. Alcibiades's desires for himself came to focus on Dalila. He believed he needed her in order to live and be happy. Certainly this was destructive. Hellmuth's increasing desire was toward that greater society: wealth and respect, and this was destructive to all my grandmother's wishes. Dalila's desire, I think, was to change this close society of family and friends, to become a power within it, perhaps even to become its center. And this, too, was destructive. And, of course, she wanted to get even with her husband and with my grandmother, who, she believed, had insulted her by ignoring her, by believing she was trivial, which perhaps she was.

When it became clear to me some years ago that my husband wanted to leave me, I threw myself more and more into the life of my daughter, Ruth, who was about four at the time. She became my friend and accessory and, without consciously intending it, I tried to turn her away from her father, because if I was right, then certainly her father must be wrong. My daughter obviously responded to my attention and loved being with me. It's not difficult to charm one's own child. But my husband also had his relationship with our daughter and even after he moved out, he would visit on Saturday afternoons and take her to the park and push her on the swings. Ruth would return from these occasions so happy and so full of life that to see her was to have slivers of glass within my heart. And yet I wanted her to be well! As time went on Ruth came to sense my anger and she stopped talking about her father. They continued to see each other; they see each other still. And each time when she returns home her eyes are bright, her cheeks are flushed as if she had been running. I realize she has a relationship with her father that I cannot imagine and from which I am excluded. I try to accept that and wish only for her happiness. I try not to see her love for her father as a betrayal or let it anger me.

Yet my grandmother hated my own father and both she and my mother felt betrayed by him. I truly believed he had died doing something heroic but, really, the manner of his death was not as important as the awful fact of his death. My mother and grandmother's response to what they saw as the shameful circumstances of his death was not to talk about him, not to think of him, and presumably they believed I wasn't thinking of him either. They had shut him out of their lives and they hoped he was out of my life, too. But here he was sitting in my room! During those long days of my sickness, my father sat on the straight chair with the cane seat, which was placed against the wall to my left, and sometimes I saw him clearly and sometimes I saw only a vague outline, but he was always there. And although I couldn't hear him, I would watch his lips move and sometimes I knew he was saying my name and sometimes he told me that he loved me and sometimes he told me to be brave. And I knew he had come to lead me into Heaven because Heaven was a large place and now, because of the earthquake, there must be crowds of new arrivals and a great deal of commotion and pushing and shoving and my father had come to make my passage easier. And if I had told my mother and grandmother that my father was sitting with me and that he continued to love me, how surprised they would have been.

Now I believe that my grandmother also thought I was going to die and perhaps even wished for it, although not entirely consciously. Given her ideas about the earthquake and her ambitions about Heaven, death was perhaps the best thing she could have asked for me. In my highly rational twenties, I saw this as madness and it made me angry at her, but I think my grandmother viewed my illness as a kind of good fortune that would take me off to Heaven while sparing me the trauma of the final earthquake. And perhaps she was beginning to feel some anxiety about that earthquake. When was it coming? She was surely aware of the increasing restlessness of her family. Hugo's departure for Puerto Montt had upset her and she made angry remarks which suggested he might have jeopardized his place in Heaven. These remarks frightened me because Spartaco had encouraged his cousin and if Hugo's future in Heaven was in danger, then perhaps Spartaco's was as well and I couldn't imagine being in Heaven without Spartaco. My grandmother had no sense of my anxiety. She would come and sit by my bed and tell me about my uncle Gabriel and explain how wonderful it would be to live in a Heaven that included us all.

"He loved horses," my grandmother told me one afternoon, "and one time he got up on a horse all by himself. Oh, weren't we surprised! Someone had ridden up from town and had tied his horse right outside the kitchen door. It was the kitchen girl who told me. Not Ana, of course. Could it have been her mother? Anyway she came running and I looked out the window and there was Gabriel sitting on that big horse as proud as anything. I got him down right away. After all, he might have fallen. No, it wasn't Ana's mother because I sent this girl away right after the accident. It was her job to watch Gabriel. Even that day when he climbed up on that horse she should have been paying closer attention. Everything was always so busy in those days and there were many distractions. I remember when I found his little body there was an awful bruise on his face where the horse had kicked him, some old farm horse that had been tied up in the stable, but his whole cheek and eye . . . But I wonder if in Heaven he's been made whole again. Father Opilio says that of course he's been made whole, that in Heaven we all look our best, but I don't know if Father Opilio knows any more about Heaven than I do. Oh, to think, Lucy, that you might be getting there first. Tell them all we're coming, tell them to be ready! Think of all the kissing and welcoming! What a glorious time that will be. And not just Gabriel, but my mother and father. And cousins, lots of cousins . . ."

And I wanted to tell her that my father would be there as well, but I still couldn't speak and my head hurt. Even so, I glanced over to where my father was sitting and he read my thoughts and smiled and, yes, he would be there, too.

"I've often wondered if people live in houses in Heaven," continued my grandmother. "You know, when all's said and done, we know very little about it. Of course, one imagines mile after mile of fleecy white clouds, but do people sleep on those clouds? For that matter do people sleep in Heaven? But if there are houses, then I hope Gabriel has a nice one. Really, we'll be very lucky if you go on ahead of us, because you can tell Gabriel we're coming and he can get his house ready or at least set aside a place for us. Father Opilio says that the whole family will be there, with some exceptions, but he didn't know about houses or anything. I expect that since one is above the clouds, it doesn't actually rain and so one wouldn't really need a roof, but sometimes it's nice to live in a house just because it's so cozy."

My grandmother could go on like this for quite some time and truly it was hard not to be caught up in her enthusiasm and expectations. Often Bibiana would be with her and she, too, would have her theories.

"I should think one of the hardest things about Heaven," Bibiana liked to say, "would be to get used to not eating. Year after year, no eating. What could you eat? To eat something means to kill something. Even grass. No eating and probably no drinking either. And probably no sleeping! I think the people in Heaven must have meditation like those swamis, but Father Opilio doesn't think so."

"And what do you know about meditation?" asked my grandmother.

"Oh, I know more than you think. Whenever you say, 'Bibiana, what are you doing staring out that window?' that's what I'm doing."

"What nonsense are you talking about?" asked my grandmother with mock seriousness.

"I'm meditating," said Bibiana, "I'm meditating like a swami." And Bibiana bent forward with laughter and gasped and was unable to catch her breath and sometimes it was almost frightening to watch her as she heaved and strained and patted her eyes until the giggles subsided and she leaned back against the wall and sighed happily, her small dark eyes as bright as porcelain buttons.

I felt quite proud about being the first of us to go to Heaven. Certainly such a thought owed a great deal to my fever, but my grandmother's talk and the image of my dead father—was it only a hallucination?—made me think that my passage into Heaven as an envoy or herald was perfectly reasonable, and I also imagined meeting Jaime Alverez who would express his appreciation that I had cared for his *animita* so devotedly. Would he be a cheerful man or would he be somber? I tried to ask my father if he knew him but the words grew lost in my throat. But my father smiled and his face was so kind that I felt certain that despite the great size of Heaven, he knew Jaime Alverez and they were friends.

One afternoon I awoke to find my uncle Hellmuth standing beside my bed. I looked up at him and my attention seemed to take him by surprise and he stepped back. His hands were cupped together and after a moment he reached forward and put a number of the chess pieces which he had been carving on the blanket covering my chest. When he leaned forward, his glasses slid down his nose and he pushed them back. He wore a brown suit and a striped tie but the suit was rumpled and the tie all bent.

"I thought you might like these," he said. "They're chess pieces. Not a whole set, of course. I thought I might finish it but now I don't think I will. Have you ever played chess?" He waited a moment with his eyebrows raised expectantly, then continued. "My grandfather taught me to play a long time ago. Maybe I was about your age."

He reached forward again and lined up the chess pieces on the blanket: two kings and a queen, three bishops, three rooks, a knight and half a dozen pawns all with individual faces. The pieces were clumsy but clearly human and their faces looked puzzled and wondering like tiny prehistoric people at the brink of their first religious experience. His large hand moved them about, putting the two kings and queen in the middle.

"You can make up stories with them," he said. "It will help pass the time. If you want, when you get better, I'll carve the rest. I hope you get better soon. Is there anything I can get you? Perhaps something to eat?"

I didn't say anything but continued to look at the chess pieces. The wood was blond and splintery. I wondered what kind of stories they might appear in. Perhaps adventures, perhaps romance. The pawns all looked like rogues and the queen had a hook nose and a sharp chin. Could the two kings be in love with her? I felt touched by my uncle's gift, but when I looked up to try and thank him, I found he was gone.

On one of those days during the first week of June, maybe Thursday or Friday, there was another earthquake, not a tremor or shock but a real earthquake, and the moment I heard the birds I knew it was coming and I felt glad: hundreds of birds filled the air with their cries. Then, from town, came the ringing of bells, with the deep bells of the Church of the Sacred Heart of Jesus ringing the loudest. The wet sheets began to tremble in the window and my bed began to shake. All the objects in the house began to whisper together and shuffle in their many places. Then their whispering grew louder and even though I lay perfectly still, I began to bounce on the brass bed. I heard my mother call to Bibiana and the door slammed. More people shouted, raising their voices over the creaking and banging of the house, over the cry of the birds. I looked at my father and he nodded and smiled at me, although he was very transparent and it was difficult to pick him out against the wall. But I knew he was urging me to prepare myself, to get myself ready for my long journey and I wished my hair was better combed and that I was wearing a clean nightdress and not some old one that had been found in the trunks upstairs.

Then Alcibiades burst into the alcove with the workman with big ears and they each picked up one end of my bed with me in it and began carrying me through the bedroom. Several of Hellmuth's chess pieces had been on my chest and they rolled off onto the floor. Ahead of me I could see Hellmuth and Walterio and Aunt Olivia carrying the other bed with my great-uncle Teodoro, who kept crying out to them to be careful and to hurry. The room was swaying and pictures fell from the walls and it was hard for Alcibiades and the workman to keep their balance and I felt this must be what it feels like to be carried on an elephant, carried on an elephant right up to Heaven, and I tried to look for my father but I couldn't see him. I only knew he was waiting to escort me to the other world. Alcibiades and the workman rushed through the doorway, banging the bed against the frame and the workman scraped his fingers and cursed and in a second they had me outside in the dim afternoon light where it was raining and cold; and there waited my family huddled under a tarpaulin and only my grandmother looked glad, but I felt glad, too. I knew that my time had arrived and as the rain fell against my face I squinched my eyes against the drops and stared upward to where I thought I could already see the blessed saints and angels, see St. Lucy the Virgin Martyr herself, looking down as if from the roof.

Alcibiades and the workman put the bed down and it shook and shook as if it meant to throw me from it and my gladness was like a brightening light and I wanted to call to the others, Do not fear for me or for yourselves. Oh, even now that radiant expectation sweeps over my memory and it truly seemed as if I was being raised from my bed, as if I was being lifted up, and for years I believed that if it had only lasted another minute, then I would have crossed over because I could see the golden door and the luminous clouds behind it and even the bearded faces of some of the saints and beneficent dead looking through as if looking through a window and I was almost ready to recognize their faces but then the door began to lose its luster and I realized that the bed was shaking not quite as violently and I could see expressions of relief pass over the faces of my family, over everybody except my grandmother, and I wept and wept and the rain beat down upon me and after a while Alcibiades and the workman carried me back inside where once again everything was dusty and there were many broken things, and my father was still sitting in the chair in the alcove as if he had never left and he looked very philosophical. What could I say to him? I felt how I must have disappointed him, that somehow I hadn't been quick enough. I pressed my face into my pillow and squeezed my eyes shut and I must have fallen asleep because when I opened them again hours had passed and it was completely dark and there were angry voices coming from the bedroom.

It was that same afternoon that Alcibiades had gone off to town with Dalila, ostensibly to view the damage of the newest earthquake. Rosvita followed them and, because she wanted a witness, she took Spartaco. My brother didn't particularly like Rosvita and didn't particularly trust her, but she clearly had one foot already planted in the adult world while he was not even near the fence. She was womanly without being a woman and she could flirt and tease and make Spartaco feel quite confused. So, although he had no wish to go with her, he found himself somehow ensnared and short of breath and his skin felt all prickly and he had no choice. Alcibiades and Dalila set off down the hill and two minutes later Rosvita and Spartaco set off after them, while staying close to the hedgerow and out of sight.

It was raining and frigid and whenever the sky cleared for a moment one could see that the snow had crept further down the sides of the volcanoes. Rosvita wore an old lambskin coat she had found in the attic with the sleeves rolled up and she also wore a beret. Spartaco wore my father's leather jacket buttoned to the neck. Even though Alcibiades and Dalila never once looked behind them, Rosvita insisted on creeping along and running from tree to tree and whenever she saw that Spartaco wasn't properly concealing himself she hissed at him and called him a boy. Spartaco hated sneaking and all subterfuge so he tried to strike some balance between walking along the side of the road and concealment, even though, as he said, there appeared to be no reason for concealment.

"Rosvita kept stopping in front of me and squeezing my cheeks and saying, 'Oh, what am I going to do with you?' " Spartaco told me later.

More houses had collapsed and there was a fire near the post office. Although many people were living in tents, some houses had survived almost intact and in these there often lived large groups of people who were all related. In fact many people lived as we did: families and friends coming together to wait for they knew not what. And that afternoon they all stood outside under black umbrellas and looked depressed. The paved roads were still impassable because of the tilted panels of cement but along the side there was often a track where carts had passed. Dalila appeared to be talking constantly and Alcibiades would nod his head, bending toward her to hear her words. Dalila wore a dark coat and hat and carried an umbrella which she kept twirling round and round. Alcibiades had on his leather jacket. Dalila's umbrella kept him at some distance but even so he continually bumped into it. Wherever the path was particularly rough Dalila would take Alcibiades's arm and on each occasion Rosvita would poke Spartaco and nod significantly, "Although I could never see what she meant," said Spartaco.

Dalila and Alcibiades walked past the church where the main spire was bent and tilted toward the street. One of the young curates was ladling out flour and sugar into the bags of people waiting in line. Despite the weather many people were wandering somewhat aimlessly and looking at the damage. Occasionally Dalila and Alcibiades would stop to speak to someone and there would be much uncertainty and shaking of heads.

They turned left on San Francisco and into town. Most of the damaged stores were boarded up. The market was nearly empty, although there was some fish and small trussed-up bales of sea lettuce and bunches of *cochayuyo*, seaweed that looks like brown rubber rope. Like us, many people were living out of their larders, and those who couldn't were depending on the Red Cross or the church or the Americans. Uncle Teodoro claimed that people were driven to eating their dogs and cats, but I don't know if it really came to that. Spartaco wanted to stop to visit the families of several of his friends, but Rosvita pulled him along and said they weren't making this trip for pleasure.

Alcibiades stopped in front of his men's clothing store which was boarded up. Spartaco and Rosvita stood at the corner and watched. There were soldiers and police and signs warning people to stay out of the buildings. Alcibiades stood in the wrecked street with his hands on his hips.

"He was grinning," Spartaco said. "Rosvita said that Dalila had told him a dirty joke, but I think he felt good because the store was wrecked. The whole street was a mess and there were wet papers everywhere. Somebody's car lay on its side and in the middle of the street was a mannequin that looked just like a naked dead body—well, almost."

After inspecting the store, Dalila and Alcibiades walked the several blocks to where Dalila's house had once stood. The hillside which it had slid down was slick with mud and the house lay in broken pieces at the bottom. Dalila started to go inside but Alcibiades stopped her and made her wait. Then he went into the house himself, although it wasn't a house but walls and roof beams and floors all jumbled together with rubbish scattered all around. And it wasn't just her house because several other houses had also slid down the hill and there were broken trees as well. Some people called to Alcibiades warning him of the danger but he only waved to them.

"He was just looking around," said Spartaco. "Rosvita said he was looking for some private place where he and Dalila could be together, but I don't think that's true. She said that Dalila was flirting with him and that she knew what was what, but Dalila was just being friendly, although in front of her house she looked sad. After a while Alcibiades came out and he was carrying some stuff: clothes it looked like and some old-fashioned shoes. That's when he saw me and waved. Rosvita wanted to run away, but I didn't see why we should, so I went to see what Alcibiades was doing and Rosvita came, too, after a little bit. She said Dalila was disappointed to see us, but that's not how it seemed to me. She just looked sad about her house. I wanted to go into the house because it was really interesting and the rooms were piled on top of each other, but Alcibiades wouldn't let me. There was some jewelry that Dalila wanted and she sent Alcibiades back several times, although all he could find were some earrings and a brooch. Then we walked back up the hill. Rosvita was very rude and wouldn't walk near Dalila and kept pretending that she wasn't there but Dalila didn't even notice. Alcibiades kept saying how he didn't see how the town would ever be put back together. How could life ever start up again? I said the army could fix the roads, but Alcibiades said why should they even bother when the earthquakes kept happening again and again. And maybe they would never stop, he said. Even if there was no great big final earthquake, there've been lots of smaller ones and they all make the roads worse and the railway tracks are useless. What's the point of fixing anything if it just gets broken again? How can the chimneys be put back up? How can anybody cook?"

Hellmuth had been out himself and returned to the farm after Dalila and Alcibiades. He was in a bad humor and didn't say where he had been. The evening was very cold and my grandmother heated rocks in the fire and wrapped them in towels for all of our beds.

When I woke up in the darkness and heard angry voices, it was Hellmuth's voice which rose over the others. "I won't permit it, do you hear me? I won't permit it."

This was followed by one of those silences that feels so full of attention and people listening as to seem actually noisy.

Then I heard my grandfather's voice, "Hellmuth, if you have to quarrel with your wife, then do it in the shed. It'll stay put now and won't fall down."

Then the silence came back again, thick and dark, and through the window I heard one of the dogs scratching vigorously and the jingling of his chain.

During those first weeks of June the weather grew worse and there was much hardship. The earthquake had blocked Lake Rinihue east of Valdivia and it was feared that the water would break through the barrier and destroy the city. Bit by bit Valdivia was totally evacuated and teams of volunteers from Santiago worked day and night to dig a new channel. The rain was constant and there were more stories about looting and people being shot. Although aid was now coming into both Valdivia and Puerto Montt, many people who stopped by the house told stories about corruption and stolen supplies and piles of food rotting on the landing strips. Added to this was the bad news that President Eisenhower's brother would not be visiting the damaged areas after all. He was an elderly man and his health would not permit it. And some people said it was a shame and blamed the canceled visit on looters and other bad elements and said we lived in a barbaric time.

The earth kept shaking. A day of quiet would go by, then another, and just when one began to hope that the earthquakes had finished their business another fierce one would oversweep us and people would rush from their houses or crouch in their tents. I kept thinking of what Alcibiades had said: how was it possible to rebuild the chimneys? Without a chimney there couldn't be a fire and, of course, there was no electricity and so all the cooking was done outdoors. Many people had chilblains and there was much sickness and people envied the refugees from Valdivia who were flown to Santiago.

Several times a day I heard trucks coming along the back road from Puerto Montt, trucks loaded with canned food and firewood and more tents and blankets. And there were planes and helicopters as well. Although many people were helped, many more were still needy. I often thought of a story someone had told from the early days of the earthquake: when the tidal wave had swept through Valdivia some people were saved by clinging to the spire of the cathedral and when the water went away a baby was seen tied to the very top of the spire with no mother or father and nobody knowing whose baby he was. Of course it was very difficult to get him down and they couldn't do it right away so the baby remained way up in the air for several hours and of course he was unhappy and his cries drifted down over the damaged city. The baby's predicament struck me as similar to the predicament of us all, as if we were all tied to a church spire high above the ruined world with no way to get down and nothing nice down on the ground even if someone managed to rescue us, and it was raining and cold and the baby cried and looked out at its surroundings with confusion and despair and how could anything ever be made better? And although I asked several people, no one remembered actually seeing the baby being rescued and so even while I was sick, I kept thinking of the baby and thinking he might still be tied to the spire as if his predicament were a signpost, the flag by which we were known.

On Saturday a man from Puerto Montt brought another letter from Freddy Piwonka Gray.

Dear Wife: Thank you for sending Hugo down to me. He is a great help as long as he does not talk and does not eat too much and keeps his mind off the girls. But you know your Freddy, I can keep him in line. It was to my great astonishment that he told me that Hellmuth and Alcibiades are doing nothing except playing chess. My own business in Puerto Montt is expanding rapidly and I now own twenty cars plus several pieces of property. One of my warehouses is full already. Nobody has more candles than I do. And blankets! Please tell Hellmuth and Alcibiades that I have all the work they could possibly handle and I will give each one a car as an example of my good faith even if there is no place where they can drive. But soon the earth will quiet itself and work will begin on the roads. Dear wife, if you happen to hear stories about me and a certain business having to do with missing American supplies, I want you to refuse to believe them. I am surrounded by vicious calumnies. There are many chances to be seized and many people are jealous of your Freddy. I was never a person who could sit around and do nothing. Again and again I have been in the right place at the right time. Tell Hellmuth and Alcibiades to hurry.

Your loving husband,
Freddy Piwonka Gray.

Hellmuth was very struck by this letter. After Miriam read it, he read it to himself several times. Among the others there was some argument about the ethics of the situation.

"Freddy's always been a crook," said my grandmother. "It's one of the things that makes him so charming. But he'll have to pay. There's no such thing as not paying in this world."

"He could even, you know, go to jail," said Walterio.

"But he's still out there making money," said Teodoro. "You've got to respect him. If my leg weren't broken, I'd join him in a second. I just hope he doesn't get the rest of us in trouble."

"It's silly, though," said Walterio. "All those cars."

"People are going to need cars," said Hellmuth.

At the time it wasn't clear to us just how plainly Hellmuth

began to see his chance. Our minds were very much on the past. We were all thinking of the earthquakes and not about what might happen afterward. But Hellmuth was a deeply disappointed man and so he was always looking around him. He found nothing satisfying in buying and selling cattle. It was a job he had accidentally stumbled into and if it hadn't been for my father, he probably would have failed at it. Hellmuth liked chess. He liked situations where everything could be calculated and understood. But in the daily world, events were not so clear and Hellmuth had many doubts. Now and then people would come to the house asking for food and Hellmuth was reluctant to give them anything just because he wasn't certain of the value of what he had. He hated the thought of giving up something that he might need later. And so he didn't act. Everything might be of value and so he was reluctant to part with anything. Every action took him in a particular direction but who knew if that was the right direction? He stood with his head lowered turning this way and that and was unable to make up his mind.

It was my grandmother or one of her sisters who gave people food. And she gave out blankets as well. Hellmuth would shake his head and suggest it was dangerous and then go back to his chess board. But he was a very proud man and he was very proud of his new Opel. And he knew the sort of life he wanted for himself if only he could find his way to it. But wasn't he surrounded by pitfalls and possible mistakes? How could he act? These dangers were like deep water and way off on the other shore he could see the person he wanted to be: wealthy and respected and a power in the community. He knew everything there was to be known about that distant person except how to get there and so he would pace back and forth, walking on his heels in a way that made the house shake, and he would roughly push his heavy glasses up to the bridge of his nose and push back his hair which made his widow's peak even sharper and more severe and he would think and think and at last he would give it up and return to his chess board where reason and intellect were enough and beautiful women didn't wait to ensnare him and the pitfalls and booby traps were not guided by a random maliciousness.

Yet here came Freddy's letter with its promise of riches. Hellmuth was very impressed and it made him think that perhaps there would be a future after all. And perhaps Freddy could help him. Freddy was forceful and decisive and wasn't afraid of mistakes. My father's death meant more to Hellmuth than just the end of buying and selling cattle. It meant that Hellmuth now had no one to advise him and help him to see what was important. Couldn't Freddy fill that gap?

Miriam herself felt torn by her husband's letter and angry that Hugo had left her to join his father. Over and over she kept saying that Freddy would get in trouble, but she, too, would have joined him immediately if he had asked. In retrospect, I think she was nervous that Hugo might have mentioned her drinking. I didn't think much of it at the time but when I was older I realized I couldn't remember Miriam during those weeks without a glass in her hand. She was never drunk but she was often wobbly. And now Hugo might have told his father and perhaps that was why he didn't want her in Puerto Montt.

"I could be very helpful, too," she kept saying. "I'm just not sure I want to go down to that messy place. Think of the dust. And you know who'd have to clean up, don't you?"

Alcibiades said little about Freddy's successes. He was impressed by his brother-in-law but didn't envy him and I think he had no desire to join him. Also, by that point, his thoughts were entirely on Dalila.

"But aren't the houses all fallen down there, too?" Dalila

kept asking. "And mud slides and hardship and no electricity. So what if he has more candles than anybody? Who wants silly old candles?"

"He's thinking about after," said Hellmuth.

"When's after?" demanded Dalila with a little stamp of her foot. "Even the beauty parlors are closed. When's it going to stop?"

"That's not the point," said Hellmuth.

I would hear these conversations from the alcove and try to imagine their faces looking serious or bemused or uncertain. I would have many theories and ideas which years later I came to realize were wrong. I couldn't see why Hellmuth wanted to leave and jeopardize his place in Heaven. I didn't see why they didn't rush down to Puerto Montt and rescue Freddy and Hugo from their awful self-deception. I would look at my father and he would look back and I knew he wanted to help Hellmuth and his face was very sad. And all during the day members of my family would look in on me. The twins would dash in to see how I was. Spartaco would sit with me and read to me books of adventure and great battles which made my feverish head spin. My mother would perch on the edge of my bed and sigh and stroke my brow. Manfredo would peek around the corner and if I glanced back at him, he would look embarrassed and flee. Walterio would bring me presents of cookies, which, of course, I couldn't eat, and the next day he would retrieve them and eat them himself and the crumbs would tumble down on my blankets and his chewing seemed very loud. And sometimes absolute strangers would look in on me and shake their heads.

Miriam's partial training as a nurse gave her a certain authority, while Great-aunt Olivia's knowledge of homeopathic cures and herb teas gave her authority as well, or at least she claimed authority. These two women constantly bickered over what was best for me. Miriam would give me aspirin while Olivia shook her head and looked sullen. Olivia would try to get me to drink some foul-smelling concoction while Miriam looked scornful and complained to the others.

Occasionally the doctor would come and take my temperature and dribble his cigarette ash around the room. "Aspirin can't hurt," he would say. "But she must take nourishment."

On Monday there came a letter from Olivia and Teodoro's son in Castro, a town of about 3,500 on the island of Chiloé fifty kilometers south of Ancud. There, too, a tidal wave had struck and many people had been lost and were last seen floating out to sea on the roofs of their houses. Their son, Tomás, had survived but he had fallen and broken his ankle.

"Just like me, the rascal," said Teodoro. "I broke my leg and he broke his ankle. I wonder what he's trying to prove?"

Tomás described how food and blankets and tents were being brought in by boat but there was thievery and much complaint.

"Some people are getting rich," he wrote. "I feel it is very unfair, especially since I am laid up and can't get about. There's much money to be made in the salvage business right now."

"There must be money all over," said Hellmuth. "I wonder if Freddy knows about Castro."

"Why should you care about other people's money?" said my grandmother. "You think too much about money. It's happiness that counts and feeling secure in the Lord."

But Hellmuth didn't answer and after a moment I heard Clotilde say, "I once knew a boy in Castro, but he's probably dead now. He had a wonderful smile."

"All those boys are dead," said Bibiana, "or they're so old that they should be dead. Think how they smile with no teeth. Think of their rosy gums." And she laughed and laughed.

Each day my grandfather would come in and sit with me for

a while. Depending on my fever I would either be half awake or off in a dream, but I remember him sitting next to me and holding my hand. His hands were rough and cool. He always wore his hat but he would push it back on his head so I could see his blue eyes. He would tell me what he had been doing: repairing a wagon, fixing a wall, mending the roof. He wanted to put a pot-bellied stove in the bedroom and run a metal pipe through the window but people kept asking what would happen if an earthquake overturned the stove and the house burned down.

"A foolish question," my grandfather said. "Do they think we'd just watch the fire burn?"

So he had put the stove out in the shed and had made a place which he said was quite cozy and warm and where he could smoke his pipe. Walterio and Miriam and even my mother would go out and sit with him sometimes but my grandmother didn't like it. "She says it's dangerous," said my grandfather, "but when you get better you can visit me, too."

And one day he told me, "You can't pick up everything all at once, but you can fix one little thing and then you can fix another. That's how things get done."

And on another day he told me, "Don't you think you should start getting well? People miss you. They want to see you smile. Are you sure I can't get you something to eat?"

And another day he said, "You need entertainment. It must be boring in here. Maybe you're sick because you're bored."

Actually, I had lots of company. After several days Clotilde had more or less moved back in. She didn't sleep in the alcove but she spent much of her time sitting in a soft chair which was right next to my father's. Her wedding dress was getting gray, despite the apron and the care she took of it, and she was developing a stubbornness which years later I decided bordered on madness. I expect she thought I was going to die and she wanted to be first in line to retrieve the alcove whenever I did. She kept a breakfast tray in her lap and all day long she played solitaire and my father watched her. I would wake up to hear her shuffling the cards and slapping them down. "What a pity," she would say when she lost or "How agreeable!" if she won. Whenever she turned over a king, she would say, "Now there's a handsome bridegroom," and when she turned over a jack she would say, "I wouldn't want to be married to that one. Just look at his sinister eyes." Often she would give me an inquiring look and sometimes she would tell me stories.

"You know," she told me one day, "my problem was that I wasn't aggressive enough. I was too shy. Many times young men would look at me and I would just look at my feet and I thought if they were really interested then they would find some way to speak to me, but they never did, or hardly ever. Even today I can remember many occasions. There were times in church or on a picnic or perhaps even walking down the street. One day Jaime Muñóz stopped and took off his hat and stared at me. I hurried past quite flustered. Yet at the end of the block I turned to look. He'd put his hat back on and was walking away. I was so disappointed. But you know, they were shy, too, all those boys. I didn't think of it at the time. I was shy and they were shy and there was no way to make a bridge between us. I'm certainly not shy anymore, I can tell you. I've been ready for a long time, but, of course, there's no one left."

During those weeks, I still imagined Death as Clotilde's intended bridegroom, as if she had dressed up in this bridal gown for Death himself and he would come and take her away on his black horse. And, of course, when she first put on the bridal gown, she had expected to wear it only for a day or so: just until Death came and rescued her. Then she had to keep wearing it, because to take it off would be a sign of defeat, although she stopped wearing the veil. Hour after hour she would play solitaire, slapping the cards down on the wooden tray and discussing her fortune and bad luck. "Shyness," she kept saying, "what's the point of it now?"

I would glance at my father and wonder if he had any theories but his face was blank and I could see it was a mystery to him as well. And I felt disappointed because how could things be a mystery to the dead?

One morning when my mother was sitting with me, she began to talk about my father. "Your grandmother says I shouldn't miss him," she said, "but I do. He had faults, of course, but he was also kind. When you live with a person, those faults seem to get bigger and bigger until they fill the whole house, but once the person has gone away it's amazing how unimportant the faults become."

I watched my father but he was looking at the floor, then, after a moment, he looked up at me and raised his hands, palms toward the ceiling, raising them higher and higher, then he let them drop to his knees and shrugged.

Is it my present situation that brings these memories back so vividly? I think of my ex-husband and how our disappointments grew and grew. I remember at parties watching him talk to some young woman. His eyes would be all sparkly and I would think how he no longer wore that same expression with me. If at this moment I were happily married or happily divorced I would probably have a whole different series of memories, as if our mood or state of mind creates for us a particular past, as if we had many pasts and how we move between them depends on our present happiness and disappointments. These days I remember my great-aunt Clotilde's disappointment, Miriam's sense of rejection, my mother's sense of betrayal. They all had much love to give and felt that life had been unfair to them, as if one could order a husband like ordering clothes from Santiago. Yet Hellmuth and Alcibiades and Dalila were also disappointed. Each of us had an ideal, a sense of what we could accomplish if we were loved or if our love were properly returned. And set against this ideal was the frustration which in each case seemed destined to be the winner. Are our desires so impossible to achieve? Really, they seem so modest.

On Tuesday or Wednesday Alcibiades and Dalila walked down to the cemetery. The twins followed them. Of course the twins were in the pay of Rosvita. That sounds more sinister than it really was. They were eager helpers and I'm sure that Rosvita only had to make the suggestion. In any case, during the afternoon Rosvita came to tell me about it. Or perhaps she came to tell Spartaco who was reading to me. Clotilde was playing solitaire and she heard as well.

"They snuck away to the cemetery," said Rosvita, "but the twins were watching."

"Did they really sneak?" asked Spartaco. "Or did they just walk down the road?" Spartaco sat on the edge of my bed and closed the book with his thumb still marking the place. The book was Robert Louis Stevenson's *The Suicide Club*.

"They walked down the road," said Rosvita. "Hellmuth was with Grandfather and didn't see them. Why should they go walking in the rain?"

"Maybe they were taking flowers to my father's grave," said Spartaco. "He was their friend and they must miss him. And other people have died. There're lots of graves they could have been visiting."

I looked at my father but he was very faded and I could see the wallpaper through his body. His hands lay clasped in his lap. I wondered if he was lonely and if his grave was very cold and if the water seeped into his coffin. In the other room

Bibiana was telling Walterio about some kittens she had found. From somewhere came the sound of hammering and I knew it was my grandfather or the workman with big ears.

"Why do you insist on changing the story?" demanded Rosvita. "They went to the cemetery because they wanted to be alone." Rosvita was wearing a peach-colored dress that looked none too clean and her wild hair was tied back with a blue ribbon. "They walked right to the cemetery and never once looked behind them."

"And what happened in the cemetery?" asked Spartaco in a bored sort of voice.

"Ah, now that's what's interesting. On their way down it was raining only very slightly but once they got to the cemetery it started to pour. You know how some of those tombs are cracked open. Well, Alcibiades and Dalila ran into one."

"Whose was it?" asked Clotilde. She had stopped playing solitaire to listen to the story.

"The twins didn't know."

"So what happened?" asked Spartaco.

Rosvita stood at the foot of my bed with her hands on the rails and her lips curved down in disappointment. "I'm not sure," she said.

"Didn't the twins tell you?"

"They kept under a tree. They said that Dalila and Alcibiades stayed in the tomb for a long time or at least until the rain let up which was about half an hour. I think he kissed her in there. Think of kissing someone right next to a dead body. Doesn't it make your flesh crawl?" Rosvita shivered.

"You have no proof of that," said Spartaco.

"Maybe not," said Rosvita, "but when they came out of the tomb, they were holding hands."

"Holding hands?" asked Clotilde.

"That's right but Alcibiades dropped her hand right away."

"I bet he was just helping her," said Spartaco. "You know, he gave her his hand to help her out the door."

"That's not what the twins said. They said how they were both laughing."

"Then what happened?" asked Clotilde.

"Nothing. They walked back up the hill. But Hellmuth saw them and he was angry. He and Alcibiades spoke sharply to each other and Dalila went to sit with Grandfather."

"I don't think anything happened," said Spartaco. "You're just making up a silly story."

"I am *not* lying," said Rosvita, standing up very straight.

"I'm not saying they didn't walk to the cemetery," said Spartaco, retreating a little. "I just don't believe in that kissing stuff."

But I'm not sure that Spartaco was correct. Whatever happened in the cemetery, it was something that increased the intimacy between Alcibiades and Dalila and led them to seek out more occasions to be alone. It also drove the wedge more deeply between the two brothers. At this point in time it seems not only sad but also slightly comic. Alcibiades and Dalila were doomed. Rosvita's jealousy guaranteed that they would have no privacy. And plainly Hellmuth was suspicious as well. For years I thought that Dalila had been especially foolish for acting with no concern for the consequences, but now I think she wanted to be caught. She wanted something destructive to happen.

In the meantime my illness continued. It wasn't clear what was wrong and the doctor had no theories. My grandfather, however, set his mind to cure me. I needed to think of something other than dying. I needed to be entertained. He did this by singing to me.

One morning he came into the alcove and stood at the foot

of the brass bed with his hands on the rails. His hat was shoved back on his head. He winked at me and took a deep breath and began to sing. The song was a humorous folk song written after the earthquake in 1939 when 30,000 people were killed. The quake struck the town of Chillán with such ferocity that ninety percent of the buildings fell down. Thousands were taken by surprise and buried alive.

> Chillán, Chillán city of crazy locomotion
> where the dead traipse around beneath the concrete
> and naked little children are lost in the streets,
> Ay! Jesus, Joseph and Mary, what a cruel malediction.
>
> Don Pedro Aguirre Cerda and his lawful wedded spouse
> are sorry to have missed such a marvelous party.
> The cataclysm was so sorrowful, so scary,
> Ay! 120 percent of the people were certainly squashed.

My grandfather tilted back his head and sang to the ceiling. His voice was cracked and because of his deafness he must have thought himself too quiet for he practically bellowed, especially when he came to the "Ay!" which sounded very woeful. Clotilde stared at him with astonishment. I looked at my father and he, too, seemed surprised, although these days he was quite faded and it was hard to see his face. My grandfather kept beating time on the railing so the whole bed shook. Hellmuth's chess pieces were lined up on the night table and they trembled and their faces looked startled. When my grandfather had finished, he gave me a smile and asked if I would like anything to eat. And I think on that first occasion he got me to drink a little beef tea.

The next morning my grandfather returned. He stood at the foot of the bed and tilted back his head so far that his hat fell off and rolled across the floor to Clotilde's feet.

The hospitals were jammed with the bruised population,
beneath the streets the cadavers were dancing,
above the streets crept the battered living,
Ay! they couldn't cope with such a huge situation.

The statues tumbled down in all parts of town,
Don Pedro de Valdivia fell from his bronze horse,
the doctors and priests, they're all dead of course;
Ay! only some dogs hung around to gobble their bones.

Spartaco and Manfredo came to watch. Clotilde stared down at her game of solitaire and seemed depressed.

My grandmother pulled back the curtain. "Can't you see you're disturbing the poor girl," she said. She stood behind her husband but he refused to look at her.

"I don't think so," said my grandfather and he began singing again, raising his voice and making such a racket that he started Peppo barking out in the yard: "Ouch, ouch, ouch!" Bibiana peeked around the corner and tapped her forehead significantly.

The next morning my grandfather came back again and the whole scene was repeated. This time Clotilde got up and marched out of the alcove. Manfredo came a little closer and stood next to my grandfather. Miriam and the twins also came to listen. When my grandfather sang, he so twisted his face that it became a mass of passionate wrinkles and he rolled his blue eyes up to the ceiling. Whenever he hit his hand against the railing at the foot of the bed, a little shock went through my body. Once more his hat fell and rolled across the floor. Manfredo picked it up and held it respectfully.

This earthquake, like a ferocious jackal,
has thrust its fangs into the bruised destiny
of Chile, leaving Chillán a shattered frenzy,
Ay! Concepción and Cauquenes, San Carlos and Parral.

In the ghost of Chillán everything is silent,
but under the pavement the corpses are dancing,
to the fox trot and Charleston and tango they're prancing,
Ay! who could have guessed destruction so violent.

I don't know if this made me better. Presumably I was already getting well and my grandfather's singing coincided with my recovery. But I came to look forward to his singing, his passionate squawking, and his urging me to eat. On the third morning I had a piece of toast and a boiled egg. Even so, I still saw myself as sick and was only waiting for Death to take me across the dark divide to Heaven. What changed my thinking was both astonishing and very simple.

On the fourth day that my grandfather sang, Manfredo stayed behind after my grandfather had finished. Mostly Manfredo had acted guilty with me, as if he were the cause of my illness, and he always hurried away when he realized I was staring at him. He was a very small six-year-old and anxiety was a great force in his life. My grandmother had been dressing him in old clothes, which had once belonged to my uncles, and all were too big for him, so that not only did Manfredo appear small, he appeared shrunken. On this morning he approached my pillow and looked at me very hard. Then he spoke.

"Are you really going to die, sister? You have to wait for the rest of us."

I am sure this was the first time he had spoken since the earthquake, yet his words sounded perfectly natural. I don't know what I expected. Perhaps I thought his voice would sound rusty in some way or as if it would creak like a creaking door. But I was quite astonished to hear him speak and in my surprise I looked across to my father's chair to see his reaction. But there was no reaction. My father was gone.

8

I AM SURE there are excellent reasons why the final earthquake didn't plunge us deep underground: reasons having to do with molten lava pushing up from the earth's core and pressures and counterpressures and fault lines. And perhaps in the real world there are no final earthquakes, no final anything. The page is turned, another chapter appears and the only closure is the final closure of one's own eyelids: one's own death. Perhaps it is only sentimentality that makes those distant cataclysms like Pompeii so attractive: the great numbers of comfortable dead seemingly fallen asleep on the streets.

But for years I blamed my great-aunt Clotilde and believed she was the reason why the final earthquake never happened. In her wedding dress and finery she had made herself ready to receive Death as her bridegroom—her last eligible prospect—but Death had crept up to the house, looked through the window and shook his head. Too old, he said. Too dried out. She was destined to be disappointed, destined to be a spinster. As all the younger men had rejected her, so did Death reject her and her destiny saved her family. Who could imagine Death snatching us up but leaving Clotilde behind? And years later when she finally died, it was from cancer: a debased and vulturish death that sucks and eats us from the inside like the rotting of a pear and is not like a bridegroom at all.

But my grandmother also felt it was her destiny to be disappointed, as if disappointment were the title of her life's book. Her marriage was a disappointment; the farm was a disappointment; her children were a disappointment. And the refusal of the earth to pitch us into oblivion was just one more in a long series, as if Death had approached close enough for her to see him, standing on the hilltop and showing his cold profile, and then had withheld himself just to spite her. For the rest of us, we were all balanced between the pull of darkness and the pull of light and as more time went by without the final earthquake, the pull of light grew stronger.

These days I find it curious what sort of things remind me of that period. For instance, we have now a very fast Volkswagen truck and there have been many accidents and people have been killed and so the truck has been nicknamed the Road to Heaven. And whenever I see one of these trucks I think of us all sitting in my grandmother's bedroom as the earth began to shake, as if the bedroom itself could be named the Road to Heaven. And doesn't it sometimes seem that the objects and events of this world exist only to become metaphors which tell us about ourselves and describe our past?

The shocks continued through June and July and even August but slowly our world was put back together and by September there was again electricity. School resumed in August and of course spring was coming, although it still rained nearly every day. But there were daffodils and crocuses and the birds made hopeful noises. By September I was in Santiago in the house of my father's sister and attending a new school and again studying the piano. We had been gone from my grandmother's house for a month, my mother having decided to leave shortly after my uncles' fight.

Still, it took a long time to get past the earthquake. Just recently a woman told me how for months afterward whenever there was a loud noise, her father would run away. And I've already mentioned the long lines of people in front of the church waiting for confession. Many people had trouble sleeping. Others would begin to weep for no apparent reason. Some people became cynical and fatalistic; others took new hope. The people on the island of Chiloé came to see the earthquake as their good fortune, despite the wreckage and many deaths, because it made the government admit that Chiloé was part of the rest of the country. Before the earthquake travelers had to show their passports in order to take the ferry to Chiloé. After the earthquake the law was changed and the Chilotes felt they had won a great victory, as if their dead were the soldiers they had lost in their battle for recognition.

I remember the discussions that Hellmuth had with Walterio and Teodoro and sometimes Alcibiades about Ana, who worked in the kitchen, how every morning she would sweep up the leaves and flower petals that had fallen during the tremors of the previous twenty-four hours. Hellmuth couldn't understand it. Why should she bother, considering our imminent destruction?

"Perhaps, you know," said Walterio, "she doesn't want to jeopardize her place in Heaven. She's showing St. Peter that, well, she's a good worker."

"She's an Indian," said Great-uncle Teodoro. "She has no inner resources."

"I think it's just stupidity," said Hellmuth.

But they were all wrong. Ana lived as she had always lived, not simply out of habit but because she didn't see why the imminence of her death should change the way she lived her life. If death came while she was sweeping up the petals of the flowers, then that was how it was destined to happen and it would be foolish to prepare for it.

But for my uncles everything was frozen by the magnitude

of the first earthquake and the seeming inevitability of a worse one. They were like men standing motionless with their hands cupped waiting to catch something heavy. When life started up again it was not because people thought that the destruction wouldn't happen, it was because they had learned to live with its inevitability, to live with the fact that the inevitability of destruction is not sufficient reason to stop living. And, of course, they were seduced by the possibilities of alternative futures where there was money to be made and love to be had. Also, they were bored with waiting for something to happen, even death. They could hear the planes and trucks arriving with help from other countries. Money was still flowing and someplace else people were alive and making big profits. How could they get their fair share if they sat idle and did nothing? And so they chose life.

And hadn't I also walked down that dark passage and hadn't I also chosen life? And once I had chosen it I was eager for it and embraced it. Of course, I didn't leap from bed immediately. I was very weak. But I began to eat and sit up. I talked and laughed at people's stories. Manfredo felt certain he had cured me and brought me food. After two more days I tried getting out of bed and took a few steps and, perhaps rashly, I told Clotilde that she could have the alcove, that I wanted to go back to my bed next to Spartaco. I was eager to get moving. It wasn't Manfredo who made me well, of course, just as it wasn't my grandfather's singing, but these things encouraged me and something changed within me. Instead of looking backward, I began to look forward. I wanted a future. I still want a future. And I also grew better, I think, because in my sickness I became able to release my father and get beyond my grieving. He was with me every day and I grew used to his being dead and saw that he did not seem uncomfortable with it.

But also the barrier between us was too great for me to wish myself across. How could I step over it with the world clinging to me so tightly? I got better because of the pull of light. I was curious. I wanted to live. But it was more than choosing life, it was also a matter of saying no to Heaven. Perhaps we all said no to Heaven. We didn't want perfection and bliss. We wanted life with all its groveling and rain and uncertainty, with its small triumphs and surprises, with its sudden beauties that take one's breath. Life is our special property; Heaven belongs to someone else. And perhaps I was wrong about my father. I had thought he had come to lead me up to Heaven, but perhaps he had come to return me to the world.

Of course, both Miriam and Olivia also claimed to have cured me and quarreled with each other and Miriam made remarks about how witches used to be burned at the stake, while Olivia said that wine never cured anything. The doctor claimed to have cured me with aspirin. The priest said it was his prayers, although I heard him tell my mother that he had truly expected me to die, that my recovery was nothing short of a miracle and he puffed out his chest and stroked his chin and felt quite proud that a miracle had occurred within his parish. By the time I was fully recovered I began to look back on my sickness and my father's companionship almost as if it had never happened, but certainly it had happened and certainly I had seen my father. I looked back on his presence, however, with some aversion as if he were a friend of whom I was now embarrassed and not someone who had arrived to help me through a difficult time. And I turned away from him and hurried forward because in just a few days it would be the shortest day of the year and after that everything was bound to get better.

When I had recovered my strength, I made a trip out to the highway to visit the *animita* of Jaime Alverez. Manfredo and

Spartaco came with me. Since Manfredo had begun to talk again, he was with me often and he talked constantly about the strange things around us and how only a short time before he had been afraid but now he was afraid no longer.

"And pumas," he said, "I used to be afraid of pumas. What if a puma snuck into the bedroom at night? It might take me or it might take the twins. We're the youngest. I used to pray it would take the twins but now I'm not scared anymore."

"A puma wouldn't like the twins," said Spartaco. "They make too much noise. Hugo said he had seen a puma and he said he knew a boy who could wrestle pumas and beat them, but I don't know."

"Even jaguars I wouldn't be afraid of," said Manfredo.

"There aren't any jaguars this far south," said Spartaco.

"But even if there were, I wouldn't be afraid of them," said Manfredo. "The only thing that might scare me would be swarms of rats. But I'd fight them. I'd get a big shovel and fight them right to the end."

"We'd give you a beautiful funeral," I said. "And I would paint your face and cover all your wounds."

It was a gray day and misty and the mountains were invisible. Our boots were all too big for us and it was hard work crossing the muddy fields which pulled at our feet and made sucking noises. Manfredo wore a brown wool jacket from the attic with the sleeves rolled up and which hung to his knees. Spartaco wore my father's leather coat. I wore my mother's jacket and a green dress, which Alcibiades had rescued from my parents' house, and my father's black hat. In a tin can I carried fresh water and some crocuses from the garden. From somewhere came the drone of an aircraft.

"Aren't you really afraid of anything?" asked Spartaco and there was an element of teasing in his voice.

"No, maybe just the rats and sometimes it frightens me to see my mother cry."

"I'm afraid of Rosvita," said Spartaco, joking. "She's a pain."

"Does she pinch you?" asked Manfredo. "Sometimes the twins pinch me and I hate it."

"Nothing like that. She's always after me to watch Dalila and Alcibiades. She thinks they're going to run away together. It's too boring."

There was still a soldier at the Copec station but this time he seemed friendly and waved. Even so we didn't go near him. The *animita* was covered with volcanic ash and my brothers and I washed it off with rainwater from the puddles. Then I wiped off the photograph of Jaime Alverez. Did I feel any regret about not seeing him? I don't think so. I loved him and wished him good cheer but I had no wish to join him. I had said no to him just as I said no to my father and Uncle Gabriel and I hoped he wouldn't be sad. There must be many diversions in Heaven and many interesting people to talk to. But years later, after my separation from Javier Albañez, I sometimes wondered if my ex-husband was not Jaime Alverez's revenge on me, as if the similarity of names hadn't led me to this man who made my life such a misery. If his name had been Sanchez or Rosales or Winkler, perhaps the two lines of our lives would never have come together. But then wouldn't my daughter be still waiting to be born? Who knows how many spirits are floating above us still hoping for their chance upon this earth?

Afterward we trudged through the fields over to Calvary Hill where my brothers had a war with eucalyptus nuts and Manfredo got hit in the eye. Then Spartaco bathed his wound with rainwater and Manfredo forgave him. The trees were covered with many new placards of all different colors and we looked to see if we knew any of the names. I had also thought of writing a placard but when I looked at the statue of the suffering Jesus I began to feel guilty. Hadn't I said no to him as well?

"I'm not sure if he's happy or sad that I didn't go to Heaven," I told Spartaco. "He might even be cross with me."

"He never looks happy," said Spartaco, "except in those picture books when he's surrounded by children."

"There's lots of children in Heaven," said Manfredo, staring up at him. "After all, he's got Uncle Gabriel."

"Maybe he wants more," I suggested, and briefly we all wondered why he wanted so many children, but then I explained that he must be happy I had gotten better, and he must have watched over my recovery, because he, too, was born on this earth and, of course, he loved it as we did. I thanked him and thanked St. Lucy the Virgin Martyr and I said a short made-up prayer at the base of the cross while my brothers waited respectfully a few feet behind me and held their hats in their hands. And afterward Manfredo and I collected more eucalyptus nuts and threw them at Spartaco who dodged away from us behind the trees so we kept missing.

Then we stood on the edge of the hill by the stone benches and looked out over the town but the cloud and fog and rain had eaten it up and not even the spires of the Church of the Sacred Heart of Jesus were visible, and I wondered if while we had been away an earthquake hadn't indeed come and swept everyone into Heaven, leaving us behind on Calvary as the only island of life, and I was surprised at how relieved I felt. But when I told this to Spartaco, he said not to be silly and that the town was full of people, and then he said we should go down to the edge of town and see if we could find any Americans because Manfredo hadn't seen them yet. So we went down the hill and we were happy because we three were together again and it seemed we were knitting our family back together and we didn't know that there is no *back*, no returning—after all, we were children—there is only forward and forward until the end.

We walked along Avenida Colón with its broken panels of concrete and it began to rain again. Near the turnoff to my grandmother's house we met Spartaco's good friend Adolfo Ossa who was also waiting for Americans. He was a thin red-headed boy and he wore a poncho and black rubber boots. An American canteen in a camouflage pouch hung from his belt and he was very proud of it. And over several weeks the Americans had given him six Hershey bars which he had shared with his younger brothers.

"I had a Hershey bar," said Spartaco, "but my uncle stole it."

"Hershey bars always make me think of the Wild West," said Adolfo.

"And gunfights," said Manfredo, flapping his long sleeves. "I wouldn't be afraid of gunfights."

Adolfo asked if we had seen another friend, Olaf Birker, whose left arm had been sliced off by a falling plate-glass window, "as neat as a slice of bread," said Adolfo.

We hadn't.

Adolfo described the stump which was bright orange and had an interesting scab. Olaf was being very brave. In no time Spartaco and Manfredo decided to visit Olaf and see his stump and I could tell that Spartaco was a little jealous of Olaf's occasion for bravery and he looked at his own left arm in a speculative sort of way. Olaf was in the tent hospital in the city park and Adolfo said he would take us. I was not eager to see the stump and besides we had been away for well over an hour and I was afraid our mother might be worried so I turned back to climb the hill.

When I reentered the farmyard I found Hellmuth pacing up and down under the tarpaulin saying that he thought it was about time to get moving, that he had things to do, while my grandmother kept saying that she needed him at the farm with her.

"But I don't do anything here," said Hellmuth. "I just sit." He had his hands clasped behind his back and he didn't look at his mother when he spoke.

"What can you do anyplace else?" asked my grandmother. "There's no work, there're no roads." She stood near the stove stirring a large pot containing stew. Hellmuth paced up and down in front of her. When she spoke to her son, she leaned toward him and squinted in order to see him with her bad eyes. Hellmuth kept taking a few steps back, perhaps so he couldn't be seen so easily, as if those few steps were meant to accustom my grandmother to the idea of departure. Bibiana sat under the tarpaulin listening and giving Ana directions on peeling potatoes. Inside I could see Miriam and Walterio playing cards. I didn't know where Alcibiades and Dalila were.

"I'll go join Freddy," said Hellmuth. "He said he would give me a car."

My grandmother laughed in an unfriendly fashion. "You already have a car and you can't even drive it anywhere. If you join Freddy and he goes to jail, then you know where you'll be, don't you? You'll be in jail, too."

"It must be cold in jail," said Bibiana. "And they say the bread is all moldy."

"No one's going to jail," said Hellmuth. "Don't you see there's money down there? It's a wonderful opportunity!" Although he sounded enthusiastic, his face looked grim, as if he were trying to instill in himself feelings that he didn't have.

My grandmother stared down at the stew pot. "I need you here," she said.

What she didn't say was that she needed her son, needed all of us, in order to exit from this world. She needed Hellmuth to accompany her to Heaven, but Hellmuth no longer had any interest in Heaven.

Hellmuth looked at her with a hurt expression, then said, "You're impossible!" and stamped away into the house where he began to complain to Miriam and Walterio, an angry muttering which we couldn't quite make out.

I had felt happy coming back up the hill and now everything seemed difficult again. From the shed I could hear my grandfather whistling and singing snatches of a song about a girl who was turned into a fish. My grandmother continued to stare into the stew pot and the smoke rose around her skirt. It made me sad to see her but I could think of no words to explain my sadness or even to say that I was sorry. I backed away, then hurried through the door of the shed. I found my grandfather cutting out panes of glass to fix the bedroom windows. The workman with big ears sat by the stove smoking his pipe and blowing smoke rings. The shed was warm and smelled of sawdust and tobacco.

"Hellmuth wants to go away," I said.

"You can't blame him," said my grandfather, stopping his work. "Time's slipping by."

My grandfather had spilled a jar of nails on the floor and I began picking them up. "Why can't he stay here?" I asked.

"He can stay as long as he wants," said my grandfather, "but he doesn't want. He's got to build himself a new house."

"What about the earthquakes?" I asked.

My grandfather pushed his hat back on his head. "He's got to build a new house even if it gets knocked down again. That's the way things work. It's like gravity. You have to keep going forward. Did Rosvita find you? She's been looking for you."

I said she hadn't, but I was thinking about gravity.

"She's a sneaky girl," said my grandfather. "I love her but

she never looks a person straight in the eye. She always looks at you from around corners."

I handed my grandfather the jar of nails. "She's trying to learn French."

My grandfather nodded. "Maybe that explains it," he said.

A little later I found Rosvita in a second-floor bedroom staring out the window toward the orchard. Walterio had told me where she was. "I don't see them anyplace," she said.

"See who?"

"That nasty Dalila and Alcibiades." Rosvita had her hair tied back with a ribbon. She wore a shirt, jodhpurs and boots as if ready for action.

"You shouldn't talk about her like that," I said. "She's your aunt."

Rosvita glared at me scornfully. "She's a thief. She's trying to ruin his life. Alcibiades is too pure for her. He could be a saint if he wanted. After all, she's his own brother's wife!"

"What does it matter if they're friends? You're just jealous he wants to be with Dalila instead of you." It seemed that many times when I wanted to talk to Alcibiades, he had been talking to Rosvita and I hadn't liked it either.

Rosvita looked back out the window. "Sometimes I hate children," she said.

It took me a moment to realize she was talking about me. "Men don't have to be friends only with men."

Rosvita gave me another exasperated glance, then led me to a bed and sat me down on it. She stood in front of me with her hands on her hips. The bed and the entire room were filthy with plaster and volcanic ash and broken glass. "It's not just being friends," she said. "She wants him to give her a baby. She wants them to be naked together."

It occurred to me that Rosvita was crazy in the way her

brother Hugo was crazy, as if all there was to talk about was sex and nakedness and men and women doing things together: the fabulous *It* of Hugo's conversations.

"She's married to Hellmuth so she can't have Alcibiades's baby," I said.

Rosvita made a groaning noise. I disliked that she treated me as a child and I disliked how her age gave her some authority in these matters. She wore a trace of lipstick that she had gotten from Clotilde and it was like a barrier between us.

"Dalila is a kind of witch," said Rosvita, "a sex witch. It's not just friendliness; it's sex."

"That's silly," I said.

But I was mistaken. Not that Dalila was a sex witch; I was wrong about Dalila and Alcibiades wanting to have sex together. I didn't know what sex was. My books were full of romantic love and this had nothing to do with romantic love. Alcibiades was full of desire and Dalila had encouraged him. Actually, I don't believe they ever had sex. They never had the opportunity. The twins were too vigilant and we were too much of a crowd. In truth, it might have been better if it had really happened instead of the destruction that took place. And I was partly responsible for that. Because I doubted Rosvita, she was determined to show me that she was right. We were children, but Rosvita was less of a child even though she still had a child's tenacity. She thought she knew what Alcibiades and Dalila were up to and her own adolescent jealousy made it terrible for her. She had fantasies about how they kissed and touched each other. She would show me proof and make me apologize for having doubted her.

Did Alcibiades really love his sister-in-law? I don't know. But he had become infatuated and, more important, he saw in Dalila a way to change his life, just as his brother once had. He was thirty-five and still unsettled. Part of him couldn't imagine being married and having a stable life with children and a woman whom he would come home to every night. In some ways he felt too young. He was afraid to close the door on his choices. He dreaded being in a situation where the situation would make all his decisions and he could only shrug and nod his head and go along with it. Even so, he hated his present life and Dalila was offering him an escape. Certainly, he knew it was wrong to run away with his brother's wife, but this was the end of the world. Everything was disrupted, wrecked, turned upside down and the old rules no longer made sense. Perhaps if Hellmuth himself had seemed to love his wife, then Alcibiades would have held back. But Hellmuth was rude to Dalila and Alcibiades couldn't see that Hellmuth was rude because he was hopelessly in love with her while thinking her a fool and thinking himself a fool for loving her. How many times do we try to explain the actions of our neighbors by assuming they are rational? Really, so little is rational. And so Alcibiades imagined he would be rescuing Dalila from an unhappy marriage.

I, of course, understood none of this and the whole story only came to me as I grew older. It seemed that whenever I saw Miriam or Alcibiades or talked to my mother or even Walterio some part was expanded, my knowledge was increased. And also my own experience taught me. Hadn't I married a man for whom infatuation was a kind of hobby? Hadn't I discovered that you can love a person without liking him at all? When my husband and I separated, my mother wrote to Alcibiades and told him I was having morbid and self-destructive thoughts and Alcibiades came down from the north to help me. Doesn't that seem ironic? His personal life was a failure, had never developed, and he was still waiting just as Clotilde had waited for the event that would never happen. Both had aged without ever having entered the adult world, without having grown up. Yet he came down to help me because my mother had written that I was in trouble and partly he helped me by showing me more about his own life, his own failure in love. Alcibiades was sixty-one and very gray, this man whom I had always thought was so handsome.

He had little money and stayed in a hotel near the train station. There were prostitutes and when we approached one on the sidewalk Alcibiades would lead me to the other side of the street, hoping perhaps that I wouldn't notice her, wouldn't be contaminated or perhaps even surprised. He wore a blue jacket, gray pants and a white shirt just like most of the other men that we saw. The jacket was old and the lapels were shiny. We sat on a park bench in the Plaza de Armas and he asked me about my husband. It was near Christmas and Indians in ragged Santa Claus suits stood sweltering in the heat. Several had ill-natured llamas attached to rudimentary sleighs where children could be photographed. The llamas would bare their yellow teeth and might have bitten people if they weren't so melancholy and lazy. The Indians had hand bells which they rang over and over, making an unmusical clanking sound.

"Has he mistreated you?" asked Alcibiades.

"He ignores me. He sees other women."

"Ahh."

"I'm not sure I want to live anymore."

Alcibiades held my hand. "It will pass. Everything goes by sooner or later. You just have to get used to this first part."

"But I still love him."

A photographer wanted to take our picture, then a young man wanted to polish Alcibiades's boots. We walked over toward the river past the dusty shops that sell buttons and needles and zippers and thread. The sidewalks were crowded and Alcibiades kept stepping off the curb. Twice he was nearly hit by taxis. "Are there always this many people?" he kept

asking. The air was blue from the exhaust fumes of the buses.
I told Alcibiades of my husband and my unhappiness. Really,
what could he do? My husband was tired of me and wanted to
live his life without me. He wanted other women. Could Alcibiades change that? When we reached Forestal Park we sat
on the grass and he bought me an ice cream and made me sit
on his jacket so my skirt wouldn't get dirty. Children played
in the fountain and got wet. There seemed to be many lovers
but perhaps it was only my loss that made them so noticeable.
What we desire and can't have, we see everywhere. I kept
weeping and he wiped away my tears with a gray handkerchief.
I was thirty-four years old and thought my life was over.

Actually I was nearly the same age that he had been during
the earthquake. Had he thought his life was over? It had hardly
begun. All during the afternoon we walked and walked. At
some point Alcibiades telephoned Manfredo at the hospital but
he was too busy to meet us. They talked for a few minutes,
then Manfredo was called away. Later we had tea in a cheap
restaurant near the fish market.

"Do you still miss Spartaco?" he asked.

"All the time."

"That's a shame," he said. "I miss my brother as well."

We waited for the waitress to bring us our order.

"Why didn't you run away with Dalila?" I asked.

"Dalila?" And it seemed for a second that he didn't recognize
her name. "That was just foolishness. Where would we have
gone?"

"Did you love her?" I asked. The waitress put a container
of Nescafé and a pot of hot water on the table. There was fresh
bread as well.

"I don't know. I loved her hair." His eyes seemed to blur
as he looked back all that way. "When she talked to you, she
had a way of making you feel very special, but when she was

in another room or someplace else, then it was hard to think of her. It was a way she had of focusing on you."

"You could have gone away together."

Alcibiades's smile was like a light illuminating his face and it reminded me of Spartaco. "Hellmuth loved her," he said. "I didn't know that. And I realized that she was also attached or loved or belonged to him. And it occurred to me that all her flirting with me was because of him. I wasn't a person; I was a pretext. I was like a pawn she was pushing around her own private chess board."

"But at the time?"

"For a short time I thought she was wildly excited about me and I was amazed because no one had ever been so excited by me before. But maybe it was only the power that excited her, the power to make someone want her, especially someone who wasn't supposed to."

A waiter was mopping the marble floor with a string mop and we had to lift our feet as he reached under the table. It was late afternoon and he wanted us gone. A parrot in a cage by the window kept shouting out numbers.

"Did you ask her to run away with you?"

"No. I mean, there was Hellmuth. But *she* kept asking *me* to go away with her. She was the one who kept insisting. We'd been in the cemetery and were caught in a rain storm and took shelter in a tomb. She put my hand on her breast. I would have done anything she asked. She wanted to cross the mountains and go to Buenos Aires. But what would we have done there? We had hardly any money."

"Do you regret not going away with her?"

Alcibiades looked out the window and stroked the ends of his gray mustache with his thumb and index finger. Out on the street blind people were selling Christmas ornaments. "I don't know," he said. "I didn't see how we could live. Maybe I shouldn't have had so many doubts. Later I decided that she never wanted to run away. She was just trying to create a scene with Hellmuth. Then when the scene occurred, everything was over. I was no longer important to her. Of course, I knew Hellmuth was angry. He had even warned me. But I didn't think we would fight. I wouldn't have been able to imagine hitting him, my own brother."

"Did you try to contact her after Hellmuth died?"

"No. I saw her at the funeral, of course. I was struck by her weeping and I had my own grief as well. After all, I hadn't seen Hellmuth since the time of the earthquake. But too many years had gone by. It didn't occur to me. Sometime later I began to think of her and considered writing, but then I heard she had remarried."

I don't know when it occurred to me that Dalila cared nothing for her brother-in-law, that he was, as he said, a pawn. No, not a pawn. That's too subtle. He was her club, her blunt instrument. She wanted to get even with Hellmuth, to punish him, and because she was somewhat tawdry she hit upon a tawdry way of hurting him. But perhaps that is unfair. She, too, had her pain. How we see people is a composite of all the times we have ever seen them. We add to them in our minds, like making figures from papier-mâché, and occasionally, when our emotions take over, the figure in our minds looms hugely over the rather small person who lived on this earth. At times I wonder how big Hellmuth and Dalila truly were, or how small. I didn't go to Hellmuth's funeral. I was in school in Santiago and still too young and consequently, although I often heard about Dalila from Miriam and my mother and grandmother, I never saw her again.

Actually I still have some of the chess pieces that Hellmuth gave me during my illness: a queen, king, a rook, the knight that looks like a dog, some of the pawns. Others I lost. For years I carried one of the rooks in my purse as a good-luck symbol: a small castle to set against the world. Its top was all jagged and one would hardly think it was a rook unless one knew its story. Then one day I just stopped carrying it.

Think of the ways we are linked to the people around us, like hundreds of strings visible and invisible. Even three years after my separation from my husband I keep discovering new strings. I find them and cut them, find them and cut them. How deeply Dalila must have been connected to Hellmuth and how impossible for an outsider to see them clearly. Partly his control came from the fact that he was fourteen years her senior. What was it like for her to be taken by him when she was only seventeen, this huge bull-like man with his hands that smelled of cattle? Hellmuth saw Dalila as his property. He owned her in the same way a person owns a lamp or a car. And she got back at him by doing what would hurt him most: by letting another man handle her and put his fingers on her. She chose Alcibiades because he was convenient. Perhaps anyone else might have done, although one couldn't imagine her choosing Walterio.

Yet I remember Walterio talking about her at my great-aunt Bibiana's funeral in 1981. I went even though I was pregnant. It was a very small affair and Alcibiades didn't come. Freddy Piwonka Gray was angry that his plan to have the farm divided into building plots had been thwarted and so he didn't come either. There was just Miriam and the grown-up twins and Walterio and some other second cousins. And a few friends, of course: women from church. Walterio was the manager of a fashionable women's clothing store in Puerto Montt. He wore a cravat and had tucked a baby blue silk handkerchief up his sleeve which he kept pulling out and waving when he spoke. He was fifty-one and quite stout. The cousins who had taken over the farm were shocked but he hardly noticed. He smelled of talcum and perfume and when he walked he kept rising up on his toes like a dancer and his black toes were narrow and very shiny.

He spoke of the silk lingerie which his store received from Paris. "Whenever I unpack it," he said, "I think of, you know, Dalila. Hellmuth told me that she had, well, drawers and drawers of it, but it was all destroyed in the earthquake. Every bit went cascading down their hill. And afterward, as a punishment, he wouldn't let her buy any new lingerie at all. Can you imagine? She had to wear plain cotton. What beautiful hair she had, what beautiful skin. I don't expect she bought any lingerie after Hellmuth's death. At first she was still in mourning and then she had neither time nor occasion. Think of all those babies! They practically poured from her."

Was it the next day that our world fell apart? I think it was a Tuesday, the day after we had visited the *animita*, and we had now been at the farm for over four weeks. It seems ironic looking back that the day was bright and blue with a mild breeze even though it was the second day of winter. It was as if the blue sky and sunlight had arrived especially to make us see our troubles as sharply as possible. The volcanoes Osorno and Calbuco rose benignly in the distance, while the column of steam above Osorno looked as gentle as an ostrich plume. Because of the good weather only Clotilde and Great-uncle Teodoro appeared to remain inside and the rest of us were scattered all over. Even Clotilde had brought her chair into the doorway so she could sit with her face in the sun and the wedding dress sparkled despite the dirt and ash which were turning it gray.

I was with my grandfather in the shed when Rosvita found me. Right away I knew something was wrong. Her face looked so eager! My grandfather was repairing a window frame and even he was struck by her expression and he put down his hammer and stared at her curiously. She wore a blue dress and a blue sweater and she looked as if she had just won a prize.

"Come with me!" she said.

Her tone was so urgent that I didn't stop to think but ran after her. I suppose I knew what she wanted or what she had discovered. After all, during those days she only had one obsession. But she was very quick and I hardly kept her in front of me as she ran around the shed and the corner of the house. When I rounded the corner, I nearly bumped into her. She was standing by a ladder that was propped against the wall and went right up to the roof. I believe I said that the house had had a huge water tank on a platform above the roof which had fallen during the first earthquake. My grandfather had been rebuilding the platform and the ladder had been leaning against it. Now the ladder stood between the platform and the third-floor window which looked into the loft where wheat was stored.

"Climb," said Rosvita.

"But why?"

"Just climb and look through the window."

Again I felt commanded by her tone and I pulled myself onto the ladder, which had been made at the farm and wasn't awfully sturdy and whose sides were sharp with splinters. I wore leather-soled shoes and they kept slipping on the rungs.

"Climb!" said Rosvita.

When I had climbed about ten feet, Spartaco and the twins came running around the corner.

"What's going on?" asked Spartaco.

Rosvita wasn't pleased to see them. "Shh, keep your voices down."

"We want to climb, too!" said one of the twins.

"Shhh!" hissed Rosvita.

I continued to climb. As I got higher, the volcano Calbuco came into view over the edge of the roof. The ladder shook and looking down I saw Rosvita climbing after me.

"Don't make any noise," she said.

The sun reflected from the yellow shingles of the house was warm and bright. I moved slowly and the higher I got the more nervous I was about falling. Looking down, Spartaco seemed very far away. He had been joined by Manfredo and they were talking quietly. I looked down at the tops of their heads and their black hair shone in the light. The twins stood at the foot of the ladder holding onto it.

My head was approaching the level of the window which was about a foot to my left. When the wheat was cut in the fall, it would be spread out on the floor of the loft to dry. It was a place I never went. There were rats and many times when I had been sleeping upstairs I would hear them scurrying on the floor boards above me. Sometimes Spartaco would play in the loft and then I would have to pick the wheat out of his hair.

When my head was above the sill, I leaned over to look. The ladder was still shaking but my curiosity pushed away my fear. I still couldn't see so I climbed another rung. I was almost at the top of the ladder. Rosvita was only a little below me and her hands were on the rung beneath my feet.

"Look through the window!" she said.

I leaned over again. At first I didn't see anything because of the darkness, but then I saw the window at the other end of the loft. Then, in front of the window, I saw Alcibiades and Dalila. They were standing, or rather she was standing and he was kneeling or crouched down. My first impression was that they were involved in some sort of game. Dalila was wearing a long old-fashioned skirt. A frilly white blouse lay beside her in the wheat. Her arms were behind her and she was undoing the buttons of an ancient-looking corset. Her bare arms and shoulders seemed very white. Below her on the floor, Alcibiades was wearing a dark suit with a vest. He picked up her blouse and pressed it to his cheek.

"Are they still there?" whispered Rosvita.

I nodded.

"What are they doing?"

"They're play-acting."

"Let me see."

But there was no way that we could both stand at the top of the ladder. Even so, I climbed up one rung, then another, and Rosvita climbed up behind me so that her head was at the level of my knees and she could just peer over the sill. When I looked again Dalila had finished unbuttoning the corset. Slowly she removed it, held it out with one hand and dropped it into the wheat. Beneath it she wore a slip and brassiere. Her black hair was pinned up in a sort of chignon.

"They're not play-acting," said Rosvita. "They're going to have sex."

Dalila let the straps of the slip slide from her shoulders, then she reached behind her to unhook her brassiere. Alcibiades remained about a meter in front of her and down on one knee. Both were in profile to me and were at the top of the stairs going down to the second floor. I thought of the rats scurrying under the wheat and I shivered.

"Don't make the ladder shake," said Rosvita. She had climbed up one more rung and her head was almost at the level of my waist. My shoulders were above the top rung of the ladder.

Dalila let the brassiere slip down her arms, then she flicked it to Alcibiades who pressed it to his face.

"Isn't this great?" whispered Rosvita. "We've got them, the witch."

Dalila's breasts were strong and pushed out firmly even without a brassiere. Her nipples were large and very dark. Alcibiades reached out to touch them and Dalila stepped back. Then she put her hands on top of her head, lifting her breasts a little more. She stood there for a moment, then she began to turn slowly in a circle. She turned and turned, picking up her knees so that I could see her shoes which were also old-fashioned and buttoned up the side. Rays of sunlight came through chinks in the roof and speckled her bare skin and were turned golden as they passed through the dust of the wheat. Dalila's fingernails were bright red. In retrospect I suppose they should have been long and rapacious, but they seemed short and stubby. Beneath her hands her black hair seemed to snatch up the light and suck it away. She unpinned her hair and let it tumble down across her shoulders. Alcibiades again reached out to touch her and again she stepped back.

"Why does she keep stopping him?" asked Rosvita with irritation.

But it seemed to me then and seems to me now that they really were play-acting, or at least Dalila was. Did she mean to take off all her clothes? I don't know.

Down below the twins were extremely impatient, especially since our fascination with whatever we were looking at was so obvious. They began to climb the ladder as quickly as possible, first one, then the other. As I felt the ladder shake, I looked down, then grabbed the rung and held on tight. Rosvita bumped against my hips.

"Get down, get down!" she said.

Then a terrible thing began to happen. The ladder started to tilt back away from the wall of the house. I looked down in horror in time to see Bibiana and my mother coming around the corner from the farmyard. Bibiana looked up at us and opened her mouth and clapped her hand over it. At first the ladder moved very slowly but there was nothing I could grab onto to pull it back and Rosvita kept jostling me. The heat reflected from the yellow shingles was very strong and as the ladder moved away from the house I could feel the air begin to cool. Rosvita slid down one rung, then another. I couldn't move but stared at the yellow shingles of the house getting farther and farther away. The ladder was standing straight up, then began to topple back.

I looked down again. "Spartaco!" I cried.

He, too, had been frozen, staring at the ladder with a dreadful fascination. When I cried out, he stirred himself and leapt forward. Dashing the few meters across the grass, he threw himself against the ladder. The shock would have knocked me off if I hadn't been hanging on so tightly. As it was, one of the twins fell, although it wasn't far and Spartaco broke her fall. The ladder hit the side of the house with a crash, bounced, and hit the house again. I began to climb down as quickly as possible and got splinters in my hands. Through the window I caught a glimpse of startled white faces and saw Dalila grabbing for her clothes. Then it seemed everyone was shouting.

When I reached the ground, I threw myself at my mother and embraced her. Manfredo embraced us, too. I was sobbing violently but whether from fear or from the sense that what I had seen foretold the destruction of everything, I don't know. Bibiana hovered nearby clucking and shaking her head. Rosvita and the twins had already rushed around the corner into the yard where Peppo was barking over and over. Spartaco stood next to me. We all knew that he had done a heroic deed and he was very proud of it and was waiting politely for us to mention it. And in a moment my mother embraced him, too.

Shortly we all went around the side of the house and found Clotilde standing in the doorway, not letting anyone enter. Her blue apron had slipped off and was lying on her chair. She was very upset.

"Rosvita's told everyone," she said. "Hellmuth has gone inside. He's furious!"

And from where we stood we could hear Hellmuth bellowing and it reminded me of the cattle that used to be kept in the pens by the railway yard. Rosvita was eager to go into the house as well but her mother wouldn't let her. Even so, Rosvita kept tugging and trying to pull herself away. The twins were standing at a window peering over the sill but I don't think there was anything to see, or rather, all the shouting appeared to be coming from upstairs, and all they could see was Great-uncle Teodoro who looked as startled as anyone. Then my grandmother hurried through the gate from the orchard and Ana the kitchen girl came with her. My grandmother was going quite fast for someone her age, a rolling, swaying walk with her elbows pumping at her sides and her head pushed forward and her eyes squinched up. She had lost several hair pins and a strand of white hair had fallen from her bun and bounced against her cheek.

As she hurried past us, I heard her say, "Foolishness, foolishness, foolishness." Then she disappeared into the house.

What would have happened next, I have no idea. Certainly Hellmuth was still shouting. But added to all the commotion came the sudden honking of a horn. Automobiles had been out of our lives for so long that at first I looked dumbly at Hellmuth's mustard-colored Opel as if in some way it was having a sympathetic response to its master's rage. But no, the honking was coming from outside the farmyard and somewhere down the hill. But it was coming closer. Spartaco turned from us and ran to the edge of the kitchen to look and at that moment a red Jeep bounced and jostled its way into the yard and behind the wheel was Hugo looking very pleased with himself.

He drew the Jeep to a stop by the stove with much squeaking of brakes and sliding across the wet ground. The engine continued to shake and bounce for a moment and then shut itself off with a long sigh and a puff of exhaust. Across the yard, both dogs were tugging at their chains and Peppo was putting all the indignation he could gather into his peculiar bark. Although the red Jeep was spotted with mud, it was also very shiny as if newly painted.

Hugo stood up in the Jeep. "Where's Hellmuth and Alcibiades?" he cried. He took a piece of paper from his shirt pocket and began to wave it back and forth over his head. My grandfather had come hurrying from the shed followed by the workman with big ears and Walterio had waddled out from the kitchen with his mouth and fingers all sticky so we were becoming quite a crowd. Through the bedroom window I could see Great-uncle Teodoro knocking on the new glass with one knuckle and demanding to know what was going on. Hugo kept waving the piece of paper.

It was Alcibiades who came out of the house first, looking flushed and angry and still wearing the old-fashioned dark suit which seemed a little small for him. Then came Hellmuth walking so heavily that his feet would have sunk into the earth if he hadn't been wearing big boots. Then came Dalila and her face looked bright and shiny and she stared around at us boldly and her eyes seemed to flash. She was still wearing the old-fashioned skirt and frilly white blouse and the hem of her skirt trailed in the mud. My grandfather peered at her and took off his hat and scratched his head and she stared back at him and looked defiant and proud. Lastly came my grandmother flapping her hands in front of her as if she were shooing geese.

Alcibiades had no interest in Hugo and the Jeep and the piece of paper which turned out to be a letter from Freddy. He walked past us all without a glance and went into the orchard. Seeing him made my heart ache, he looked so deep into himself and unhappy. Dalila went to sit in the Opel, her one piece of territory. Hellmuth went straight to Hugo. He seemed puffed up with injured dignity as if swollen with water. His heavy glasses kept sliding down his nose and he roughly shoved them back. His thinning black hair stood up like sharp spikes.

"How'd you get here?" he demanded.

"The back road's open if you watch where you're going."

Hellmuth took the letter, unfolded it and read it while standing by the hood of the Jeep, holding the paper with two hands. Hugo stood on the running board and looked around very importantly as if he had come to buy something but saw nothing worth his trouble. The twins had run over to him first thing, very proud of their brother, and had scrambled into the backseat. They were bouncing up and down trying to see which one could bounce higher and the springs squeaked and squeaked. Even Rosvita took a few steps toward the Jeep as if to indicate that her allegiance was with the outside world and not with us.

Hellmuth finished reading and lowered his hands. Glancing around, it seemed that he, too, had changed, or at least that his mind was now focused on other things, faraway things.

"What does he say?" asked Miriam. "Does he mention me?" She had been sipping wine all day and was unsteady on her feet.

Hellmuth gave her the letter, then entered the house, pushing past the rest of us without looking at us. Miriam stared at the letter in her hand.

"Read it," said Bibiana.

"He doesn't mention me at all," said Miriam. "He doesn't even think of me." Her eyes welled with tears. Then she grew angry at herself and wiped them away with the back of her hand. She began to read.

" 'Dear Hellmuth and Alcibiades and Walterio, too, if you are interested . . .' "

"I might, you know, be interested," interrupted Walterio, still nibbling something. "It depends on what he has to say."

"Hush," said my grandmother.

Miriam resumed reading: " 'I keep expecting to hear from you but I hear not a word. All I hear is that you are doing nothing. What do you expect, that the Americans will put your lives back together for you? Don't you understand that I have work, real work? I am busy every day from six in the morning to midnight but I can't do it all myself. Just ask Hugo. There is much buying and selling and trading. There is property to be bought and repairs to be made. Many people from Chiloé are eager to obtain things. Not only am I a buyer and seller, I am a middleman. I am like the neck of an hourglass and all the sand passes through me. But I need people I can trust. Can you imagine there are those who want to steal from me? I need your help, even Walterio if he is not too busy stuffing himself. Hugo will drive you back to Puerto Montt, just don't let him go too fast. The Jeep is new. Each hour you waste means money thrown away. Your affectionate brother-in-law, Freddy Piwonka Gray.' "

Miriam threw the letter down on the ground. "What about me?" she said. "There's not a word about me." And again the tears appeared in her eyes.

Walterio picked up the letter and smoothed it out with his fat hands. He was sweating and all his clothes were tight. "I suppose there are things, you know, I could do," he said, "although I wouldn't want to work from six in the morning until midnight and I definitely don't like that remark about stuffing myself."

"You do stuff yourself," said Olivia.

My grandmother took the letter from him. "You could end up in jail," she said. "How would you like to eat nothing but porridge and feel lucky if you got even that?" She looked at the letter but her eyes weren't strong enough to read it. Then she glanced around at the rest of us. She, too, seemed defiant but also very sad. Later I realized that she saw Hugo's arrival and Freddy's letter as the end. People would be leaving, separating, and she felt angry at all of us for putting the world between us and her wishes. She was saying, Do what you want, I will stay here no matter what happens. But at that particular moment her defiance and anger were overwhelmed by the events around us: what we had seen in the attic and Hugo's arrival. These things actually made her seem small. There was also Hellmuth's fierce intention which we couldn't as yet guess at. But perhaps that is false because didn't we know that he would go down to Puerto Montt even before he told us?

Then I noticed my grandfather watching my grandmother. During the reading of the letter, he had cupped one hand over his ear and leaned forward in order to listen. He, too, looked sad but he seemed sad for his wife as if he wanted to approach her and put his hand on her arm and comfort her. At least that is what I thought at the time. Certainly he understood her disappointment. But the lines of their relationship were already drawn and there was little comfort exchanged between them. In any case, after another moment he gave his hat a tug and trudged back to the shed. The workman with big ears went with him.

"Well, I've made up my mind," said Walterio. "I'm going to go. I mean, I'm really going." And he began brushing the crumbs off the front of his sweater.

"And I'm going, too," said Miriam, "even if he doesn't want me. We'll all go."

Hugo looked embarrassed and didn't say anything. The twins jumped up and down in the back of the Jeep. "We're going, we're going!" they shouted.

"Hush up," said Hugo. He looked uncomfortably at his mother and it was clear he was not happy with this new development. Later he told Spartaco that Freddy had a new girl-friend in Puerto Montt and he was afraid that Freddy would be angry if his mother came down as well. But certainly she wouldn't be stopped and when they all left she went with them and it must have been all right or at least not terrible because I never heard of any trouble that came from it. In any case, Miriam had already learned to accommodate herself to Freddy, and mistresses could be no surprise to her.

But that was the next day because it was too late to leave now since it would mean arriving after dark and there was no electricity and there was still a curfew and they couldn't drive within the city of Puerto Montt itself where the pavement had all been destroyed. They could only drive to the very end of the dirt roads and that was at the edge of town.

Even so Hellmuth came out of the house again with a bag of his clothes and he put them into the back of the Opel. Dalila got out and glared at him and again her long skirt dragged on the ground.

"You don't expect me to go down there, do you?" she said.

Hellmuth didn't even glance at her but clearly he did expect it and even demanded it because she belonged to him just as his car belonged to him.

He slammed the trunk shut, then looked at her old-fashioned

skirt and white blouse. "Get rid of those stupid clothes," he
said.

The rest of that afternoon and evening was filled with wran-
gling and discussion and my grandmother was very unhappy.
Alcibiades didn't return until late. By that time Hellmuth had
taken Dalila to the shed and had made her bring their bedding
and pillows because he refused to sleep in the same room with
the rest of us and he said he had business with his wife. Dalila
clearly didn't want to sleep in the shed but she was afraid of
her husband and for a long time I heard Hellmuth shouting at
her out in the darkness even though I couldn't hear the words.
It was angry and violent and made the dogs bark. But I had
been surprised whenever I saw Dalila before Hellmuth took
her to the shed because even though she appeared uncertain
and even frightened, she also looked pleased.

By the time Alcibiades got back, the twins and Manfredo
were sound asleep. It was raining again and Alcibiades's
leather jacket was soaking wet. He looked around, I guess for
Dalila and Hellmuth, and then went to his bed without speaking
to anyone. By now Rosvita had told everyone what we had seen
in the attic. Bibiana and Clotilde and even Olivia were very
indignant and unforgiving and Olivia had suggested that she
wouldn't be able to sleep in the same room with Alcibiades,
but after he arrived she made no attempt to move. Great-uncle
Teodoro was equally indignant and made it clear that if he had
the use of his leg, he would take some action, although he
didn't say what it would be, only that action was plainly needed.
He kept looking at my grandfather and saying that somebody
should do something, but although my grandfather obviously
knew what had happened he chose not to get involved and that
evening his hearing aid appeared to break and he couldn't hear
anyone at all. I expect he felt sorry for Alcibiades and didn't
want to add to his troubles. Certainly one only had to look at

Alcibiades to see how badly he felt. My grandmother also stayed out of it—indeed, she was far more upset that people were leaving—and I came to decide later that she probably blamed the whole matter on Dalila, seeing her son—both her sons—as victims of a conniving and selfish woman.

Alcibiades sat on the edge of his bed and struggled with his boots. I'm sure we were all looking at him while pretending our attention was elsewhere. Only Walterio looked at him directly and after a moment he waddled over and gave him Freddy's letter.

"I'm going down, too," said Walterio. He wore green pajamas that were big enough for a tent and his breathing was rapid and shallow, like the panting of a dog on a hot day. "All three of us can, you know, work together helping Freddy."

Alcibiades handed back the letter. "I'm not going," he said and his tone was harsh.

There was a nervous sort of silence. Then my grandmother said, "He's going to stay with me, stay right here with the rest of us."

Alcibiades looked at his mother and didn't speak. But I could tell from his expression that he had no intention of remaining at the farm.

We began to get ready for bed. Clotilde had already withdrawn into her alcove and had pulled the curtain. My grandfather appeared to be asleep. I brushed my mother's hair and liked how the static popped and made little sparks in the dark. Spartaco came back inside from brushing his teeth.

"Oh, I hope we're not shaken out of our beds tonight," said Bibiana. She stretched and groaned, then pulled up the covers over her soft body. There was a clinking noise as Miriam poured herself a little more wine.

Walterio had retrieved the letter and put it away. I don't

know why he decided he was its particular keeper. Then he did a strange thing. He bent over and began touching his toes, up and down, up and down, although, of course, he couldn't actually reach them. It took me a second to realize he was exercising. Bibiana giggled and even my mother stared. It struck me that he was preparing himself for his trip to Puerto Montt. Then from the shed I heard Hellmuth's upraised voice. I looked over at Alcibiades but he was already under his blankets and had his pillow over his head. I couldn't even see his yellow hair. I lay down and covered my own head and soon I was asleep. What did I dream of? Rushing mostly: hurrying and hurrying and arriving too late.

In the morning we were all up early. It was cold and gray and rainy and the sunny warmth of the previous day felt untrue, a dream from a restless night. My grandmother was in a fury and spoke to no one except Ana the kitchen girl and then she only spoke in order to shout. Bibiana bustled around her and Clotilde remained in her alcove with the curtains shut. Hugo worked to put the canopy on top of the Jeep but he only got it partly right and it leaked and it was clear they would all get wet. Walterio began to look uncertain and several times I again saw him doing his exercises, but although he grunted and strained he never once reached his toes and I thought of all those cookies being broken to dust in his huge stomach as he heaved himself up and down. He packed a bag, as did Miriam and Rosvita, but they couldn't take much because the Jeep was so small and the twins would have to sit on the adults' laps. Hellmuth and Dalila remained in the shed until at least nine, even though my grandfather was eager to get back to work. Alcibiades kept coming into the yard and looking around and, although he tried not to show it, I'm sure he was trying to catch sight of Dalila.

When Hellmuth came out at last, Dalila walked very close beside him. Her head was lowered and she walked directly to the Opel. She wore a purple coat and her hair was covered with a dark scarf. Alcibiades came out of the house and said something which she ignored. I didn't hear the words but his tone was urging and sad. Dalila got into the front seat of the Opel and stared straight ahead. Alcibiades walked quickly to the Opel and opened the front door.

"Can't you even look at me?" he asked.

Before he could say anything else, Hellmuth had sprung on him and yanked him away, pushing him so that Alcibiades fell against the house. Then Hellmuth raised his fist and ran at him. There was a lot of commotion. People were calling to them to stop. Rosvita stood with her hands over her face. Before Hellmuth could do anything, my grandfather rapped his cane against Hellmuth's arm.

"Have you no manners?" he said in a loud voice. "You can't fight in front of children, in front of your own mother!"

Both Hellmuth and Alcibiades were glaring at each other but Hellmuth looked the angriest and he kept bunching and relaxing his fists. They were large and looked like red meat.

"Come with me," he told his brother. Then he turned and splashed across the yard toward the orchard. Alcibiades hesitated, then followed. Before passing through the gate, Hellmuth took off his glasses and handed them to his sister Miriam. He walked without looking back. Alcibiades followed him and the two brothers disappeared into the orchard. We were all very quiet. I looked at Dalila sitting in the front seat of the car. I wish I could say she was smiling or looking triumphant or even sad but she stared straight ahead at the wall of the house and her face showed nothing at all. I stood with Spartaco and held on to his arm and felt frightened although I hardly knew what was happening. The wind flapped the edge of the tarpaulin so it snapped and made a racket. Only the twins had taken shelter from the rain.

From inside I could hear Teodoro calling from his bed, "What's happening? What's going on?"

Glancing back toward the orchard, I saw that Hugo had climbed onto the roof of the shed and was peering over the top into the trees. He was very excited and kept looking back at us and grinning.

"They're going to fight," he said. He crouched down and stared into the orchard. "He's hitting him! Hellmuth is hitting him!"

I listened for some noise, the sound of huge and awful blows, but the only noise was the wind blowing the rain across the yard and buffeting the tarpaulin. The dogs were cowering in their houses, as if they knew something was wrong, and the chickens had crowded under the Jeep. Walterio and Miriam and my mother stood near the stove. Walterio kept shaking his head.

"He's hitting him," Hugo repeated. Then he stopped grinning and jumping about and just stared. "Come on," he called into the orchard, "do something! Hit him!"

My grandfather hurried toward the shed. "Get down from there," he called. "You have no business up there!"

Hugo apparently didn't hear him and kept staring into the orchard, and his whole face seemed to wince as if he himself were the one being hit.

"Get down from there!" called my grandfather again. Then he picked up a stone and threw it at Hugo. It bounced on the roof.

"Hey!" called Hugo and he looked at his grandfather in surprise.

My grandfather threw another stone and another. "Get off that roof!"

Hugo shielded his head with his arm. "Cut it out!" he cried. Then a rock hit him in the leg and he began hopping up and down.

"It's not your business," shouted my grandfather in a rage. "You've no right up there!"

The roof of the shed was quite steep, although the edge was only about six feet off the ground. But, of course, the wooden shingles were slippery from the rain. My grandfather threw another stone and this one hit Hugo in his other leg, which crumpled so that Hugo fell backward and began to slide down the wet shingles on his behind.

"Heyyy!" shouted Hugo. Then he slid over the edge and plopped down into the middle of a puddle and made a big splash so that drops of muddy water even reached us three meters away. My grandfather chuckled and looked quite happy with himself and clapped his hands together several times. The twins, of course, thought it was extremely funny. Even Manfredo laughed. Miriam ran over to Hugo and helped him to his feet and tried to wipe the mud from his clothes. He didn't seem to be hurt, only shaken up, but he was very upset and I expect he would have cried if he didn't have such a sense of himself as the oldest grandchild.

At that moment, Hellmuth came out of the orchard. His hair was mussed and I saw blood on the knuckles of his hands. He retrieved his glasses from Miriam, carefully set them on his nose, and walked straight to his Opel. Then Alcibiades came out as well and, oh, his face must have hurt. There was a cut under his eye and his mouth was bleeding and a trickle of blood ran down his chin. His whole body seemed clenched and bent. I squeezed Spartaco's arm. I was standing near Hugo and I heard him keep telling his mother, "He never hit back, he never hit back."

Hellmuth climbed into the front seat of his car and tried to start the motor. The ignition made a grinding noise that cut above the sound of the wind. It whined and whined. Hellmuth stopped, then tried again. Dalila sat next to Hellmuth but kept her eyes focused straight ahead. The ignition whined, then caught. The car coughed several times, then stopped. Again came the grinding of the ignition. This time it caught properly. Hellmuth pressed down on the accelerator and the engine roared higher and higher, making a screaming noise so the twins covered their ears and the chickens burst out from under the Jeep, flapping their wings and running for the shed. Clouds of blue smoke poured from the exhaust pipe.

Hellmuth put the Opel in reverse and backed away from the house. We hurried out of its path, all except my grandmother who refused to move. Then Hellmuth changed gears and turned onto the driveway which was bumpy with ruts and which had been twisted and broken by all the aftershocks. He never once looked at us. The car moved forward, bouncing over the ruts, how violent it was, bounce, bounce, bounce over the twisted earth, and within it I could see Hellmuth and Dalila trying to face straight ahead but going bounce, bounce, bounce, going up to the very roof, as if their bodies were fighting the air around them, fighting the silence and the wind and their own angry feelings and after another moment the car bounced around the side of the kitchen and was gone and there seemed to be a hole right in the middle of the air where the car had disappeared.

Alcibiades walked to the pump, grasped the handle and began pumping it up and down so the pump made a hee-haw sound like a metallic donkey. A stream of clear water poured out into the yard. Alcibiades washed the blood from his face, using his handkerchief. None of us went near him. There was even blood in his blond hair. Through the bedroom window I could see Great-uncle Teodoro's pale face staring at us with a mixture of uncertainty and irritation.

Walterio went up to his brother and tried to take his arm. "Are you . . . you know . . ."

Alcibiades shook him off. Then he looked around at us. What did his face look like? I've had it in my memory for thirty years and I still can't get it right. It looked out of order somehow, not just from the bruises. It looked fragmented from the inside. It looked like it rested at the top of a huge darkness. It looked heavy, his whole face looked heavy as if it were pulling him down to the ground. He wiped the water from his mustache and glanced around for his jacket. Rosvita ran and brought it to him. He nodded to her and put it on, then began to walk out of the yard.

"Alcibiades!" called my grandmother.

He turned to face her. Again there was that expression, a clear expression like an open window so that one could see all the darkness piled up inside him. He started to raise his hand as if to wave good-bye, then dropped it again and turned and walked off, walking right through the puddles. I ran after him to the corner of the garden and watched him walk down the hill to town. I waved and waved but he never looked back. I thought maybe he would return that night or even the next day but he never did.

These were two dear brothers who had been the best of friends and were destined never to see each other again. Sometime that winter Alcibiades moved north. Hellmuth went to work for Freddy Piwonka Gray and became quite wealthy and built a new house, but five years later he drove into the River Maullín and was drowned. It wasn't the mustard-colored Opel but one of Freddy's trucks. There had been a heavy rain and the river was swollen. Apparently he didn't see the bridge.

People said he was drinking but I don't know if that is true. Dalila never contacted Alcibiades, although she saw him at the funeral, and a year later she married a pharmacist from Valdivia and moved there. Almost right away she began having babies. She had four children but then died giving birth to the fifth. And, of course, those children grew up and are right now seeking their fortunes, their private happiness. Sometimes Miriam mentions them.

The others of my family all moved toward their deaths, their separate deaths: my grandmother in her bed, my grandfather of a stroke in the barn, Clotilde of cancer, Teodoro falling dead from his tractor, Bibiana just wasting away. It comes back to me sometimes, my grandmother's wish that we could all die together. How sensible it seems. But the earthquake that was to take us to Heaven left us alive while destroying our family. The earthquake did indeed sweep us away. It swept us into separate lives. Alcibiades was swept all the way up into the desert where it never rains and the only trees are in the carefully watered city parks and the sun sucked all of the moisture from his face. Does he think of Dalila as he walks through that city where each building is like a bright light? What does he think of his dear brother? And how much time does he have left?

It's the separateness that hurts me now. Some people have long lives and some short. Think of the distance that grows between us as we get older and move apart. Think how the real world intrudes on whatever we dream for ourselves. Think of the great distance of the dead. My brother, Spartaco, was last seen during the military coup. He was a graduate student in engineering. His best friend told me that he had run out to help some woman lying in the street. Maybe she had been shot, maybe she had been knocked aside by a Jeep. Spartaco helped her to her feet, helped her toward the corner. He glanced up and saw his friend standing at the window and waved—whether in greeting or farewell, who knew. It was past curfew and nearly dark: a warm spring evening. The woman wore a white scarf over her head and there was no telling her age. Spartaco turned the corner, the woman still clinging to his shoulder. They were never seen again.

FOR THE BEST IN PAPERBACKS, LOOK FOR THE

In every corner of the world, on every subject under the sun, Penguin represents quality and variety—the very best in publishing today.

For complete information about books available from Penguin—including Pelicans, Puffins, Peregrines, and Penguin Classics—and how to order them, write to us at the appropriate address below. Please note that for copyright reasons the selection of books varies from country to country.

In the United Kingdom: For a complete list of books available from Penguin in the U.K., please write to *Dept E.P., Penguin Books Ltd, Harmondsworth, Middlesex, UB7 0DA*.

In the United States: For a complete list of books available from Penguin in the U.S., please write to *Dept BA, Penguin*, Box 120, Bergenfield, New Jersey 07621-0120.

In Canada: For a complete list of books available from Penguin in Canada, please write to *Penguin Books Canada Ltd, 10 Alcorn Avenue, Suite 300, Toronto, Ontario, Canada M4V 3B2*.

In Australia: For a complete list of books available from Penguin in Australia, please write to the *Marketing Department, Penguin Books Ltd, P.O. Box 257, Ringwood, Victoria 3134*.

In New Zealand: For a complete list of books available from Penguin in New Zealand, please write to the *Marketing Department, Penguin Books (NZ) Ltd, Private Bag, Takapuna, Auckland 9*.

In India: For a complete list of books available from Penguin, please write to *Penguin Overseas Ltd, 706 Eros Apartments, 56 Nehru Place, New Delhi, 110019*.

In Holland: For a complete list of books available from Penguin in Holland, please write to *Penguin Books Nederland B.V., Postbus 195, NL-1380AD Weesp, Netherlands*.

In Germany: For a complete list of books available from Penguin, please write to *Penguin Books Ltd, Friedrichstrasse 10-12, D-6000 Frankfurt Main 1, Federal Republic of Germany*.

In Spain: For a complete list of books available from Penguin in Spain, please write to *Longman, Penguin España, Calle San Nicolas 15, E-28013 Madrid, Spain*.

In Japan: For a complete list of books available from Penguin in Japan, please write to *Longman Penguin Japan Co Ltd, Yamaguchi Building, 2-12-9 Kanda Jimbocho, Chiyoda-Ku, Tokyo 101, Japan*.